# A MATTER OF HONOR

"I am Chih-li, Imperial Grand Minister of Internal Security, First Rank," the man barked. "Your very presence insults my honor."

His words hit Worf like a slap across the face. "What do you know of honor?" he demanded.

Chih-li raised his chin proudly. "The safety of the Dragon, his family, his guests, and his property is my responsibility and mine alone. To suggest I require foreign assistance is to besmirch my honor in the most heinous manner imaginable."

Worf's steady gaze never left the blades in Chih-li's hands. "Honor demands I obey the commands of my captain. I cannot do otherwise."

"I see," Chih-li said. He fixed Worf with a penetrating stare. "Then our course is set." He raised both swords in front of him.

# Look for STAR TREK Fiction from Pocket Books

## The Original Series

# Star Trek: The Next Generation

# Star Trek: Deep Space Nine

# Star Trek: Voyager

# STAR TREK
## THE NEXT GENERATION®

# DRAGON'S HONOR

## KIJ JOHNSON
## and GREG COX

POCKET BOOKS

New York   London   Toronto   Sydney   Tokyo   Singapore

This book is a work of fiction. Names, characters, places and incidents are products of the author's imagination or are used fictitiously. Any resemblance to actual events or locales or persons, living or dead, is entirely coincidental.

An *Original* Publication of POCKET BOOKS

POCKET BOOKS, a division of Simon & Schuster Inc.
1230 Avenue of the Americas, New York, NY 10020

STAR TREK is a Registered Trademark of
Paramount Pictures.

A VIACOM COMPANY

This book is published by Pocket Books, a division of
Simon & Schuster Inc., under exclusive license from
Paramount Pictures.

ISBN: 0-671-50107-0

First Pocket Books printing January 1996

10  9  8  7  6  5  4  3  2  1

POCKET and colophon are registered trademarks of
Simon & Schuster Inc.

Printed in the U.S.A.

# DRAGON'S
# HONOR

# Chapter One

*Captain's log, stardate 47146.2. Following orders from Starfleet, the* Enterprise *is en route to Pai, throneworld of the insular and enigmatic Dragon Empire. Until recently, the humanoid inhabitants of the Empire have avoided any direct contact with the Federation and other civilizations. All previous negotiations and attempts at diplomatic relations have been conducted via subspace communications. It is my understanding that my crew and I will be the first outsiders to visit Pai in over a dozen generations. . . .*

"CAPTAIN PICARD," DATA ANNOUNCED abruptly. "Sensors detect a large vessel approaching the *Enterprise* at warp speed." Seated at his bridge station, the golden-skinned android inspected the data flowing into his monitors. His fingers deftly manipulated the sensor controls. "It is on a direct intercept course," he confirmed.

1

Jean-Luc Picard leaned forward in the captain's seat. He had not expected a welcoming party so soon. The *Enterprise* was still several dozen light-years from the Dragon Empire, and the Pai, he knew, rarely if ever ventured beyond the borders of their own solar system. Indeed, there was some question as to whether the Empire possessed warp capability at all. "Mr. Data," he asked, "can you identify the vessel?"

Data did not look up from his console. "I believe so, Captain," he responded. "Preliminary readings suggest that the vessel is a G'kkau warship, approximately seven and a half years old, possibly of the *S'sssr'ss* class, with a crew complement of roughly one hundred and fifty-five G'kkau raiders." Data paused for a second and peered more closely at his sensor readings. "Further analysis is required before I can give you a more exact answer to your question."

"That's more than enough, Mr. Data," Picard said. He glanced around the bridge. With the exception of Geordi and Beverly, who were at their posts in Engineering and sickbay, respectively, all his senior officers were on hand. The only new face was at the conn: Lieutenant Tor, a young Andorian who had recently transferred over from the *Nisqually*. Along with the others, she awaited his orders. First things first, he thought. He wasn't sure what the G'kkau were up to, but he had no interest in playing chicken with another starship at warp speed. "Shields up," he commanded. "Slow to impulse."

The *Enterprise* immediately dropped out of warp drive. As always, Picard thought he could feel the starship decelerate beneath his feet, but he knew the sensation was purely psychological. Human senses were not designed to register the transition from faster-than-light travel to mere sublight speeds.

Seated at his right, Will Riker let out a grunt. "The G'kkau," he said, scowling beneath his neatly trimmed black beard. "What are those butchers up to now?"

"I don't know, Number One," Picard said, "but I intend to find out." His mind quickly reviewed what he knew of the G'kkau. The reptilian conquerors had long been a threat to peace in a neighboring sector of the galaxy. Ever since achieving starfaring status several centuries ago, the G'kkau had systematically pillaged many weaker and less advanced species. They were little better than a race of pirates, really, and no genuine menace to the Federation, the Romulans, or any of the galaxy's known superpowers, but Picard had heard many horror stories of the atrocities the G'kkau had inflicted upon unsuspecting peoples and planets. The massacre on Snokomie IV, during which an entire race of intelligent avians was executed and *consumed,* was only the freshest and most memorable example to come to mind. Starfleet had feared the G'kkau might have designs on the Dragon Empire. Could they be making their move already? If so, Picard realized, then his mission was even more urgent than he had assumed.

"Mr. Data," he asked. "What is the status of the G'kkau ship?"

"It has come to a full stop, Captain, directly between us and Pai."

*That cannot be a coincidence,* Picard thought grimly. "Weapons, Mr. Worf?"

The Klingon security officer stood at his station

above and behind Picard. Beneath the bony ridges of his forehead, dark eyes smoldered with barely banked fire. "The warship is fully shielded, Captain, and its phaser banks are armed."

"Hail the other ship," Picard ordered. "Onscreen." If worst came to worst, he thought, the *Enterprise* could handily defend itself against the alien vessel in an all-out battle. He had never personally encountered the G'kkau before, but Starfleet intelligence suggested that their weapons were not quite up to Federation standards. Still, intelligence reports had been wrong before, and Picard didn't feel like taking any unnecessary risks, especially since the nearest reinforcements were several days away. In any event, he always preferred to try diplomacy first.

"The G'kkau are responding to our hail," Worf stated. Picard thought he heard a rumble of disappointment in his security officer's deep voice; no doubt the Klingon had looked forward to a glorious battle. Then a visual transmission appeared on the bridge's main viewer, replacing the starfield that had previously been displayed there. Picard sat up straight in his chair as he got his first look at one of the occupants of the other ship. Seated at his left, Counselor Deanna Troi let out an involuntary gasp. Was she reacting to the G'kkau's appearance, he wondered briefly, or had her empathic senses alerted her to the G'kkau's hostile intentions?

"Counselor?" he inquired in a low voice.

"Aggression," she whispered. "Pure, undiluted aggression."

"I see," Picard said. Staring at the face that had materialized on the viewer, he understood her reaction perfectly. Distinctly reptilian, the alien being somewhat resembled a Gorn, except that the G'kkau seemed even less humanoid. Iridescent green scales glittered over its exposed head and shoulders, which took up most of the screen. A long, flat snout, much like a Terran crocodile's, protruded from the creature's skull. Pendulous dewlaps hung from the G'kkau's throat. A pair of yellow eyes, marked by thin black pupils, were lodged above the origin of its snout, beneath a sloping, scaly brow. A transparent third eyelid blinked rapidly over the G'kkau's lizard-like eyes; the nictitating membranes seemed to flash, as if in Morse code, an unending message of warning and hostility. Picard could not see the rest of the G'kkau's body, but from the placement of its shoulders he guessed that it routinely traveled on all fours rather than erect—assuming, of course, that it had *merely* four limbs. At the moment, Picard could not recall the specifics of G'kkau anatomy; he made a mental note to himself to consult the Federation's biological database as soon as it was convenient.

"I am Master Kakkh of the *Fang,*" the being on the screen declared. The ship's Universal Translator gave Kakkh's voice a masculine timbre. "What are you doing in this sector?" Rows of sharp, serrated teeth clacked together as he spoke; evolution had clearly provided the G'kkau with the deadly jaws of a carnivore. Picard called on his Starfleet training, and years of experience dealing with all manner of sentient entities, to suppress the instinctive foreboding that the sight of those ferocious fangs instilled in him. Both humans and Klingons, he reminded himself, had evolved from predator species, and yet both peoples had proven themselves capable of acting in a civilized manner . . . even if, Picard silently conceded, Klingons had a somewhat different idea of what constitutes civilization. He hoped the G'kkau could do the same, despite the grim record of the past few centuries.

"I am Jean-Luc Picard," he began, a stony expression upon his face. "Captain of the *U.S.S. Enterprise*, representing the United Federation of Planets."

"We know you, *Enterprise*," Kakkh said harshly. A forked tongue flicked in and out of the G'kkau commander's snapping jaws. The cabin behind Kakkh was dimly lit by human standards; Picard glimpsed only shadows and swirling, purple mists. "What are you doing in this region?"

"I might ask you the same question," Picard said. He rose from his chair and strode to the front of the bridge, stepping closer to the viewer.

"The affairs of the G'kkau are none of your concern, human," Kakkh said contemptuously, dimming Picard's hopes of peaceful negotiation—and confirming the worst suspicions of his gut instincts. *Never smile at a crocodile,* he thought, remembering an old Earth song.

"They are if your intentions endanger the people of the Dragon Empire," Picard answered him, opting for the direct approach. Given Kakkh's belligerent attitude, there appeared to be no point in mincing words. The sooner he determined the G'kkau's true intentions, the better.

"The Pai do not belong to your foolish Federation yet," Kakkh said, swishing his tail. The tip of the heavy, green appendage swept across the screen, behind Kakkh's fearsome visage. "You have no place here, and your mission is doomed to failure. If you are wise, you will return to your own space at once."

"Is that a threat, Master Kakkh?" Picard said, scowling. The G'kkau clearly knew more about the *Enterprise*'s present assignment than Picard would have liked. This encounter was definitely no accident. Still, Kakkh was deluding himself if he thought Starfleet would back down so easily. Picard could feel Worf's presence at the weapons station; he did not need to look back over his shoulder to reassure himself that the Klingon was ready and willing to defend the *Enterprise* if necessary.

"The G'kkau do not threaten, human," Kakkh said. "They strike. Consider my words a warning, and heed them."

"If you know as much of our mission as you imply," Picard replied, "then you know how important its outcome is to both the Federation and the Dragon Empire. While I appreciate that you may have your own . . . interests . . . in this region, we fully intend to continue our journey to Pai, and to conclude our business there." He stared at Kakkh, hoping that the reptilian commander could read the determination in his expression and his posture. "At the moment, your vessel obstructs our course for Pai, but we can and will go around you if necessary."

Kakkh did not reply immediately. A long silence ensued during which the cold, unreadable gaze of the G'kkau never left Picard's face. The steady winking of Kakkh's inner eyelids ticked off the seconds as regularly as a metronome. What was Kakkh thinking, Picard wondered. With a discreet wave of his hand, he signaled Worf to mute the audio component of their transmission. "Counselor?" he asked Troi.

"I detect definite hostility, Captain," she answered, "and perhaps a measure of anxiety, but I cannot be sure. His emotions and body language are quite alien to me."

"Will he attack, do you think?"

"I'm sorry, Captain. I can't be positive."

Picard sighed and signaled Worf to restore sound transmission. There were times he wished Troi's empathic abilities were more precise, but, in the long run, he was glad she never pretended to an infallibility she did not possess. Empathy was an art, not a science; even full Betazoids had been deceived on occasion.

Suddenly, with neither a farewell nor a final threat, Kakkh's image disappeared from the viewer. A starfield replaced the lizard's head and shoulders; in the distance, Picard spotted a glittering, metallic object that was probably the *Fang*. Even the name of their ship was threatening, he observed. "Transmission cut off at the G'kkau's end," Worf reported promptly.

"Their communications manners leave something to be desired," Picard commented. He took his seat in the captain's chair. "Keep a watch on that ship." What was Kakkh up to, he wondered; could the G'kkau be so ferocious—and so foolhardy—as to launch a full-fledged assault against a Galaxy-class starship? "Full magnification on the screen," he ordered. "Let's get a look at them."

The tiny metal dot on the viewer expanded instantly, transforming into the unmistakable form of an alien spacecraft. The *Fang,* Picard noted, actually resembled its namesake. Curved like a scimitar, the ship was wide and cylindrical at the rear, where he guessed the main engines were, then tapered to a sharp point at its prow, which glowed with a constant ruby radiance. The rest of the ship, like the G'kkau themselves, was a bright, opalescent green. From the *Enterprise*'s current orientation, the blood-red tip of the *Fang* appeared to point downward, as though poised to strike.

"Their engines are powering up," Data informed him.

Picard kept his attention at the *Fang*'s glowing point, where he guessed the ship's primary weapons were lodged. "Stand by, Mr. Worf," he said. Phasers, disruptors, photon torpedoes . . . who knew what kind of venom could spit from this *Fang?*

"I don't like the look of this," Riker said gruffly.

"Neither do I, Number One," Picard agreed. Not for the first time, he wished Starfleet had given him more time to prepare for this assignment. He should have studied and anticipated the tactics of the G'kkau. "Lock phasers on target, Mr. Worf."

"Done," the Klingon said instantly.

"The ship is moving," Data told him. Picard saw a flash of crimson light at the rear of the *Fang*. He leaned forward, his body tense. Then, to his surprise, the ship spun horizontally on its axis, turning its back to the *Enterprise*. Red-hot, the flat, circular stern of the G'kkau ship glowed as if afire. The *Fang* shot away from the *Enterprise*, its image shrinking on the viewer as the ship disappeared into the distance. "The G'kkau are retreating rapidly," Data confirmed. Picard let out a deep breath, but not so obviously as to concern his crew.

"What was that all about?" Riker wondered aloud.

"Kakkh blinked," Picard said, remembering Kakkh's nictitating membranes, "in more ways than one."

"They are cowards and without honor," Worf said, pronouncing judgment on their entire species. Doubtless he regretted a missed opportunity to test his martial skills against the G'kkau.

"That may be, Mr. Worf, but I suspect we have not heard the last of Kakkh and his ilk. Cowardice does not rule out cunning and ambition." Picard watched the red glow of the *Fang*'s engines grow smaller and smaller until finally it vanished from view entirely. "Mr. Data, can you track the course of the G'kkau vessel?"

"I am trying, Captain," the android said, "but its apparent destination is the Dragon Nebula itself. Once it enters the nebula, the ionized gases will generate considerable interference with our sensors. I'm afraid that 'noise' from the nebula will effectively mask the *Fang*'s location unless we pursue them immediately."

Picard shook his head thoughtfully. "No. Our business is with the Pai, not the G'kkau. Not yet, at least." He glanced toward Lieutenant Tor. Her blue antennae swiveled slightly in his direction. "Proceed to our original destination at full speed," he instructed her.

Stars streaked by on the main viewer as Picard settled back into his chair. Now that Data had called it to his attention, Picard could see the celebrated nebula from which the Dragon Empire took its name. A sprawling arc of delicately colored, coruscating gases, the Dragon Nebula spread across the center of the screen. The planet Pai, too distant to be seen just yet, orbited a medium-sized, yellow star at the fringe of the nebula. From certain angles, Picard knew, including the perspective of the Pai, the entire nebula resembled the mouth of an enormous fanged beast: a dragon perhaps, or, he had to admit, a G'kkau. *How ironic,* he thought, *that Starfleet has sent me to save the humanoid citizens of the Dragon Empire from a voracious race of real-life dragons.*

At the moment, Picard didn't feel like St. George. This brief standoff with the G'kkau warship troubled him more than he let on. Ultimately, it was probably good to be aware that the G'kkau were already lurking about, but their unwanted presence did not promise to make his mission any easier—or anything less than crucial. More than merely future relations between the Federation and the Pai was at stake; unless Picard succeeded, the Dragon Empire itself faced annihilation at the claws of the G'kkau.

*And to think,* he mused, astounded at the very notion, *it all depends on a wedding. . . .*

"The importance of this wedding cannot be overstated," Picard began.

His entire senior staff, including Dr. Beverly Crusher and Chief Engineer Geordi La Forge, was seated around the conference-room table. Picard sat at the head of the table, occasionally glancing down at the data padd beneath his fingertips. Part of him felt uneasy about leaving the bridge under the command of the support staff while an enemy warship might still be hiding somewhere in the vicinity. The *Fang* had fled, however, at the first sign of opposition from the *Enterprise;* perhaps he'd succeeded in scaring Kakkh away for a while. If more trouble did arise, he reassured himself, the bridge was only a turbolift away.

Besides, now that they were less than an hour from Pai, it was absolutely vital that he brief his officers as much as he was able. They had to be fully prepared for anything that might occur, both here and on the planet's surface. He only wished there had been time to inform the crew earlier, but Starfleet had made it clear that time was of the utmost importance. *Easy for them to say,* he thought with touch of irritation. *They don't have to understand the intricacies of an entire civilization with minimal preparation and study.* The diplomat in Jean-Luc Picard was offended by the very notion of negotiating from a position of relative ignorance; the Starfleet captain resolved to make the best of a bad situation.

"The Dragon Empire consists of slightly less than a dozen planets, all orbiting the same sun," Picard continued.

Worf made a derisive snort. "One solar system hardly constitutes an empire," he said.

"Perhaps not by the standards of the Klingons or the Romulans," Picard conceded, "but it has a long history, dating back to the earliest days of human interstellar communication. Many researchers theorize that the Empire was originally settled by colonists from Earth's Asian continent, sometime after the genetic wars. Indeed, our best data indicates that their society bears a strong resemblance to that of medieval China; it may be a deliberate re-creation of an old Terran culture, not unlike the Native American communities established in what is now the Demilitarized Zone. Unfortunately, records from that era are sketchy, and historians from Earth have not been allowed on Pai since its rediscovery by Starfleet." Someday, Picard thought, if all went well with his current mission, he wouldn't mind leading an archaeological dig on Pai; it would be fascinating to compare the historical traces of the planet's original settlers with comparable artifacts from twenty-first-century Asia. All that depended, of course, on there being a Dragon Empire left to visit. The G'kkau were not known for their sense of historical preservation.

"For several years now," he explained, "the Dragon Empire has been divided by civil war. The Emperor, also known as the Dragon, faced a serious uprising led by Lord Lu Tung, a powerful noble. Not long ago, the Dragon's forces put down the rebellion, but Lu Tung's supporters remain numerous enough that the Dragon cannot deal with Lu Tung as decisively as he might like."

"In other words," Riker said, "he can't just stake Lu Tung out on an anthill somewhere."

"Precisely," Picard said. "So a compromise has been worked out to prevent another war. The Emperor's eldest son, the Dragon-Heir, will marry Lu Tung's only daughter. This union will join the families and bring peace to the Empire. The bride, by the way, is known as"—Picard consulted his padd—"the Green Pearl of Lu Tung."

"My God," Beverly said, obviously amused, "this sounds like something out of *The Mikado.*"

"Indeed," Picard agreed. He recalled that Beverly had recently staged an amateur production of that operetta as part of her ongoing Gilbert & Sullivan Festival. "Despite its humorous ring, though, this is a deadly serious business. Starfleet believes it is only a matter of time before the G'kkau invade Pai, expanding their own power and producing massive casualties throughout the Empire. Our own encounter with the G'kkau adds credence to this scenario. Starfleet has warned the Empire, and offered protection if the

Empire elects to join the Federation; but the Federation is understandably reluctant to admit the Empire until their own internal conflicts are resolved. Via subspace, the Federation has hammered out a treaty with the Empire, all pivoting on the wedding as proof of the Empire's newfound unity."

"But why are we here?" Riker asked. "With all due respect to your own diplomatic accomplishments, this doesn't sound like a job for a starship."

"No offense taken, Number One," Picard said sincerely. *I have my vices,* he thought, *but vanity is not one of them.* "The treaty needs to be signed in person by a representative of the Federation, and the Dragon insisted on a Starfleet commander rather an ambassador; apparently, they place great stock in an individual's military prowess."

"Ah," Worf said approvingly, "an honorable people." Troi, seated between Worf and Riker, could not suppress a smile at the predictability of the Klingon warrior's response.

"I hope to find them so," Picard said. "And yet it is not clear that the Pai fully comprehend the danger facing them. The treaty is not yet ratified and there is some concern that, even if the wedding goes off as scheduled, the Dragon might have second thoughts about joining the Federation. Sending the *Enterprise,* the flagship of the fleet, to the wedding is a high-profile goodwill gesture intended to ease the treaty's passage. More importantly, it also gives me a chance to meet with the Dragon in person, and to convince him of the utter necessity of accepting the Federation's aid against the G'kkau."

"Do you think the G'kkau will try to interfere with the wedding?" Riker asked. Picard was glad to see that his first officer had already worked through all the implications of their assignment. He could count on Will Riker to make sure nothing caught them by surprise.

"Given our 'chance meeting' with Master Kakkh of the *Fang*," he said, "I think we can practically guarantee it. Without the marriage, the civil wars are likely to resume. Without a unified government, the Dragon Empire cannot join the Federation. Without Starfleet's assistance, the Pai will be wiped out by the G'kkau."

"For the G'kkau," Riker observed, "that's a pretty good incentive for breaking up the wedding."

Picard nodded. "It may prove just as well that the Federation sent the *Enterprise* to this event instead of a strictly diplomatic delegation."

"Captain," Deanna Troi asked, "suppose the G'kkau were to attack before the wedding could be completed?"

"Within limits the Prime Directive would apply," Picard said grimly. "Unless they request our aid the Pai would be on their own." He hoped it wouldn't come to that. The Prime Directive was a wise and necessary principle, essential to the evolution of entire societies, but it could exact a cruel toll on an individual's conscience. As captain of the *Enterprise*, he had too often found himself forced to stand by helplessly when faced with tragedies both small and great, all to preserve the Federation's ancient doctrine of noninterference. In the greater scheme of things, it was the right thing to do; still, his sleep was sometimes troubled by memories of history's innocent victims. *Not this time*, he promised himself. *I will see the wedding concluded, and the Pai delivered into the safety and security of the Federation, even if I have to perform the ceremony myself!* "Any questions?" he asked the assembled officers. "Suggestions?"

Geordi shrugged. "From a technical standpoint, there's not much I can do to engineer a happy marriage. If we want to make a good impression, though, perhaps I could put together some sort of high-tech entertainment for the wedding. A really snazzy fireworks display maybe."

"An excellent idea, Mr. La Forge," Picard said, proud of Geordi's initiative. "Every little bit helps."

"Yeah," Geordi said enthusiastically, visibly brimming over with ideas. "Fireworks. That's the ticket. Some lasers, some fluorescent isotopes, and quantum discharges . . . Captain, I think I can promise you a light show that the Pai will never forget."

"A prismatic shift in forcefield frequencies might also produce an aesthetically pleasing optical display," Data suggested helpfully.

"Make it so," Picard said. Once again, he was struck by how curious it was that so much could depend on something as simple as a wedding. Or perhaps it was not so curious, he thought upon further reflection. Even on Earth, centuries past, the fate of nations had often been determined by a royal marriage or two, and a failed union could have cataclysmic consequences. *Just look at Henry the Eighth,* he thought, *not to mention Charles and Diana . . .*

"Jean-Luc," Beverly said. "Speaking of good impressions, there is one more thing we should consider. I don't know much about the Pai in particular, but I did a tour of duty on New Peking once and spent a lot of time visiting the museums and historical exhibits.

If Pai is anything like ancient China, it must be an extremely male-dominated society. Women will be treated as lesser beings, as chattel even, and expected to be modest and subservient. Not unlike Ferengi females today."

"Fools," Worf commented. Klingon society remained somewhat patriarchal, Picard knew, but, unlike the Ferengi, Klingons at least prized aggressiveness and defiance in their women. Picard could no more imagine Worf attracted to some shy, delicate flower of a woman than he could see the fierce Klingon warrior doting on a pampered poodle. Klingons expected their mates to disagree with them at every opportunity, and enjoyed the ensuing conflict. Given the growing affection between Worf and Counselor Troi, he wondered briefly what that said about Deanna.

"Gender roles in Pai society are their own affair," Picard said, "but I cannot ask my female officers to be treated with anything less than the respect they deserve. If the Dragon Empire is to join the Federation, they must accept our ways, just as we accept theirs."

"Of course," Beverly agreed. "Still, given the importance of this treaty, I'm willing to bend a little bit this time around, just to avoid shocking the Pai leaders unnecessarily." She glanced down at her at her formfitting Starfleet uniform. "Maybe we should dress more modestly, in keeping with Pai standards of propriety, if that's okay with you, Deanna."

Troi shrugged, her long black hair cascading over her shoulders. "I suppose so," she said. "There'll be time enough to raise the Pai's collective consciousness—*after* we've saved them from the G'kkau."

"I don't know," Picard said. "I am uncomfortable about requiring my female officers to conform to a different standard of dress and behavior."

"You're not ordering us," Beverly insisted. "We're volunteering. Right, Deanna?"

"Yes," Troi replied. "When you meet with the Dragon, you want him to be concerned with the treaty, not our attire. We can't afford to let anything distract the Pai from the issue at hand, namely their need for protection against the G'kkau."

"Very well," Picard said. "In that case, I thank you and Beverly in advance for any special efforts on our behalf." Rising from seat, he fixed his officers with a stern and steady gaze. "Dr. Crusher is right. Once we beam down to Pai, we must all be on our best behavior. More than a wedding and a treaty is at stake. This is a matter of life and death for all the people of the Dragon Empire. We dare not fail them, no matter how curious or backward their customs may seem to us."

"Personally," Data said, "I look forward to observing a human culture that has developed in isolation from the Federation. The Pai may provide me with many insights into the history and development of human social structures and mores."

"Easy for you to say," Riker joked. "You don't have to wear a dress."

"Well, it could be worse," Geordi said, turning his VISOR in the direction of Beverly and Deanna. "Ferengi females aren't allowed to wear any clothes at all."

"So?" Troi asked, smiling. "On Betazed, no one would ever think of wearing clothing to a wedding."

# Chapter Two

THE BRIDGE OF THE *FANG* steamed slightly, but not enough to obscure from Kakkh the sight of his second-in-command, Gar, picking his way along the ridged floor.

The G'kkau liked heat, humidity, and near darkness, more or less in that order, and designed their battleships accordingly. The control bridge of the flagship was very low, with a ceiling that followed the spherical curvature of the ship's hull, making a huge inverted shallow dish that met the floor at the edges. G'kkau crew members stood in a scattered pattern around the bridge, reptilian heads down as they smelled and watched the displays set in the slimy floor. Their scaly bellies slid over the viscous yellow goo coating the solid duranium tiles. From time to time one or another of them touched raised controls on the floor with a clawed forelimb, and the taste of the air would change slightly as new information was emitted.

Kakkh flicked his tongue out to read the air, hot and still and thick with the smells of the chemical indicators. He regretted that the humans were so thoughtless as to fail to transmit olfactory data along their communications channels; Kakkh would have liked to have sniffed Picard's fear or resolve. How could he tell anything about an entity's intentions only from its sight and sounds? Their useless transmissions were more proof, as far as he was concerned, that humanoids were a treacherous breed that deserved to be destroyed.

"Master." Gar stood beside Kakkh's raised mound in the center of the bridge, a scarlet communications gel cupped between three talons. "Our contact among the Pai has opened a channel from the planet's surface and asks for a moment of your time."

"Hah," Kakkh snarled. "At last."

Gar dropped the gel into a lubricated depression in the floor. An oval screen between Kakkh's forelimbs flamed into life, and Gar crawled to one side so they both could see it. Kakkh had to squint against the brilliance of the tiny image, that of a humanoid male dressed in multicolored robes. What Kakkh could see of the human's surroundings looked dry and painfully bright. And probably cold.

"The sooner we exterminate these people and reshape their world," Kakkh muttered, "the better." Then he switched on the automatic translator with a flick of his tail. "Greetings," he said.

The human snapped shut the paper fan he had been fiddling with. "Noble dragons, I give you welcome." The man bowed, just low enough to seem a calculated insult even to the G'kkau who, being quadrupeds, did not normally bow.

"I cannot wait to eat this one," Gar said in an undertone.

Kakkh only curled a warning talon as he responded to the man. "Is everything on schedule?"

"Oh yes," the Pai male said, sounding quite shocked at the suggestion that matters might not be in order. "Events like this cannot be planned or changed overnight, you know. The wedding is to take place tomorrow morning, just after sunrise. In fact, the wedding feast begins in mere moments, honored dragons."

"Except that there will be no wedding," Kakkh said. "Correct?"

"Naturally," the human said with a smile, baring what seemed to Kakkh to be singularly unattractive and ineffectual teeth. *The Pai have the jaws of a rodent,* Kakkh thought. *They were born to be prey.* "I will have killed the Dragon by then." His smile faded away. "I must admit, I have my regrets about this killing."

"You *what?*" Gar snarled.

Kakkh felt his throat frills swelling, but he controlled his response. "What is there to regret? You will rule the Dragon Empire," he lied.

"Well, yes." The human tapped his chin with one manicured fingernail. "But it troubles me that I must kill him without the honor of face-to-face combat."

Kakkh felt a pain in his forebrain beginning. "But

you have explained to us that the Dragon is a weak and honorless fool," he reminded the human. *By the fangs of my father,* Kakkh thought with some irritation, *surely this miserable creature could not be having second thoughts at this late date?*

"Oh, he is unworthy of this throne, that is understood. And yet . . ."

"It is your duty to save the Empire's honor," Kakkh said.

"Yes, you are quite right, revered lizards," the human said. "The honor of the realm demands a new Dragon, and I must be that man. I would, of course, wrest the Empire from him in direct battle," he stressed, seemingly as much to himself as to the G'kkau, "if that were only possible. Then he could die with honor. Alas, it cannot be."

"Why not?" Gar asked, squeezing onto the command mound. Kakkh could not blame him; Gar was younger than Kakkh, and less patient with the annoying foibles of mere mammals. "Why not just fight him now?"

The human's eyes widened in shock. "That would be *quite* impossible," he protested, clearly scandalized. "The wedding has been scheduled for a year. It must take precedence over any formal challenge."

"I see," Gar said. "A duel is inappropriate, but an assassination is acceptable."

"That is *completely* different," the man said with some hauteur.

*Enough of this,* Kakkh thought. It was important for the young to be exposed to the weaknesses of other species, but he could not risk antagonizing their human pawn so close to the fruition of their schemes.

The human's foolish assistance could spare the G'kkau considerable effort and casualties during the coming invasion. He hissed softly at Gar, who slithered away from the mound.

"Just so the Dragon dies before the wedding," Kakkh said. "As you have kindly informed us, the Dragon Empire's treaty with that decadent Federation will be final after the ceremony. That cannot happen." Kakkh swung his head from side to side, releasing a weary sigh. "It still amazes me that your ruler, once so wise and respected, would even acknowledge the existence of such barbarians."

"It scarcely seems possible," the human agreed, "but the Dragon is old and soft."

"He must be," Kakkh said, "to consider such an alliance. The honor and invincibility of the Dragon Empire is known throughout the universe. Why sully your magnificence by consorting with these foreign devils?"

"I understand and enter entirely into your sentiments in this matter," the human said. "Why, already one of their starships has violated our sacred borders. They orbit over Pai even now."

"The *Enterprise?*" Kakkh hissed sharply. As far as he knew, Picard's ship was the only Federation vessel in this sector, but he wouldn't put it past Starfleet to sneak in another ship under some transparent pretext.

The human snorted. "How should I know? The names of their ships are incomprehensible to me. Unlike *The Heavenly Dream of the Crimson Dragon's Eternal Life,* my own royal yacht."

A familiar throbbing grew stronger in Kakkh's forebrain. This human's persistent idiocy made his head hurt. He had to impress upon the Pai the necessity of his murderous mission. "The *Enterprise* cannot act before the treaty is signed. Kill the Dragon and you will preserve the sacred honor of your Empire. Your courageous blow will be remembered for all eternity."

"Oh, yes," the human said. Naked greed and ambition shone in his face.

"Do your duty, Dragon-to-Be," Kakkh coaxed. "Bring honor to your descendants for a thousand generations."

"For my sons," the human agreed readily, "and the sons of my sons." The human appeared convinced, at least for a moment. Then, to Kakkh's dismay as he watched, doubt overtook enthusiasm upon the human's pale, scaleless visage. His eyes shifted back and forth, as if suddenly fearful of observation. "I hope I do right to trust you," he said hesitantly. "Please do not be offended if I express certain reservations. You cannot deny that, even more so than the outsiders from the Federation, you are very different from us."

Kakkh drew himself up regally. "Are we not the dragons of your ancient lore?" he asked. "Are we not the very symbols of your Empire's honor?"

"I do not mean to impugn your honor, friend dragon," the human insisted. "I have no doubt that you are noble creatures, and have naught but the Empire's best interests at heart. It is merely that we have enjoyed the comfort of our solitude for so long that is difficult to reach beyond our own realm even to such venerable allies as yourselves."

"We have no desire to disturb your sacred traditions," Kakkh assured him. "Fear instead the wiles of the Federation, and strike now before they corrupt your Empire as they have contaminated so many other worlds before you. You must take action—for honor's sake."

The human nodded gravely. Kakkh thought he perceived renewed determination in the human's demeanor, but who could be sure where such worthless creatures were concerned? Nostrils flaring at the end of his snout, Kakkh sniffed the air, but smelled only the ordinary scents of a warship's bridge. He looked forward to tasting the odors of Pai itself, after they had eliminated the unsuspecting mammals and terraformed the planet to suit their own needs.

"I shall do as you say," the human said, visibly squaring his shoulders beneath his flowing robes. He bowed again, more deeply this time, and the screen went blank.

"Honorless dolt," Gar said. The younger G'kkau eased partly up the mound. His green scales reflected the dim interior lights of the bridge.

"When has any being not of the G'kkau ever shown honor?" Kakkh said. "They are all mere animals. Prey."

"What of the Federation?" Gar asked. "I have heard of this Picard. It is said he defeated the Borg, and more than once."

Kakkh had smelled the same reports, but was not overly concerned. Picard had a weakness: his precious Prime Directive. "He can do nothing until the treaty takes effect," he explained. "With the Dragon dead, the wedding will not occur and the treaty will be invalid. And after the Dragon is gone, nothing can stop our puppet from seizing control of the Empire.

Under his rule, the Pai will offer no resistance to our invasion and, in time, the traitor's death will be but one drop in an ocean of blood. And the famous Captain Picard, conqueror of the Borg, will be powerless to stop us."

Kakkh sniffed the air again. This time he smelled victory.

The turbolift door slid open and Beverly walked into Transporter Room One.

No, Picard decided: *walked* was too pedestrian a word. Dr. Beverly Crusher *glided* in, as beautiful and as exotic as the illustrations from a centuries-old children's book. She wore a full-length robe with huge sleeves that trailed on the ground as she entered. Beneath it were a series of other robes, their various iridescent fabrics showing at her neckline and at the openings of the sleeves. The outermost robe was pale peach and green, painted in an elaborate pattern of ribbon-entwined flowers and rings. Her thick red hair had been pulled back to the nape of her neck with a broad painted ribbon that fluttered as she moved. Her eyes were startlingly dark against her luminous skin. In one hand, she carried a small silk fan.

*Sometimes I forget just how attractive Beverly is,* Picard thought ruefully. *More fool I.* He stepped forward and applauded quietly. "You look . . . enchanting," he said. If they weren't minutes away from beaming down, he would have offered her his arm.

"Bravo," Riker said. He stood waiting, along with Data, at the foot of the transporter platform. Ensign McKenna, a blue-skinned Bolian female, was posted at the transporter controls, ready to beam the away team down to Pai. "Doctor, you'll outshine the bride herself. What gorgeous robes."

"Left over from my revival of *The Mikado*," she explained. "Judging from my historical research, all this is quite an ordinary rig for a female guest at a royal wedding. I expect I'll be solidly average down there."

"I had my doubts before," Picard said, "but I have to admit I was mistaken. This is a lovely touch, and one which the Pai are bound to appreciate."

Beverly laughed. "Maybe if they wore burlap I wouldn't have been so quick to volunteer." She inspected Picard and the others. "You gentlemen don't look so bad yourselves."

"Frankly," Picard said, scowling, "I always dislike wearing this . . . folderol." He gestured at his red-and-black dress uniform, his medals gleaming discreetly on a black shoulder.

Riker nodded sympathetically. "I know what you mean, sir. We're all more comfortable in our duty uniforms. By the way, are you sure we should be carrying phasers? It seems odd for a diplomatic mission."

"Indeed," Picard agreed. "However, the Pai insisted on dealing with warriors. According to our admittedly sketchy knowledge of Pai customs, a man of quality is expected to carry weapons at all times."

"If you say so," Riker said, shrugging.

"You think you're feeling awkward," Beverly said with a grin. "Wait until you see Deanna."

"She's on her way?" Riker asked.

"She's coming down with Worf, but she keeps tripping on her robes. Fortunately, Worf's there to assist her."

"That is . . . fortunate," Riker said. Picard heard the edge in his first officer's voice, despite Riker's best efforts to conceal it. The slowly simmering romantic triangle between Will, Worf, and Deanna was a source of private concern to Picard. So far the fledgling relationship between the Klingon and the counselor, along with her deep ties to Will Riker, had not interfered with the smooth running of the *Enterprise*. Picard hoped he'd never have to intervene in any of his officers' private lives, but he remained acutely aware of the potential for friction.

But that was a problem for another day. Right now, another union took priority, namely the crucial wedding of the Green Pearl and the Dragon-Heir. "They're going to have to be a little more brisk," he said a tad impatiently.

"Don't look so sour, Jean-Luc," Beverly said. "Weddings are supposed to be happy occasions, remember?"

"I will enjoy myself *after* the wedding," he said. "Until then, I am simply concerned that everything go well."

"Before every wedding everywhere," Beverly reassured him, "someone says that, and they mostly come off all right. There's rather more at stake here, but it's still just a wedding, after all." The transporter-room door opened behind her, making a slight *whish*ing noise. "Oh, here they are," she said, turning gracefully to see the newcomers.

Worf had elected to stay aboard to insure the security of the ship and to watch for the reappearance of the G'kkau warship, so he still wore his regular duty uniform with the broad metallic sash glittering over one shoulder, but Troi was as spectacular as Beverly had promised. Her robes were styled similarly to the doctor's, but the fabrics shimmered slightly and were colored deep blues and purples. She curtsied to the applause of the others.

"Thank you all," Troi said, still kneeling, then muttered something under her breath. Picard distinctly heard the word "hell" escape the counselor's lips.

"Something the matter?" Riker asked.

"You can stand back up now, Deanna," Beverly said simultaneously.

"I would if I hadn't stepped on my hem as I went down. Now I'll fall over if I try." Troi shifted slightly, and put out a hand to rebalance herself. "Damn," she swore again.

"Fascinating," Data observed. Picard wondered if he was intrigued by Deanna's costume, her language, or the physics involved.

Riker stepped forward to assist Troi, but Worf was already closer to her. "Allow me, Counselor," the Klingon said. He caught her arms and lifted her bodily, causing her feet to clear the floor by a couple of centimeters, before he set her upright.

"Thank you, Worf," she said. Riker stood by stiffly.

Picard decided to defuse any tension even before it began. "Mr. Worf," he said, all business. "Please report to the bridge. If anything resembling a G'kkau vessel shows up on our sensors, I want to know about it immediately."

"Understood," Worf said. The door *whish*ed open and he marched out of the transporter room. Picard and the rest of the away team took their places on the platform. Troi stumbled slightly stepping onto the cell. She tugged up the hem of her robes with obvious exasperation.

"The more I try to navigate in this thing," she commented, "the more I appreciate nude weddings."

*This mission is not getting off to a good start,* Picard thought grimly. "Ensign McKenna, energize."

# *Chapter Three*

RIKER BLINKED HARD. Even though he had successfully materialized on Pai, the shimmer of the transporter beam was still affecting his eyes. The large chamber in which he found himself glittered and twinkled with complex patterns of colored sparks that made his head swim.

"Oh, my," Beverly said. "I should have dressed up."

No, Riker realized suddenly, it wasn't the transporter; it was the room. Every available surface had decorative patterns carved or painted or embossed or enameled onto it. White satin hangings adorned with brightly painted images of birds and flowers covered the walls. Polished porcelain tiles, elaborately embellished, covered the floor, which was impeccably clean and pristine; Riker could not see a single scuff mark marring its shining surface. Glancing up at the ceiling, he saw the coils of a dragon, at least ten meters long, apparently carved from a single, gigantic piece of solid ivory. *They had to have used a replicator to generate that much ivory,* he thought. *No living creature has a tusk that huge. At least I hope not.* Every whisker, scale, and claw of the mythical beast had been executed in minute detail. Riker tore his gaze away from the dragon on the ceiling and looked around. Small pedestals made of dark, heavily lacquered wood rested in the corners of the chamber, supporting colorful china vases brimming over with roses, peach blossoms, and other floral arrangements. Even the air was suffused with rainbow-colored smoke from a series of paper lanterns that hung from the ceiling like chandeliers. The lanterns were painted with intricate designs, and the heavy scent of incense assaulted his nostrils, mingling with the odor of fresh flowers; for a second, Riker felt as though he'd been walled up inside a perfume factory.

The rich, layered look of the chamber was furthered by the solitary individual waiting for the delegation from the *Enterprise:* a man as gaudy as the room itself, dressed in brightly dyed silk robes that reached almost to the floor. He also wore a black, lacquered cap tied to his head. Riker noticed that the man did not appear startled by the away team's sudden materialization; he was evidently familiar with transporter technology, if only by reputation. He regarded the Pai official evenly, determined to make a good first impression. He hoped the robed man hadn't caught him gawking like a tourist; still, all this extravagantly ornamented elegance was hard to ignore. His eyes were still reeling from the instant sensory overload.

The Pai stepped toward them and bowed from the waist. He was a small, pudgy man almost lost in voluminous robes of emerald green trimmed with copper and pink. His face was Asian in appearance and clean-shaven except for a long, thin black mustache that dangled before both sides of his jaw. A thick ponytail hung, Manchu-style, from the back of his skull. He gripped a folded paper fan in one hand and wore, oddly enough, a monocle over his right eye. Both eyes held the anxious expression of a man whose life depended on catering to another's whims. "Welcome," he said. His voice was surprisingly high-pitched; Riker recalled that eunuchs had often served in high posts in imperial China. Frankly, Riker didn't want to know if the same applied on Pai.

Riker waited for the Pai to continue speaking, but, after a few moments, it became obvious that the man, whoever he was, had said all he was going to say.

Picard stepped past Riker, toward the little man. "Greetings. I am—" he began.

Unexpectedly, the man raised his hand in a gesture enjoining silence, and bowed again. The Pai's fingernails, Riker observed, were easily as long as the fingers they were attached to. Picard stepped back into the midst of the away team, saying softly over his shoulder, "What is *this* about, Data?"

The android's response was pitched low. "Little reliable information regarding the Dragon Empire's rules of etiquette is available, Captain. Nevertheless, a few conclusions might be drawn—"

"Try to be brief, Mr. Data," Picard interrupted him. "This gentleman doesn't seem to mind the pause in proceedings, but it's hardly necessary to extend it."

"I think I may have the answer," Beverly whispered

from under the cover of her fan. "Initially at least, equivalent ranks might be expected to deliver formal greetings only to each other, which means you can't address a subordinate directly. Assuming, that is, that you are being held the equal in rank of the Dragon himself."

"Then who *is* supposed to speak to this gentleman?" Picard asked her.

"My best guess would be Will," she said.

"Me?" Riker said softly. "I didn't plan on giving a speech."

"Then you will have to improvise, Number One."

Riker gazed at the Pai official, who now exhibited the worried expression of a rabbit. He wondered momentarily how the man had deduced the captain's rank prior to any introductions. Then he realized that Picard's age and demeanor had no doubt quickly identified him as the leader of their party.

Back straight, head held high, and feeling only a little foolish, Riker walked toward the other man. The official bowed once more. Trusting his instincts, Riker bowed back, then began to speak. "Sir. I am Commander William Riker of the *Starship Enterprise*. In the name of the United Federation of Planets, and on behalf of Captain Jean-Luc Picard—" He paused, and Picard nodded at the Pai. "—I greet you and thank you for inviting us to join your festivities."

The man looked visibly relieved that the awkward social impasse had been overcome. "Welcome, welcome," he said effusively. "This humble one is privileged to extend the Dragon's hospitality to all the honorable and esteemed officers of the *Enterprise* . . . and to the ladies as well. This insignificant one is the Dragon's Grand Chamberlain, who has the small honor to go by the name Mu, granted to his grandfather a hundred summers ago after the unfortunate incident involving the *tan shui*. Please convey to your exalted captain my lowly salutations and devout wishes for his pleasure and satisfaction on Pai, Throneworld of the Empire, Jewel of the Solar System, Pride of the Nebula, Heavenly Treasure of the Universe, Principality of the Dragon-Heir, and Divine First Residence of the Revered and Illustrious Dragon."

Riker had to shut his eyes for a second. With all the ornate patterns covering the Pai's clothing, every move the man made seemed to strobe gently. Listening to the chamberlain's seemingly endless recitation of superlatives didn't help his disorientation; in fact, Riker couldn't help being reminded of Deanna's mother, Lwaxana Troi, Daughter of the Fifth House, Holder of the Sacred Chalice of Rixx, and Heir to the Holy Rings of Betazed. Lwaxana would fit right in here, he thought, considering the garish decor and ostentatious ceremony. Besides, he'd always figured her for something of a dragon lady.

"These are my fellow officers," Riker said, pointing out his companions. "Lieutenant Commander Data, Dr. Beverly Crusher, and Ship's Counselor Deanna Troi." The chamberlain regarded Data curiously, then raised his eyebrows at the titles of both female officers. Rather than bowing, he gave both Troi and Crusher a hasty and rather embarrassed-looking tip of the head. *Looks like Beverly was on target,* Riker surmised, *regarding sex roles on this planet.* Mu didn't seem to know what to make of the two women; he swiftly turned his attention to Riker and Picard.

"Please grant me the honor of guiding you to the

divine presence of the Dragon," he said, bowing deeply. Mu continued to bow while backing toward a wide, gilded arch at the far end of the chamber. Riker took the lead as the Starfleet officers followed Mu toward the door. The spacious chamber was wide enough for ten to walk abreast, but the crew fell into pairs to make a stately and disciplined entrance. Picard walked beside Riker.

"Is he going to back all the way to the arch?" Deanna whispered from behind Riker. "Still bowing?"

It appeared so. The chamberlain appeared to be engrossed in studying the porcelain floor tiles as he led them across the room. Approaching the arch, Riker heard music coming from a short distance away. The tinkle of copper bells mingled with the twang of some sort of string instrument to produce an exotic melody that reminded him of a traditional Chinese restaurant he'd once visited on Deep Space Six. As a rule, Riker preferred classic Earth jazz and blues, but he had to admit that this music fit the colorful Oriental decor.

Looking around, he found it easy to imagine that he had somehow been transported through time and space to the Forbidden City in Peking during the height of the Ming or Manchu dynasties. Riker had to remind himself that the historical feel of his surroundings did not rule out the presence of advanced technology; many cultures chose to keep their high-tech hardware unobtrusive and out of sight. Even in the twenty-fourth century, not every locale resembled the bridge of a starship.

Blue-tinted smoke curled in tendrils through the

doorway, smelling as heavy and sweet as cheap Ferengi potpourri. Mu hesitated at the very brink of the exit, then sighed and took a deep breath. Head down, his gaze still glued to the ornate floor, the chamberlain addressed Riker in a low voice. "Honored Commander, I was not going to speak further of your lovely ladies, but I find I must."

"Please," Riker said, anticipating trouble.

"By tradition, no women are allowed at a state banquet of this nature, except for entertainers. It would be inappropriate to the dignity of the occasion. And yet these women are, as you say, officers and thus must be considered honored guests."

"They *are* officers, sir," Riker said firmly. He glanced at Picard. The captain's face was stern.

"If you say so," the chamberlain agreed hastily. "Then of course they must attend. I will have someone escort them and your Lieutenant Commander Data to a small table—"

"Near the kitchen," Troi murmured.

"—not unduly far from the celestial magnificence that is the Dragon. Through this door, if Lord Commander Riker would condescend so completely to honor us all (not to mention his exalted master Captain Picard), the Dragon awaits their honorable presence."

Riker was annoyed at the chamberlain's assumption that Data and the two women were entitled to less honorable treatment. Still, he was reluctant to raise a fuss before the captain could even lay eyes on the Dragon himself. He remembered the G'kkau warship lying in wait somewhere within the Dragon Nebula and concealed his irritation. *Sorry, Deanna,* he thought, recalling his own humiliating experiences on the matriarchal world of Angel One, *I know how you must feel.*

"We will be the honored ones," Riker said. "After you, Captain."

Picard found himself facing an enormous courtyard easily five times as large as the chamber they had beamed into. A flight of shallow marble steps led to a wide pavilion bordered on all four sides by vermilion towers capped by conical roofs painted a bright and sunny shade of yellow. Ming yellow, Picard realized: the sacred color of the ancient Chinese emperors. Each floor of the towers had an overhanging yellow roof, stacked atop each other in descending size, growing smaller and smaller as they approached the sky. More painted paper lanterns hung from the lower roofs, bestowing light upon the sumptuous scene before Picard. Bronze incense burners, the size of warp engines, rested at both ends of the stairway, turning the warm night air faintly blue. The floor of the courtyard was paved with reddish bricks of terra cotta, except where a rectangular marble frieze had been embedded in the exact center of the yard; the frieze depicted a dragon mating with a phoenix. A fertility symbol, Picard guessed; appropriate for a wedding banquet, if a little graphic in its presentation for his tastes.

Two rows of tables were placed on the right and left sides of the pavilion, leaving a wide space open between them. Female musicians, modestly attired in satin gowns buttoned to their necks, performed in the opening, standing at the four corners of the dragon frieze. Dozens of guests knelt behind the tables on padded cushions. Dressed much like the chamberlain, the guests ranged in age from young men to wizened elders, but all looked proud and prosperous. Picard assumed the men, guests at an imperial wedding, to be the leaders of the Empire: judges, scholars, dignitaries, and their sons. Their robes looked like the finest silk, adorned with intricate embroidery. None of the men wore yellow, however; that color, Picard recalled, was reserved for the Emperor and his heirs.

There was much yellow at the opposite side of the courtyard, facing Picard. A long dais, draped in golden silk, had been erected at the top of another flight of marble steps. Huge jade dragons mounted on marble pedestals flanked the dais; the dragons had been carved rearing up on their hind legs, their forelimbs reaching out to claw the smoky air. Glancing upward, Picard saw, above the golden rooftops of the surrounding towers, the Dragon Nebula itself: a wisp of violet mist speckled with stars. Picard looked again at the dais, where four men sat awaiting him. Even across the impressive length of the courtyard, he could see that three of the men wore robes of yellow.

A servant, his dark plait of hair trailing down his back, led Data, Troi, and Beverly away. Picard watched as the women and the android were guided along a gallery to his right, beneath the overhanging eave of the eastern tower. Soon they disappeared into the shadows behind one of the huge jade dragons.

Mu clapped his hands loudly, and the music came to a sudden stop. Clutching their instruments, which included a harp and two flutes, the musicians scurried out of sight, leaving the center of the courtyard unoccupied. "Please," the chamberlain said with yet another bow, "follow me." Head bowed, he walked down the steps and into the courtyard. Picard and Riker marched a few steps behind him.

As they passed by the seated guests, each mandarin and soldier would bow until his head rested on the table before him. "Extraordinarily flexible, it seems," Picard whispered to Riker, "despite all the robes."

"Perhaps," Riker speculated, "the fanciness of the robes indicates the status of the wearer. If so, these are all highly esteemed gentlemen."

Picard looked at Riker, his only ornaments the tiny pips on his dress uniform's collar. "I trust they will not think us the least popular men in the Federation."

Less than a yard away from the foot of the dais, Mu suddenly dropped to floor, lying flat on his belly atop the polished bricks. Picard hoped he and Riker were not expected to abase themselves in the same way. For the moment, he chose to remain standing before the dais.

In a voice surprisingly loud for one whose face was pressed against the floor, the chamberlain said, "Most excellent and exalted Dragon, most estimable Heir and estimable Second Son, honorable Lord Lu Tung, allow this insignificant one to introduce to you His Excellence Lord Captain Jean-Luc Picard of the *Starship Enterprise,* the honorable Lord Commander William Riker. And other, er, officers," he finished vaguely and gestured in the general direction of the jade dragon. Glancing over, Picard saw Beverly and the others being seated at a small table lurking inconspicuously in the shadow beneath a gilded rooftop. Caught by the sudden swivel of heads in their direction, Beverly brought up her fan to conceal her face while Troi visibly struggled to sit down without tripping over her robes. Data, unflappable as ever, bowed to the assembled guests before sitting.

Every head in the courtyard slowly swiveled back to regard Picard and Riker. "Lord Captain, Lord Commander," the chamberlain continued his introductions, "His Excellent and Exalted Majesty, the Dragon Emperor of the Dragon Nebula and Environs. Chuan-chi, the estimable First Son and Heir to the Dragon Empire and Keeper of the Throne Planet of Pai. Kan-hi, the also estimable Second Son. The honorable Lord Governor General Lu Tung."

"Bring them forward," a voice from the dais said imperiously. Picard easily identified the Dragon by both his age and the extravagance of his robes. The ruler of the Dragon Empire was, like his vizier, a small round man. A full beard, white as snow, partially concealed a face that fell easily into laugh lines. "Now, Mu!" he added in a much sharper tone; his visage fell as easily into a horrible scowl. Swaddled in heavy robes of yellow silk, embroidered with gold and silver thread, the Dragon resembled a gilt statue of a dissolute and irritable Buddha.

The chamberlain lifted his head from the floor. "Most Excellent and Exalted One . . ." he began.

"What are you doing down there?" the Dragon interrupted him. "Looking for something? Get up, get up. And have them bring stairs for the gentlemen. Sometime tonight would be nice." He glared at Mu, who scrambled hastily to his feet and vanished into the shadowy recesses of the western tower. He returned with a pair of servants clad in simple blue garments. The men brought a set of portable stairs over to the dais. Then they abased themselves as

Picard and Riker ascended. "Sit, sit," the Dragon said enthusiastically.

The dais was furnished with six couches laid out in a horseshoe, its open end facing the floor. Two couches stood free. Picard seated himself gingerly on the one beside the Dragon. Riker found a place nearer a younger man whom Picard assumed to be one of the Dragon's two sons. "Excellence," Picard began, relieved to be able to speak at last, "I am honored to extend the greetings of the entire Federation to—"

"So, Picard, hmmm?" the Dragon broke in. "I have heard good things about you. You are a true warrior and a man of honor. Good, good. You look like a warrior. I told those soft courtiers at your Federation, those old women who chat ceaselessly over subspace, that I wanted a warrior here, someone who would understand my side of things, a real man. You look one, yes?" The Dragon tapped his own balding pate. "Lots of thoughts, hmmm? Lots of experience makes the follicles die. We are men of the world, you and I."

"I expect we will find we have much in common," Picard began again, "as do the Federation and—"

"Indeed," the Dragon interrupted. "I look forward to hearing your poem."

"Poem?" Picard echoed, caught off-guard. "I'm afraid I don't understand."

"The wedding poem, of course," the Dragon said. "It's traditional."

*I'm sure it is,* Picard thought, making a mental note to worry about it later. *Just one more thing my briefing left out.* "As I was saying, Excellence, the Federation and the Dragon Empire share many interests—"

Scowling, the Dragon tilted his head toward the

courtyard. "Why is there no music?" he said abruptly. "Mu!"

The chamberlain approached the foot of the dais. "Most Excellent and Exalted One?"

"Start the entertainments again. Are we to sit here like peasants?"

The chamberlain flinched visibly, then clapped his hands together. Almost immediately, the four musicians returned to their posts and commenced playing. They were followed by a ten-meter-long, dancing dragon made of brightly dyed paper and cloth; at least a dozen performers operated the dragon from beneath its fiery red coils. The dragon capered back and forth across the courtyard to the accompaniment of the music of bells, flutes, and harp.

The Dragon smiled with satisfaction. "Much better," he sighed. "Allow me to introduce to you my humble eldest son and heir, the eager bridegroom: Chuan-chi."

The Heir sat between Picard and Riker. *Eager* was not the word Picard would have used to describe him. Chuan-chi looked to be in his early forties, tall and thin, with a large nose and, currently, a sour expression that might indicate indigestion. A school of scarlet fish, of over a hundred exotic breeds, were embroidered on his yellow robes.

"Gentlemen." Chuan-chi sounded as dyspeptic as he looked. He brought his hands together and bowed, with the air of a man submitting himself for a painful and humiliating physical inspection. "You bring honor to my father's palace."

As the formal introductions had apparently been concluded, Picard assumed he could now speak freely. Certainly, the Dragon himself did not seem to be standing on ceremony. "The honor is all ours," Picard said to the Heir, "and my congratulations on this happy occasion."

"Happy for the Federation no doubt," Chuan-chi replied. There was no mistaking the frosty edge to his voice. Did the Heir disapprove of the treaty binding the Empire to the Federation, Picard wondered. That could be a problem, depending on the extent of his influence over his father.

"My second son," the Dragon said, "and a vexation in my old age: Kan-hi." The vexation in question was a beardless youth, no older than twenty, sprawled indolently on a couch opposite his brother. The young prince was handsome enough, but his hair was disheveled and his yellow robes in some disarray. He saluted Picard with a crystal goblet almost overflowing with red wine. "You must forgive my esteemed brother, Captain," Kan-hi said. "He is constitutionally incapable of appreciating his own good fortune."

Chuan-chi glared at his younger brother. Picard could tell there was little love lost between the Dragon's sons. "Enough!" the Emperor said brusquely. He shook his head and rolled his eyes heavenward. "A willful and disobedient child," he explained to Picard. "It is my own fault. His mother was my favorite concubine. I doted on her and she spoiled him in turn. Still, I delude myself that he might someday still bring honor to his illustrious ancestors."

Picard was unsure how to respond to the Dragon's open disapproval of his own son. "We are all willful in our youth," he volunteered, hoping to alleviate the tension. "Isn't that so, Number One?"

"I'm sure I gave my father plenty of cause for aggravation when I was that age," Riker said, grinning roguishly. "Still do sometimes."

Kan-hi, the object of the discussion, appeared unembarrassed. "You sound like a man after my own heart, Commander Riker," he said. "Perhaps you should join our celebrations after the banquet, the Penultimate Bestowing of the Undomesticated Seeds."

"The Penultimate Bestowing of the Undomesticated Seeds?" Riker asked, somewhat taken aback by the flowery terminology.

"Yes," Kan-hi explained, "the traditional last revels offered to an unmarried man on the eve of his wedding. Heaven knows," the prince said, staring glumly into the ruby depths of his wine goblet, *"someone* ought to enjoy himself tonight."

"My esteemed brother does himself a disservice," the Heir said sarcastically. "I have no doubt he will acquit himself well at the festivities; drunken debauchery is an art for which is he has shown much talent and aptitude."

"You ungrateful, cold-blooded—!" Kan-hi exclaimed. He started to rise angrily from his couch, but a heavy arm fell upon his shoulders, pressing the offended prince back into the waiting cushions. The arm belonged to the squarely built man seated beside Kan-hi. Unlike the Dragon and his sons, this man was clad in robes of green and blue, although the fabrics seemed no less rich and expensive than the royal gold of the Dragon. He looked at the Dragon and coughed loudly.

"Oh, yes," the Dragon said. "How could I forget? Captain, Commander, permit me to introduce my loyal and trusted subject, Lord Lu Tung, happy father of the beautiful bride."

Seated beyond Kan-hi, as far from the Dragon as possible, Lu Tung looked anything but happy. He appeared only slightly older than his future son-in-law, his dark beard and mustache peppered with gray. He had piercing eyes half-hidden under thick, frowning eyebrows, and a face as closed and unreadable as any Vulcan that Picard had ever met. How, he wondered, did Lord Lu Tung really feel about marrying off his only daughter to the son of the man he had so recently tried to depose? Would he be content to see his grandchild ascend the throne he had failed to conquer by force? Looking at Lu Tung's flat, emotionless expression, Picard wished that Deanna were close enough to consult. Perhaps the counselor's empathic abilities could determine just how "loyal and trusted" the Dragon's former adversary now was.

Indeed, there seemed to be all manner of personal undercurrents, and volatile emotions, simmering barely beneath the surface of the diplomatic pleasantries being exchanged upon the dais. Was it even possible, he mused, to unite the Pai in time for them to join the Federation—and resist the voracious depredations of the G'kkau? Diplomacy, he reminded himself, was often ten percent issues and ninety percent personalities; he had frequently managed to achieve a negotiated settlement between even more hostile and demonstrative parties. He wished, however, that he had a better idea of everyone's personal agendas. He would have to listen very carefully to everything that was said and, perhaps more important, left unsaid.

He and Riker exchanged greetings with Lord Lu Tung, who was polite but stiff in his replies. Then Riker attempted, with some difficulty, to engage the Heir in small talk while Picard turned his attention to the Dragon. Given Chuan-chi's evident distrust of the Federation, Picard was glad he would be otherwise occupied when Picard attempted to bring up the subject of the treaty. He didn't envy Riker, though; Chuan-chi struck Picard as a singularly stuffy and humorless individual. He felt a twinge of sympathy for the unlucky bride.

It felt odd, in fact, to be attending a wedding banquet at which the bride was not present. And yet, he recalled, even societies less male-centered than the Pai often kept the bride and the groom separated until the moment they took their vows. Picard wondered if Chuan-chi had ever laid eyes upon the Green Pearl of Lu Tung.

"Excellence," Picard said to the Dragon, speaking softly in hopes that the Heir would not hear their conversation. "I fully believe that the signing of the treaty will be just the beginning of a long and fruitful partnership between the Dragon Empire and—"

"At last! Food!" the Dragon bellowed. "I thought Mu was trying to starve me to death." Two more servants approached the dais, bringing the first of what seemed an endless series of tiny lacquered trays to the small tables beside each of the men.

Picard looked down at his tray, which was crowded with dozens of miniature plates and bowls. The foods were all charmingly presented, garnished with flower blossoms and small fish no larger than minnows. There were no utensils, so, following the example set by the Dragon, Picard used his fingers to pick up a tiny piece of what looked like cake and brought it to his mouth. The Dragon watched him expectantly.

Picard almost gagged at the taste. His was a palate trained by years in Starfleet to try anything, from live Klingon *gagh* to Ferengi grubs, and to find its merits, regardless of cultural preconceptions about what constitutes edible food. But this was bad, *really* bad: bitter and gamy and nasty. Even aware of the Dragon's eyes upon him, it took all his training to manage to swallow a bite.

"Ah, you like?" the Dragon said, beaming. "Extraordinary, is it not?"

Picard took a deep drink of his wine; in accordance with ancient Chinese tradition, the drink was both warm and strong, with a distinct resiny taste, but it failed to wash away the foul aftertaste of the noxious morsel. "Yes," he managed at last, "it is certainly that. What is it?"

"A great delicacy. Thousand-year-old *lao shu.*" Picard felt obliged to take another bite and swallowed heavily. On top of the awful taste, he now noticed the disgusting texture of the thing, which succeeded in being gritty and slimy at the same time.

"Quite so," Picard said with difficulty. "I am not familiar with your *lao shu.* An animal, I take it." His Universal Translator had been stumped for a more descriptive synonym.

"It is a small beast, native to Pai, so big—" The Dragon held his hands a few inches apart to demonstrate the size; Picard noted the Emperor's overlong fingernails, which made the vizier's elongated nails look trimmed. "—not including the tail. Much like your rat, but with gills. We take a small *lao shu* and bury it for a millennium in an earthenware pot packed with spiced preservatives. When we dig it up, it has dissolved into this delightful substance." He pointed a nail at the half-eaten cake in Picard's hand. "You like it?"

"It is quite delicious," Picard said, perjuring himself without hesitation. Given a choice, he would have rather eaten a Denebian slime devil.

The Dragon laughed and reached across to slap him on his back. "I see you are a man of no little refinement! Excellent! I have too few people to share these gourmet delights with. You will not believe this, but most people, including my own sons and my most educated mandarins, would sooner die than eat *lao shu*. Can you imagine that?"

"I am trying to," Picard said.

"Mu!" the Dragon hollered. As if by magic, the chamberlain popped into sight again.

"Yes, Most Excellent and Exalted One?"

"Our guest is a true connoisseur. Inform the high chef of this. Command him to exert himself for the captain's supreme delectation. Only the most exotic of repasts are worthy of his rarefied sensibilities."

*I don't like the sound of this,* Picard thought. "Really, Your Excellence, there is no need to go to any extra trouble on my account."

"Nonsense!" the Dragon said, dismissing Picard's objections with a wave of his hand. "It is my pleasure . . . no, it is my great good fortune to have this unlooked-for opportunity to finally share the highest refinements of Pai cuisine with someone capable of appreciating them." He patted his generous belly. "Oh, Captain, the sublime, unfathomable tastes we two shall savor this night . . . !"

Picard's heart sank, perhaps to console his apprehensive stomach. "Of course," he agreed. "If that is your pleasure." He peered at the remains of the *lao shu* and tried to estimate the minimum number of gulps required to finish it off. Even one more seemed too many. *Starfleet expects every officer to do his duty,* he reminded himself. Valiantly, he took another bite.

As the morsel worked its way past his gag reflex, he spoke again, hoping to turn the discussion to more serious matters: "Excellence, earlier you stated that you wished to speak with a warrior, someone who could fully understand your concerns."

"Quite so," the Emperor said. Perhaps, Picard thought, the Dragon would now broach the subject of the G'kkau; he was eager to discuss the Empire's defenses. "Those Federation mandarins are all very well, but soft. I wanted to be able to hammer out the last of our agreement with another fighting man."

*Hammer things out?* Picard grew more worried. "My understanding is that the treaty is already final, awaiting only the wedding itself to take effect."

"Well, yes, that is what the clerks and bureaucrats would no doubt like to believe—oh, well done, sirs!" Down on the courtyard floor, the dancing paper dragon had advanced to acrobatics, capturing the Dragon's attention. The head of the dragon, complete with bulbous eyes and long plastic fangs, had just jumped through a loop composed of its own tail and hindquarters. Propelled by the athletic legs of the concealed performers, the coils of the dragon formed increasingly intricate designs above the marble frieze embedded in the courtyard. It was a wonder that the mock dragon did not tie itself into knots, or else trip over its many pairs of humanoid feet, but to Picard the spectacular stunts were merely an unwanted distraction from the business at hand.

"Regarding the treaty," he said, "if there are any details I can clarify for you . . ." He hoped the Dragon's concerns were not too complicated. There wasn't time for another round of extensive negotiations, not with a G'kkau warship already prowling the Dragon Nebula.

"Oh, the details are fine, I'm sure," the Dragon said, not taking his eyes away from the feats of the acrobatic dragon. "It's the treaty itself that bothers me."

Picard felt success slipping away, along with peace and safety for the Pai. "How so?" he asked.

The Dragon finally turned and met Picard's gaze. "There is no honor in this treaty," he stated. "Upon reflection, I fear that joining your Federation, as worthy as it doubtless is, can only compromise the honor of the Dragon Empire and my own throne."

Picard resisted an urge to sigh wearily. It was clear he would have to reargue the Federation's case from first principles if he was to complete his mission on Pai. Briefly, he wondered if anyone in particular had placed these doubts in the Dragon's mind prior to his arrival. The Heir? The Second Son? Lord Lu Tung? The chamberlain? At the moment, it didn't matter; he had to change the Dragon's mind quickly, before the wedding tomorrow.

"Many races and worlds have found the Federation an honorable and effective mechanism for mutually beneficial cooperation," he told the Dragon.

"I am quite certain they have," the Dragon agreed amiably, "but those worlds are not, after all, the Dragon Empire." He drew himself up proudly. "Since the days of our ancestors the Empire has flourished beneath the sacred Dragon Nebula without any dependence upon other worlds. Through our ancient and venerable traditions we have achieved the very apex of civilization. Any alliance or association with lesser states can only diminish us. No offense intended, of course. We are happy to have you as our guests and to share with you the blessings of this, the most glorious and magnificent realm in the history of the universe." A look of concern crossed the Dragon's face. "In the past, I fear, we may have been too miserly with the fruits of our glory. No more! I look forward to treating you to more of the pleasures of Pai."

As if on cue, the servers returned and laid another tiny plate upon his small table. Picard barely glanced at the contents of the plate; he had to convince the Dragon of the seriousness of the situation.

"Excellence," he said, lowering his voice, "forgive me if I speak bluntly, but it is only concern for your people that compels me to be the bearer of bad news." He fixed the Dragon with a solemn stare, determined to hold on to the Emperor's full attention. "Starfleet has reason to believe that a G'kkau invasion of Pai is imminent, perhaps only a matter of hours."

The look the Dragon gave him reminded Picard of an indulgent grandfather humoring a small child. "The G'kkau, yes. Your people have spoken of them before. No doubt these nasty lizards have proved bothersome, even dangerous, to other races. But, Captain, look around you. This is the *Dragon Empire*. What have we to fear from these scaly barbarians?"

"I fear you underestimate the G'kkau," Picard objected. "It is no reflection on your honor to admit that you may face a genuine threat to your people and your way of life."

The Dragon shook his head. "No more gloomy words, Captain. This is a wedding, a joyous occasion, and you are an honored guest. Relax, enjoy yourself. Here: try this raw *kao tzu.*"

Picard eyed the pale, fleshy lumps on the plate. *"Kao tzu?"*

"It is like your slugs, but with more flavor."

## Chapter Four

"MY GOD," BEVERLY MARVELED, "look at this place. It's like going back in time."

Being an android, Data could not share in the doctor's enthusiasm, but he did find their present surroundings to contain numerous points of interest. He sat between Beverly and Counselor Troi on a low couch behind one of the great jade dragons looking out over the courtyard. He listened to the music, compared it against 375 similar melodies composed over the last 2,452 years, speculated on the composition of the performers' instruments and the effect the choice of physical materials had upon the quality of the sound, performed an olfactory analysis of the incense pervading the atmosphere and judged it to be both nonintoxicating and harmless, admired the acrobatic skill of the dancers beneath the dragon facade,

observed discreetly the captain's interactions with
the Emperor, memorized the faces and costuming of
every attendee at the banquet, and calculated the
odds of successfully completing their mission, which,
judging from the captain's expression and body language, were diminishing by the minute. Simultaneously, he socialized with Beverly and Deanna.

"In fact," he responded to the doctor's observation,
"this setting only mimics the appearance of a traditional Chinese palace. Careful inspection reveals the
existence of an advanced technological infrastructure
supporting much deliberate artifice. The dragon costume, for instance, contains several components constructed from complex polymers, while the uniformi-
ty of tone produced by both flautists suggests that
their instruments were mass-produced. Furthermore,
the ambient temperature in the courtyard is identical
to that of the interior chambers, suggesting some form
of concealed heating apparatus; indeed, meteorologi-
cal conditions on the planet's surface, as observed
from the *Enterprise,* would indicate that the actual
outdoor temperature for this region of Pai should be
several degrees lower than the conditions we are
experiencing. In addition . . ."

"We get the point, Data," Troi interrupted gently.
"Pai technology is not as primitive as it appears.
Which stands to reason, of course; the Dragon Empire
would not qualify for Federation membership otherwise." A server came and laid several fresh dishes
before them, then disappeared back into the tower.
"Anyway," she continued, "this sort of formal occasion is hardly the best way to judge everyday life
on Pai. Ceremonial events tend to emphasize tradition over convenience. Even on Betazed, we'd *never*

think of serving a replicated meal at a state banquet, although my mother once . . . Damn!" She rescued the trailing end of her right sleeve from a dish on the low table beside their couch. "These big sleeves keep getting in the way. How do you manage to keep yours so clean, Beverly?"

"Practice," the doctor said, deftly lifting a sugared rice ball to her lips.

Troi gave her a dirty look, and tried to wipe a smear of sticky amber sauce off her robe. "Maybe this is the real reason Pai clothing is so heavily decorated," she said ruefully. "Stains don't show."

"That seems unlikely, Counselor," Data commented. "A high degree of ornamentation is displayed in almost all their artifacts, even when that ornamentation is so small as to be indiscernible, as with the chamberlain's monocle."

"His monocle?" Beverly asked.

"Yes," Data explained, "the metal ring containing the lens is engraved with a very detailed rendition of seventeen nightingale-like avians flying through a tropical forest. More indirect evidence of advanced technology: a laser would most likely be required to execute the engraving with such microscopic detail."

"Which you can see?" Troi said.

"Dr. Soong provided me with excellent eyes," Data said. He scanned the courtyard, observing and cataloging the many instances of elaborate decoration on both the furnishings and the diners' attire. "It is interesting. Most cultures, having reached this level of surface ornamentation, go into a backlash of sorts, when they begin to simplify, often to as great an extreme. I wonder when—" He stopped speaking suddenly, his attention caught by a sudden glint of light near the door through which the servers came and went.

Nearly invisible in the flickering glow of the paper lanterns, something small and silvery hung motionless in midair. Data estimated it was approximately 5.87402 meters away from where he now sat—and 8.00003 meters from the Dragon and the other personages upon the dais. He stood up slowly, being careful not to overturn the uneaten delicacies arranged around him.

"Data?" Troi asked. "Is anything wrong?"

"That is what I am attempting to determine, Counselor," he said, keeping his gaze fixed upon the tiny, floating object.

The device glinted again, and Data realized that it was turning itself, as if scenting the air for something. Or someone. He stepped toward it as it began drifting away from the eastern tower, gathering speed as it moved. The object was clearly aiming for someone on the dais. He eyed the angles and made some quick internal calculations. He did not wish to create a disturbance, but . . .

A servant, bearing a tray of steaming fruit jellies, stepped between Data and the object, blocking his view. "Please be seated," the servant began, "and enjoy these humble refreshments. They are called the Blessings of Summer's Last Rejoicing, and—"

There was no time to explain. Data seized the servant by his shoulders and swung him out of the way. Startled, the man stumbled backward, eliciting a cry of alarm from Troi as the Blessings of Summer's Last Rejoicing slid off his tray into her lap. "Data!

What in the world?" Beverly exclaimed, even as Data quickly located the mysterious device once more, hovering only 1.2488 centimeters from where he had last seen it.

Abruptly, it darted forward in a straight line for the dais and its occupants. Data noted its acceleration and reacted appropriately. He leaped away from his couch, past the looming jade dragon, and snatched the object from the air less than 3.6507 meters from the dais. Holding on to it carefully, he inspected the device: a finned, needle-tipped dart no more than .99998 of a centimeter long. It wiggled between his fingers, still struggling to jump free. He immobilized it by breaking off the bottom fin.

"Data?" Picard said loudly. Data removed his focus from the intercepted dart and evaluated the reactions of the captain and the others present to his unexpected actions. Had he been human, he suspected he might have been embarrassed by the commotion. Everyone in the courtyard was now looking at him, and many of the young men had risen angrily to their feet. He assumed they would not attack unless given an order to do so, but recognized that this assumption could not be considered irrefutable. The chamberlain was cowering in the shadows at the rear of the courtyard, evidently uncertain whether to intervene. The musicians, their performance interrupted, retreated with their instruments to the four corners of the courtyard, while curious faces peered out from beneath the disguise of the dragon. He glanced behind him and saw, with regret, that he *had* created a mess as a result of the necessary swiftness of his response. The displaced servant was kowtowing

frantically before Counselor Troi, apologizing—
almost faster than the Universal Translator could
accommodate—for the viscous red goo that was now
spattered all over her elegant indigo robes. Beverly
tried to help the unfortunate servant pick up the
pieces of three shattered plates, but that only seemed
to distress the man more. Interesting, Data thought.
He trusted that the two women were capable of
handling the situation on their own. He turned his
attention toward the dais.

"Your Excellency, esteemed gentlemen." He nodded politely at the rulers of the Empire. "Captain, I
must apologize for causing a disturbance. It was in an
effort to intercept this object." He held up the dart;
the crippled missile vibrated between his fingers. He
noted that a miniature asp had been engraved along
the narrow shaft of the dart, its venomous fangs
rendered in detail far too minute for the average
human eye to observe.

*Clearly,* he deduced, *the dart was of native origin.*

His analysis of the dart was interrupted by the
sound of high-pitched humming coming from somewhere beneath the missile's metal casing. The noise
was not unlike that of a phaser on overload. Data
hastily calculated the probability that a self-destruct
mechanism had been activated and concluded that it
would be wise to put some distance between himself
and the dart. Employing the full strength of his
artificial limbs, he hurled the dart straight up into
the sky. The humming grew louder and more shrill
as the dart ascended to an altitude of approximately 15.4682 meters before detonating overhead.
The bright red explosion consumed the dart entirely,

leaving not even ashes to fall back down to the floor of the courtyard. Curiously, some of the banquet guests applauded the explosion, perhaps assuming it to be part of the evening's entertainment. Data regretted the destruction of the dart before it could be fully examined. He also reminded himself to contact Geordi regarding his planned fireworks display; the explosion had suggested to Data several other pyrotechnic possibilities. Perhaps a deliberately induced phaser overload channeled into visible wavelengths . . .

Nothing like an assassination attempt to perk up an otherwise dull party, Picard thought. He had no doubt that an assassination was exactly what Data had prevented. But who, he wondered, was the dart's intended target?

With the Dragon's permission, the android had approached the dais and briefed Picard on his actions and observations. Data remained standing before the dais, awaiting further instructions from Picard, while Mu fretfully attempted to calm the rest of the banquet guests. "Please sit down. All is in order. There is nothing to see, nothing at all," he said over and over until the various soldiers and dignitaries appeared appeased. At his command, the dancing dragon resumed its performance, although few seemed interested anymore in the make-believe creature's caperings; all eyes stayed fixed upon the dais where Riker, Lu Tung, and the Dragon's two sons crowded around Picard, curious to hear more about the mysterious dart. Only the Emperor sat apart from the others, scratching his chin through his beard and eyeing Data with open fascination.

"Astounding!" the Dragon declared. At first Picard thought he was referring to the apparent attempt at murdering one of them; then he saw that the Dragon looked more interested in the golden-skinned android. "He moved so quickly! What manner of being is this?"

"Lieutenant Commander Data is a sentient artificial life-form," Picard explained quickly. He could understand the Dragon's curiosity—Data was a singularly unique individual—but he wanted to get to the bottom of this dart business as soon as possible. Were the G'kkau responsible somehow, or was this merely the result of some internal intrigue between the Pai themselves? Either way, it boded ill for his mission.

"A mechanism?" the Dragon said.

Picard nodded. "And a valued member of my crew."

"A mechanism of great value indeed," the Dragon agreed. He winked at Picard, grinning broadly through his beard. "Your Federation was wise to send him."

"So it would appear." Picard felt like he was missing something important in this exchange, but he was anxious to divert the Dragon from his apparent fixation on Data. "Excellence, might I call your attention to this rather disturbing incident?"

"Oh *that*," said the Emperor, sounding mildly annoyed at the intrusion of such an uninteresting subject into the conversation. "What about it?"

"According to Commander Data, the device he captured appeared to be a miniaturized flying syringe, probably remote-controlled. I wouldn't doubt that the tip was poisoned."

"Poison?" the Second Son exclaimed. He seemed genuinely stunned by the notion.

"What an appalling notion," the Dragon-Heir said. "Only a foreigner could conceive of such a thing."

The Dragon shook his head. "Really, Picard, I appreciate your concern, but I fear you are making too much of this. This little toy must be a prank, nothing more."

"A prank, Your Excellency?" Picard was puzzled by the Dragon's obvious lack of concern.

"What else?" the Emperor said jovially. "Why, I have it! One of my Heir's many friends could not wait for the formal banquet to conclude before launching the evening's rowdier festivities. No doubt the dart, if that's what it was, was tipped with some mild intoxicant or aphrodisiac. A bit premature, while we old men are still around, but nothing you need worry about."

"Are you sure about that, Excellence?" Riker asked. "Such an advanced weapon, just to deliver a love potion. That seems a bit . . . extreme."

"Oh, no!" laughed Kan-hi. "It's quite common at parties, and it would take strong dose of something to get my brother to loosen up."

"Silence!" the Dragon-Heir snapped, glowering at his younger brother. "Have you no respect for anything?"

"Not for a loveless marriage of convenience," Kan-hi said. "The Green Pearl deserves better than the likes of you." Picard was struck once more by the obvious enmity between the Dragon's two sons. He also noted that Lu Tung, the bride's father, remained silent throughout this exchange. What did he think of his daughter's future husband, not to mention the assassination attempt? Did Lu Tung intend to capture by stealth what he had failed to conquer by force?

"That is enough," the Dragon commanded. "You bicker like old women in front of our honored guests. My apologies, Captain Picard."

"No apologies are necessary," Picard said diplomatically. "Yet I would not dismiss this matter of the dart so lightly. How can you be sure that the weapon was genuinely poisoned?" He wished the missile had not destroyed itself so quickly. Dr. Crusher's tricorder could have determined in minutes the nature of the toxin contained by the dart. "For safety's sake, isn't it worth considering the possibility?"

"But, my dear captain," the Dragon protested, "there would be no honor in slaying a foe in such an underhanded manner. Even Lord Lu Tung, my esteemed former adversary, would never stoop to such cowardly tactics."

A backhanded compliment if ever there was one, Picard thought, but if Lu Tung took offense at the Dragon's remark, his face revealed no sign of it. "Indeed," he agreed. "Poison is not the way of the Pai, no matter who sits upon the throne."

"Not yet maybe," Kan-hi muttered, "but just wait until my brother is Emperor."

"You will be the first to know," Chuan-chi said ominously.

An angry look from the Dragon silenced them both. Frustrated, Picard realized that the Pai nobles were too caught up in their own personal feuds to take the assassination attempt seriously and that, without any physical evidence, there was no way to prove to them that the dart had been intended to kill someone upon the dais. Very well, he decided, if the Pai could not be bothered to protect themselves, then it was up to him and his crew to keep everyone alive and well until the wedding.

"Excellence," he addressed the Dragon. "Under the circumstances, I should like to summon Lieutenant Worf, my chief of security, to the palace to insure your safety." He was reluctant to remove Worf from the bridge when the location of the G'kkau warship remained unknown, but Geordi could always take charge of keeping an eye out for the *Fang*. With an assassin clearly on the loose in the palace, he preferred Worf here.

Unfortunately, the Dragon disagreed. "What?" he said indignantly. "Are you implying that I, the Divine Ruler of the Dragon Empire, cannot protect myself?"

"Of course not, Excellence," Picard said, "but a little extra caution at this most vital of junctures can only profit us all."

"Nonsense, Picard. This is a matter of honor. The Dragon Empire does not require the protection of outsiders such as your security chief. I expressly forbid you to bring this man here. You are my guest," the Dragon stated emphatically. "Please do me the courtesy of behaving as one."

*So much for that idea,* Picard decided, unwilling to provoke the Dragon any further. Perhaps later he could devise a pretext for beaming Worf down without offending the Emperor's acute sense of honor. For now, he would have to rely on the officers at hand.

"Excellence," he said, "some small business has come up which requires my attention. With your permission, I would like to confer with my officers in private."

"Right this minute?" the Dragon asked, incredulous. "Why, we haven't been served dessert yet. Trust me, Picard, I'm sure my chef has prepared something truly special for the two of us."

*I can hardly wait,* Picard thought glumly. "This will not take long. I look forward to resuming our meal shortly."

"Well, if you must, you must," the Dragon sighed. "I know too well the demands which befall men of our exalted position. Mu! Escort Captain Picard and his honored associates to the Hall of Supreme Harmony. Do not worry, friend Picard, I shall instruct the chef to hold dessert until your return. In truth, I've always thought candied *rahgid* eyes taste better cold."

The Hall of Supreme Harmony was a spacious chamber on the ground floor of the northern tower, not far from the courtyard where the banquet wore on. Hanging silk lanterns illuminated the walls, which were adorned with large blue glyphs of Chinese design. Picard guessed that characters probably spelled out ancient words of wisdom for the edification of the hall's visitors. The air smelled faintly of oranges, and he could still hear the harps and flutes of the musicians playing outdoors. The hall held no furniture, so the Starfleet officers remained standing upon the white polished floor.

"Mr. Data," Picard said. "From what you saw of the dart's trajectory, can you tell who was the intended target?"

"I am afraid not, Captain. At the point I intercepted the dart I could only determine that it was aiming for someone on the dais."

"It seems to me," Riker commented, "that the

Dragon would be the most likely target. Why settle for a prince when you can kill the Emperor himself?"

"You're probably right," Picard agreed, "especially since the Heir appears to oppose the treaty with the Federation. The death of the Dragon would effectively scuttle any chance the Pai have of joining the Federation before the G'kkau invade. Still, we can't take the chance we're wrong. We have to assume that everyone on the dais is a potential target, including you and me, Number One."

"Lu Tung and the two princes strike me as likely assassins as well," Riker said. He quickly filled in Troi and the others on the tensions among the wedding party. "None of them has an alibi. Anyone could have arranged to have that remote-control device launched during the banquet."

"Do you think the assassin will try again?" Beverly asked.

"Yes," Picard said, "and soon. Too much depends on tomorrow's wedding. The assassin will probably try to strike sometime tonight, which means we have to keep our eyes on all the suspects *and* the likely targets." Picard looked over his officers. "Number One, I think you should take Kan-hi up on his invitation to attend the Heir's private celebration tonight. That way you'll be in a position to protect both the Heir and the Second Son. Do you think you can manage to guard them under these circumstances?"

Riker shrugged. "It's basically just a bachelor party. How rough could it be?"

"Just the same," Beverly suggested, "let me give an anti-intoxicant. Then you'll be able to keep a clear head no matter how much heavy drinking you're expected to take part in."

"A good idea," Picard said. "Make it so." He reflected further. "And take Data with you, in case the princes separate. We want to keep a close watch on both of them."

"The bachelor party is a fixture of much human history and literature," Data said. "I look forward to observing the phenomenon in person."

"Just wait, Data," Riker said with a grin. "If this party's anything like some of the ones I've attended over the years, you're in for a memorable experience."

"Not *too* memorable, I hope," Troi said pointedly. Picard noted for the first time that her robes looked rather the worse for wear. The sleeves were dripping slightly, as though they'd been dunked in something, while a gooey red mess stained the front of the dark blue robe. If he hadn't known better, he might have thought she had suffered some gory injury to her midsection. The sticky red stain smelled faintly of strawberries, however, and Picard recalled the Blessings of Summer's Last Rejoicing, one of the few edible dishes he'd consumed all evening. Conscious of Picard's inspection, Troi blushed slightly as she turned to address him. "What about the Dragon himself? And Lu Tung?"

"I will personally look after the Dragon," Picard declared. "I need to spend more time with him anyway; unfortunately, he appears to be having second thoughts about the treaty. Even if we succeed in keeping him alive until tomorrow, there's no guarantee he'll sign the treaty unless I can persuade him to later this evening. Counselor, you will accompany me. Your empathic abilities may come in useful during our negotiations."

"Certainly, Captain," she said, "although perhaps I should change clothes first?" She glanced down at the crimson jelly soiling her robes.

"Just remove the outer robes," Beverly suggested. "There are enough overlapping layers in these outfits that you'll still be decently covered by Pai standards." She helped Troi slip out of the stained blue robe, only to discover that the strawberry jelly had soaked through the next two layers of clothing as well. By the time, they were finished, Troi was clad in merely a single violet gown that revealed rather more of the Betazoid's shapely figure than before, but was still more modest, Picard judged, than her usual skintight Federation uniform.

"Good enough to guard the Dragon," he said as Beverly bundled up the discarded robes and had them beamed back to the *Enterprise*.

"That still leaves Lu Tung," Riker pointed out.

"Yes," Picard said, "and that poses a difficulty. At the moment, I can't think of any excuse by which one of us could contrive to accompany him after the banquet. And, unless customs are wildly different on Pai than they are on Earth, I can't imagine he'll be attending his future son-in-law's bachelor party."

"Can't we just offer him protection outright?" Troi said.

Picard shook his head. "It would reflect poorly on his honor, he claims." Picard deliberated in silence while Beverly administered her hypospray to Riker. "The one good thing," he said finally, "is that Lu

Tung is possibly the least likely candidate for assassination. He has already lost the war, he is not in line for the throne, and, unless I'm missing something, his death would not affect the treaty. All in all, he's more likely to be the assassin than the target."

"Speaking of targets," Beverly said, "what about the Green Pearl herself? It's a horrible idea, but I can't think of a faster way of stopping a wedding than by killing the bride."

Picard scowled. Beverly was right. They had to assume the Green Pearl was in danger as well. He hoped Lu Tung would not go so far as to sacrifice his own daughter, but the G'kkau (and maybe even one of the princes) might have no such scruples. Certainly Chuan-chi seemed less than enthusiastic about marrying the Pearl. And as for Kan-hi . . . well, any child of the Heir and the Green Pearl would inevitably come between the Second Son and the throne.

But how could they manage to protect the Green Pearl? They hadn't even been allowed to lay eyes on her yet. Picard contemplated Beverly Crusher, so elegant and dignified in her formal robes. If anyone of them might be permitted to get close to the bride, it would probably be Beverly. "Dr. Crusher," he said, "perhaps we can persuade Lu Tung to let you visit the Green Pearl tonight?"

"Fine with me," she said, "but for what reason?"

"To attend to her, er, physical well-being," Picard said, improvising. "Heaven forbid she should fall ill the night before her wedding."

"That might work," Beverly said thoughtfully, "if you can persuade the Dragon and the others that I'm a qualified healer."

"You know," Riker broke in, "while I was chatting with the Heir it came out that the Green Pearl's mother died several years ago. Chuan-chi commented that it was, quote, 'unfortunate' that she did not have her mother to help prepare her for the wedding."

"Unfortunate for the Pearl, perhaps," Picard said, "but lucky for us. After we return to the banquet, I will helpfully volunteer Beverly's services as chaperone, surrogate mother, or whatever."

"And bodyguard," Beverly added. She took a deep breath to prepare herself. "I suppose this is the closest I'll ever come to being the mother of the bride. Who knows? Maybe this experience will come in useful if and when Wesley ever gets married, not that that's likely to happen anytime soon." She glanced back toward the lavish banquet. "I just hope he opts for something a little less elaborate."

The music from the courtyard came to a halt, and Picard heard a smattering of polite applause. "We had better get back to the banquet before the Dragon wonders what's happened to us." A grim expression came over his face. He did not relish the prospect of candied eyes, chilled or otherwise. Still, duty called and his much-abused taste buds had no choice but to obey. "Keep your eyes open," he reminded his officers. "A life, and the future of the Dragon Empire, is at stake."

The *Fang* drifted through the Dragon Nebula on its stealthy approach to Pai, all but its most basic systems shut down to prevent the flagship from being picked up by sensors on either the *Enterprise* or the planet itself.

"Master?" Gar said. "The traitor on Pai has contacted us again."

"It's taken him long enough," Kakkh hissed. "Very well. Put him through."

The screen between his forward claws bloomed into life. Kakkh beheld the pink, scaleless visage of their human pawn. He thought the Pai looked apprehensive, but it was hard to tell. These humans were impossible to read by sight alone. "Yes?" he demanded. "You have been a long time in contacting us."

"Ah, well," the Pai stammered. "There has been little to report."

"Little to report? You were going to kill the Dragon. Is he dead or not?"

"At this moment, I must confess, he still lives, although not for lack of any effort on my part."

"What?!" Kakkh snarled. "What happened?"

"I did my best," the man said, bristling slightly. "I programmed a venomous stinger to strike the Dragon during the banquet, but a mechanical man snatched it out of the air seconds before it could do its deadly work."

*The android known as Data,* Kakkh realized. He had studied the crew of the *Enterprise* extensively. *Damn the Federation! How dare they interfere with the plots of the G'kkau.* "Where are Picard and the others now?" he asked.

"They are meeting privately at this very moment— in the middle of the banquet, of all things. Astoundingly rude and inappropriate."

"Then how did you manage to leave?"

The noble simpered. "The gentle call of imperious

nature. Perfectly acceptable. Unlike the shocking conduct of those Federation buffoons—barbarians, if you ask me."

"I did not ask you," Kakkh snapped. He had lost all patience with this foolish human's babbling. "All I asked for is the death of the Dragon, and so far I have been disappointed in your efforts."

"If not for the unlikely appearance of Picard's artificial creature," the Pai noble emphasized, "the Dragon would now be dead. My plan was perfect."

"Not perfect enough," Kakkh said. "You have another plan, I assume."

"Naturally," the man said with what Kakkh guessed was a display of indignation. "My next scheme is already in motion. I am rather proud of it, actually; this attempt has a classical character, really, in keeping with the traditions surrounding an imperial wedding. . . ."

"I am not interested in the details," Kakkh interrupted. "Just the results. You have failed once. Do not do so again."

For once, Kakkh was gratified to see an unmistakable expression of fear come over the Pai's insufferably smug features. "I . . . I must return to the banquet," the traitor said, "before Picard returns and I am missed."

"Go," Kakkh said, "but do not forget your mission. The Dragon *must* die." With a savage sweep of his right forelimb, he cut off the communication. His eyes swiveled in their sockets, seeking out Gar. "We cannot wait much longer for this incompetent to fulfill his purpose. We will attack Pai tomorrow, and destroy their Empire whether or not the fool has killed the Dragon."

"The Federation starship is already there," Gar warned. "How will we deal with them?"

"They can do nothing without the Dragon's signature. It would be better if our pawn assumed control before the assault, but if we strike quickly enough there will be no time to conclude the treaty."

"True," Gar conceded. "But will not the *Enterprise* fight to defend its own people on the planet?"

"They cannot," Kakkh insisted. "Their Prime Directive renders them powerless. Besides, they are but one vessel and we have a hundred G'kkau warships. If they offer any resistance, we will obliterate them utterly."

A predatory gleam sparked in Gar's eyes. His inner eyelids twitched with excitement. Kakkh could smell the blood lust exuding from his officer's glands. "In that case," Gar said, "I hope they do resist."

His fangs clashed together, eager for fresh Federation flesh.

# Chapter Five

THE WEDDING BANQUET was winding to a close, and none too soon for Picard. The *rahgid* eyes had been just as foul as he'd feared, and several subsequent dishes had only troubled his digestion more. The Dragon seemed determined to put Picard's gustatory abilities to the ultimate test. He just hoped Beverly had something in her med kit to settle his stomach afterward.

Swollen, black clouds swarmed overhead, pouring down massive quantities of rain. At first, Picard had expected the banquet to be halted on account of the rain, but apparently the courtyard was protected from the weather by an invisible forcefield. Countless droplets of water collided with the field, then streamed away toward some hidden reservoir. He admired the grace and efficiency with which the Pai had coped

74

with their environment. For all their eccentricities, the Pai could be justifiably proud of their craftsmanship and obvious love of beauty. It would truly be a tragedy if the G'kkau reduced all this luxurious splendor to ruins as they had so many other civilizations.

Nearby, Riker and Kan-hi had struck up an involved and detailed conversation comparing the drinking games of Pai and Alaska, demonstrating with frequent swallows of something that steamed whenever a server refilled their cups. Picard was glad his first officer was bonding successfully with the younger generation of Pai nobles, although he grew ever more thankful for Beverly's foresight in shielding Riker against the effects of too much local alcohol. Chuan-chi, the dour bridegroom, occasionally made token efforts to contribute to the discussion, even if he obviously wished he were elsewhere. Picard suspected that the Heir was only going along with this "Penultimate Bestowing of the Undomesticated Seeds" business because tradition demanded it. Once again, he felt sorry for the unfortunate Pearl.

To his pleasant surprise, Lu Tung had readily accepted Beverly's offer to keep the Pearl company tonight. "My honorable wife, her mother, died many years ago," the former rebel explained, "and my . . . activities . . . the last few years have kept me far too busy to seek out a worthy successor. I have my concubines, of course, as what man does not, but none of them are mature enough to provide suitable guidance to a bride of my daughter's stature. It is not right that a bride should go to her wedding unprepared and indeed, before your kind offer, I feared I would have to rely on, at best, a Concubine of the Fifth Rank to fulfill the traditional duties of the bride's mother. You say your 'Dr. Crusher' is a woman of honor and experience?"

"I cannot recommend her too highly," Picard said with total sincerity. "She is a respected physician, a valuable officer, and she has raised a fine and upstanding son." *And more than capable,* he added silently, *of protecting your daughter from any lurking assassin.*

"Excellent," Lu Tung said, although his stony expression revealed little in the way of emotion. "On the battlefield, I came to have great respect for the healing abilities of women. Their gender has a natural talent for medicine, I believe."

The stoic noble was quite different, Picard thought, from the effusive and temperamental emperor he had sought to depose. Small wonder they did not get along. Lu Tung's stern demeanor reminded Picard of Sarek of Vulcan, at least before age and illness undid that great man's emotional control. He found himself hoping Lu Tung would not turn out to be the assassin.

The Dragon, meanwhile, only had eyes for Data. The Emperor had insisted that the android join them on the dais, and was now besieging Data with endless questions about his construction and nature. Picard almost suspected that the Dragon was intent on learning how to build an android of his own. It was a good thing that Data had no true feelings, Picard thought, because the Dragon's intense curiosity was enough to make almost any other being uncomfortable very quickly.

"Amazing, amazing," the Dragon said, squinting at Data's skin. "An unusual texture. Why did they not give you a more conventional skin color?"

"I do not know, Your Excellence. My creator, Dr. Soong, never told me and I never asked him."

"And he didn't put any surface ornamentation on you?" the Dragon asked.

"No, Your Excellence. It was not deemed necessary."

"Well, that could be easily remedied." Eyes narrowed, the Dragon tilted his head to one side, examining Data as if he were a work in progress. "A little silver and bioluminescent inlay, perhaps some tiling effects on the planes of his face. The forehead definitely cries out to be engraved, and the coloring of the eyes is far too simple. . . . Why hasn't this been done before, one wonders?"

"I have not thought of it as a practical possibility," Data admitted.

Feelings or no feelings, Picard felt obliged to intervene on Data's behalf. Excusing himself from Lord Lu Tung, Picard leaned over to join the Dragon and Data. "Mr. Data is a starship officer," he explained to the Dragon. "Any excess decoration would be unnecessary, as well as contrary to his and our purpose."

"Understood, Captain," the Emperor replied, "but if he were somewhere else—a royal court, say—*then* one might think of such a thing, don't you think?"

*Oh, no,* Picard thought as the full implications of the Dragon's interest in Data sunk in. Naturally, an unquestioned ruler such as the Dragon would not consider it necessary, or even good form, to actually ask for any object he desired. It would usually be enough to simply state his admiration for a specific item and he would, as surely as if he had commanded it, be presented with the item. Certainly, the Dragon had more than expressed an interest in Data, who in his eyes must simply be just another manmade artifact. *He's probably wondering,* Picard realized with dismay, *why I haven't offered Data to him already. Unless he thinks Data is a wedding gift for tomorrow.*

"In the past," Data commented, attempting to fully satisfy the Dragon's curiosity, "my features have been modified for tactical reasons, such as impersonating a Romulan. I suppose, in theory, there is no reason why my appearance could not be altered to suit a more aesthetic agenda."

"Precisely!" the Dragon agreed enthusiastically. "That's exactly what I was thinking. Captain Picard, you *must* allow me to compliment you on this amazing creation here. Even with its current plain exterior, it can only be an ornament to any ship *or* court."

His mind racing, Picard could not think of any graceful way to extract Data from the Dragon's covetous grasp. As a matter of fact, the Federation had provided the *Enterprise* with a generous assortment of gifts to extend to the Dragon Empire, but, at the moment, the Dragon appeared unlikely to accept any substitute, no matter how attractive or well intentioned, for Commander Data. It was clearly essential, therefore, that he separate Data from the Dragon as fast as possible, before it became absolutely impossible to avoid offering the android without offending the Emperor. *Out of sight, out of mind.* Picard hoped the old maxim held true in this case.

"Mr. Data," he said sharply. "Have you forgotten? Commander La Forge requires your presence on the bridge immediately."

"Excuse me, Captain," Data began, "I was not aware . . ."

The Dragon's gaze shifted from Data to Picard. A

wary expression came over his face. There was nothing to do, Picard decided, but to press on and deal with the consequences later.

"The bridge, Mr. Data," he repeated. "Return to the *Enterprise* at once." *Come on, Data,* he thought. *You've played enough poker. Recognize a bluff when you see one.*

"But what about accompanying Commander Riker to the Heir's party?" Data asked.

"Belay that order," Picard said. Riker would have to chaperone the princes on his own. Picard didn't want Data on the same planet as the Dragon. "Do as you're told, Commander."

Comprehension of some sort dawned on Data's face. "Of course, sir," he said, beneath the probing stare of the Dragon. "I had forgotten about Commander La Forge." Rising to his feet, he tapped his comm badge, which chirped in response to his touch. "One to beam up," he said.

A second later, a familiar golden glow surrounded Data. The android's form flickered briefly, before dissolving entirely into a shimmering column of light. "Wait!" the Dragon protested, but he was too late. The glow vanished, taking Data with it, and leaving only a few lingering sparks floating in the air. The sparks themselves faded away before the Dragon could say another word.

"Forgive Mr. Data's sudden departure, Your Excellence," Picard said. "But he had urgent business aboard the *Enterprise,* business vital to the completion of our mission."

"I don't know about this, Picard," the Dragon said, pouting beneath his bushy white beard. "You Federation sorts seem to have far too much urgent business for my taste. Always running off just when I'm trying to be hospitable . . ."

"And we are honored by your hospitality," Picard interjected hastily. *I have to change the subject,* he thought, *and distract him from Data. No matter what it takes.* "And speaking of your legendary hospitality, weren't you going to tell me more about some of the extraordinary delicacies your kitchen is providing for us?"

"Delicacies? Oh, yes." The Dragon's tone lightened, becoming cheerier and less querulous. "Why, you haven't tasted anything yet, my dear captain. If you thought candied *rahgid* eyes were a treat, just wait until you try a mouthful of stuffed *ragoji* bowels! They're indescribable."

*I'll bet they are,* Picard thought sourly. He couldn't help wondering what the bowels were stuffed with.

After the banquet concluded, following the unavoidable and inevitably awful consumption of the stuffed bowels, the Dragon offered to give Picard and his remaining officers a tour of the palace. Eager to restore the Dragon's goodwill after the awkwardness with Data, Picard readily agreed to the tour. He still hoped he and Troi would get an opportunity to speak with the Dragon alone at some point, so they could convince him of the necessity of signing the treaty, but that would have to come after the tour. For now he took comfort in the fact that the unknown assassin would have difficulty killing any member of the party while they traveled as a group through the sumptuous decor of the Imperial Palace of the Dragon. Indeed, each chamber seemed richer and more spectacular than the one preceding it. No wonder, he thought, the G'kkau were so intent on conquering Pai. The treasures of the palace alone would make the Dragon Empire a tempting target for a suitably greedy and ruthless people. He was surprised no Ferengi had found his way to Pai just yet.

Starting with the Pavilion of the Emerald Peacock, the chamberlain led the party through a score of palace rooms, each more improbably named than the last, and in each instance he droned out a set speech about the room, its furnishings, and its history, with the Dragon inserting more down-to-earth comments. Lord Lu Tung begged off the tour after the Memorable Room of the Grand Couch, taking Beverly with him to his rooms to meet the Green Pearl. Picard wished her luck before she left.

The Heir, the Second Son, and Riker lasted through the Chambers of the Degraded Priests (Upper, Middle, and Smaller) and the Gallery of Hushed Meetings, but they called it quits in the Salon of the Forgotten Cap, wandering off to find the rest of the two princes' companions at the Penultimate Bestowing of the Undomesticated Seeds. Picard suspected that Riker would have his hands full protecting the Dragon's sons from each other, let alone the unknown assassin.

That left Picard, Troi, Mu, and the Dragon to stand before a pair of engraved, gold-plated doors large enough to fly a shuttlecraft through. "Prepare to enter the High Hall of Ceremonial Grandeur," Mu intoned solemnly.

"Where we keep the gifts," the Dragon. He glanced around somewhat wistfully, as if hoping for Data's sudden materialization. For his own part, Picard was glad that the android officer was safely back aboard the *Enterprise.*

"Ah," Picard said, contemplating the set of large, gilded doors facing him. Mu pressed a unobtrusive button on the handle of his fan, and the heavy, gold doors began to swing open under their own power. Somewhere beyond the doors, Picard heard a gong clang loudly. *Automatic pomp and circumstance,* he concluded, *with an Oriental flavor.* He peered through the parted doors, hoping to find something new to compliment. He had seen a number of opulently furnished rooms by now, and it was becoming harder with each new chamber to come up with something new to say about it.

That this was where the wedding gifts were being stored went without saying, for the hall was crammed with objects of every size, the smaller ones arranged on low tables around the outside of the room, and the larger ones standing in the center atop a colorfully embroidered carpet the size of Ten-Forward. Armored guards, equipped with both swords and hand weapons, were posted in the four corners of the chamber. Inspecting the treasures on display, Picard saw numerous ceramic bowls, plates, vases, pipes, boxes, and statuettes, all of the finest quality, laid on top of the many tables. Hand-painted silk hangings were piled carelessly atop each other, next to what looked like a replicator constructed of solid gold. A five-story miniature temple, complete with hundreds of tiny monks no larger than a fingernail, was carved from ivory, while a throne of fine, dark wood had been varnished until it literally shone. Next to the model temple, Picard saw the priceless Ming Dynasty vase that, along with various other artifacts from all over the Federation (and rather than Commander Data), comprised the *Enterprise*'s actual gift to the Dragon Empire. There was too much to take in all at once, but, looking elsewhere, Picard's gaze fell upon, in succession, five intricate bronze dragons, six porcelain tortoises, a pair of lacquered wooden jewelry boxes etched with mildly erotic designs, four stacks of gold-pressed latinum, and a pearl-covered computer padd. And then, of course, there was the life-sized jade elephant standing on four immense, green legs in the very center of the hall.

"Good heavens!" Troi exclaimed. As she was the daughter of one the ruling houses of Betazed, it took a lot to impress Troi, but Picard wasn't surprised by her reaction. They had literally found the hoard of the Dragon. Or one of them, at least.

"Your woman has good taste," the Dragon commented, "but, of course, females are easily bedazzled by pretty things."

Up until this moment, Picard had been aware, but not exactly surprised, that neither the Dragon nor his trusted chamberlain had spoken to Troi directly, nor even attempted introductions. Apparently, they considered it perfectly natural that Picard should have an attractive female subordinate trailing behind him as he viewed the palace. As far as he was concerned, Troi was demonstrating a degree of patience above and beyond the call of duty.

"Excellence, Grand Chamberlain, permit me to introduce Counselor Deanna Troi, an indispensable member of my staff."

The Dragon laughed heartily. "Well, I'm not sure I'd call any woman indispensable, but I can see why you value her so highly." He eyed Troi appreciatively, so much so that Picard wondered whether she had discarded more layers of clothing than was entirely proper for this culture. By Federation standards, her remaining robe was quite modest, but who knew what the Pai thought of her current attire? He hoped Troi would not go down in history as the woman who scandalized the Dragon Empire, although, to be honest, the Emperor's grinning inspection of Troi seemed more openly lecherous than appalled. "Quite fine indeed," he said. "Certainly, your Federation cannot be faulted for the quality of your women."

"The Dragon is too kind," Troi said, rather ignoring the spirit in which the Emperor's comment was intended. "I think you will find the Federation has much to offer the Pai."

"And what exactly do you have to offer, my lovely?" the Dragon said with a leer.

*Best to change the subject,* Picard decided, *before the Dragon expects me to hand over Deanna as well as Data.* He observed the armored warriors standing guard over the hoard of the wedding gifts; they stood at attention as stiff and immobile as if they were carved from jade or ivory themselves. Their armor looked to be composed of overlapping plates of polished steel embossed with ornate designs of battling dragons and griffins. Silver filigree outlined each plate, while rings of brightly painted rubber provided flexibility at the joints. A sword was sheathed at each man's side, and they held shiny, metallic rifles against their chests. Their rigid bearing and stern expressions, glimpsed beneath elaborate headdresses adorned with gold and pearls, reminded Picard of Lieutenant Worf at his most Klingon. An idea occurred to him.

"Excellence," he began. "On behalf of the Federation, I would be delighted to provide an honor guard to watch over this fine assemblage of treasures."

The Dragon looked puzzled by Picard's suggestion. "But I have my own guards to do just that," he protested, "as you can see for yourself. Chih-li, my Minister of Internal Security, has personally supervised the security arrangements for the entire wedding."

"And they are more than sufficient, I'm sure," Picard said hastily. "What I am suggesting is merely a courtesy customarily granted to heads of state such as yourself. I would consider myself dishonored if you will not permit me to offer you some small honor guard as a token of the Federation's concern for your safety and well-being."

"Oh, dear! We can't have that." The Dragon's face brightened. "I know. You can send for your Mr. Data. I would be happy to have him posted among the wedding gifts."

*I'm sure you would,* Picard thought. "Actually, I had a different officer in mind. Lieutenant Worf. As head of security, he'd seem the logical choice for—"

"Nonsense," the Dragon insisted. "Data is the perfect gift . . . I mean, guard."

Obviously, the Dragon was not about to forget his interest in Data anytime soon. Picard decided it was time to address the issue head-on. "Excellence, I must point out that Mr. Data *is* a fully sentient being, and thus he cannot be considered a potential gift."

"But we give sentient beings all the time," the Dragon said, "if you consider women sentient."

"He is also an officer in Starfleet," Picard said.

"And Starfleet wants me to be happy, do they not?" the Dragon pointed out.

Picard felt himself losing ground. "Well, yes, but—"

"Ahem," Troi broke in. "Forgive me for interrupting, but this one is compelled to recollect, as she is sure lord and master Captain Picard recalls, that Lieutenant Commander Data is suffering the inconvenience with his positronics."

*Lord and master?* Picard hoped Deanna was not laying it on too thick. "Of course," he said. "The inconvenience." *What in blazes was she up to?*

"My mandarins will be delighted to take a look at him," the Dragon offered helpfully.

*Let him in their grip and we'll never see him again,* Picard thought.

Troi cleared her throat again, while batting her eyes at the Dragon. Observing the skillful way Deanna was manipulating the Emperor, Picard realized that his counselor had learned a trick or two from her mother. "While the Most Excellent and Exalted One's scientists would no doubt be surpassingly adept at solving just such a problem, still I am confident the Federation would not wish to be responsible for any fatalities so soon before so blessed an event as tomorrow's wedding."

"Fatalities?" the Dragon and his chamberlain said simultaneously. Picard resisted the temptation to join in.

"A malfunctioning android *can* be dangerous," Troi explained. "Still, our own Commander La Forge is well aware of the risks involving in repairing Data. I am quite confident he will survive."

The chamberlain gulped audibly, and even the ebullient Dragon looked a little shaken at the prospect of a homicidal android running amok. "Perhaps I have been too hasty about this man Worf," the Dragon said. "You say he is accustomed to providing security on behalf of Starfleet?"

"His function would be purely ceremonial," Picard insisted, "and no reflection on your own honor." *But with an assassin on the loose, I want Worf close at hand. Data can take command of the bridge.* Perhaps the Minister of Internal Security was more amenable to reason than his emperor, and would permit Worf to discreetly provide extra protection for the Dragon as well as his gifts.

"Your magnanimousness is well known," Troi added, bowing slightly. Now that she had shed most of her cumbersome robes, her movements were as graceful as ever. "Please permit us the honor to at least *pretend* we can contribute in some small fashion to your security."

"Very well," the Dragon agreed. Picard could not tell whether it was his arguments, or Troi's flattery, that had persuaded the Emperor. "Have your Worf brought to this hall. Mu, notify Chih-li that a Starfleet guard will be joining our own."

*At last,* Picard thought, *I am making some progress.* With Deanna's help, he had extracted Data from an embarrassing situation and managed to have Worf placed in a position to better protect the palace. *Now, if I can just get the Dragon to focus on the matter of the treaty, perhaps I can complete my mission without any further complications.*

"I say, Picard," the Dragon said, "have I told you

how much I admire your woman?" The old man's gaze roamed over the shapely contours of Troi's single purple gown. "Beautiful, dutiful, *and* perceptive. She truly is a prize fit for a captain . . . or an Emperor," he hinted broadly.

Picard's eyes rolled heavenward. He could tell it was going to be a long night.

# Chapter Six

"A TOAST! TO THE DRAGON!"

"To Lord Lu Tung!"

"Rebel scum!"

"Son of a cross-eyed concubine!"

With an inarticulate cry of rage, one young Pai warrior lunged at another. The two men grappled amid a chaotic mass of overstuffed cushions, overturned dishes, overwrought noblemen, and underdressed serving maids. Will Riker, stretched out on a plush velvet divan between the Heir and his blacksheep younger brother, ducked as the battling pair, locked in hand-to-hand combat, threw themselves over Riker's head and crashed into the wall behind him. Tangled among the satin wall hangings, the two men continued to struggle, their arms and legs thrashing about. Apparently unconcerned with the outcome of the fight, Kan-hi rescued a bottle of wine from the men's flailing limbs.

"Have another drink, my dear Riker," the Second Son said.

The Penultimate Bestowing of the Undomesticated Seeds of the Dragon-Heir reminded Riker of some of the wilder celebrations he'd attended on the pleasure planet Risa. Over a dozen young men had crammed themselves into a suite of rooms apparently belonging to Chuan-chi himself. The rooms were broken up by paper screens draped with translucent fabrics of varied colors. The celebrants sprawled on large cushions scattered throughout the suite while smiling handmaidens, clad in wispy strips of diaphanous gauze that left Riker convinced that the Pai were humanoid in every way that mattered, wended sinuously through the party, refilling goblets of wine, serving tasty treats on small china plates, and dodging, sometimes unsuccessfully, the groping hands of the raucous young bachelors. After the voluminous robes displayed at the banquet, including the discreet costumes of the musicians, this generous display of exposed female flesh came as something of a pleasant surprise to Riker, as well as a potentially dangerous distraction. He'd have to make sure all this enticing Pai pulchritude did not divert him from his primary duty: protecting the Dragon's sons from the assassin —and each other.

He accepted more wine from Kan-hi, thankful for the immunity to intoxication that Beverly's hypospray had provided him with. The wine was emerald green in color, gently heated, and strong to the taste. He could feel the potent brew burn its way down his throat. Fumes from the goblet seared his nostrils and made his eyes water. Given the rate at which the wine was flowing, Riker guessed that he was already the only sober man at the party. Blinking away tears, Riker grinned at the Second Son and gestured toward the brawling warriors kicking and punching each other on the floor only a few feet away. "Shouldn't we break them up?"

Kan-hi shrugged. "Why bother? They'll settle the matter, one way or another, soon enough. And then there'll be another fight."

Riker had to concur. Despite his luxurious surroundings, the situation struck him as a very volatile one. These aristocratic young warriors were prickly and quick to fight, and the recent civil wars seemed to have left plenty of hard feelings—and long-simmering grievances—lurking behind the riotous good cheer. Add copious quantities of wine to the equation and Riker saw trouble on the horizon. Under the circumstances, you didn't need a premeditated assassin to provoke violence; the party alone might be enough to kill an heir or two.

"It's a barbaric tradition, really," Chuan-chi said disdainfully. Riker turned his head to look at the Heir. "I'm afraid there's nothing to be done but endure it all, Commander Riker. My first such celebration, many years ago, was just as tiresome."

"This is your second wedding, sir?" Riker asked Chuan-chi.

"My honorable first wife succumbed to a fever several years ago," the Heir explained. "It was quite irresponsible of her, but then one can seldom depend on a woman."

Riker was unsure how to respond. Luckily, the

arrival of another serving maid interrupted the discussion, sparing him the necessity of an immediate reply. Wearing only a narrow strip of saffron gauze wound around her hips, the woman knelt before the three men and offered them fresh slices of a turquoise fruit unfamiliar to Riker. Her hair, bound in a single long ponytail that fell past her knees, was dark and lustrous, and her lips, fingertips, and toenails had been painted the same color as the fruit. Beneath lush, black lashes, her sapphire eyes cast curious looks in Riker's direction. He returned her gaze with frank admiration.

"You find her pleasant to view?" Kan-hi asked. Riker detected no jealousy or resentment in his tone.

"Very much so," he said honestly, accepting a greenish blue slice from the woman's slender fingers. "The women of your world are quite attractive."

"Oh, this is but my brother's *outer* harem, and these women mere servants. You should see his private concubines," Kan-hi said, "except, of course, that no other man can ever see them. Only my father's women are said to be more lovely." The Second Son paused for a second, and an uncharacteristically solemn expression came over his face. "No other woman, however, can compare to the Green Pearl herself. Her grace and beauty have no rivals, and her heart . . ." Here the prince's voice dropped to a whisper. A faraway look entered his eyes. ". . . her heart is a greater treasure than the very throne of the Dragon."

A heavy thud announced the outcome of the drunken struggle behind them. One eye blackened, blood streaming from his nose, the victorious Pai rose and adjusted his robes, leaving his unconscious opponent stretched out on the floor. With a great show of dignity, he regained his seat among some empty cushions opposite Riker while a delectable trio of near-naked serving girls hastened to tend to his injuries with soft, heated cloths and tender caresses. Another woman quietly tiptoed over on small, bare feet to check on the fallen warrior, while the lady of the turquoise fruit slipped away, casting one final sidelong glance at Riker as she departed. Riker had to remind himself that, effectively, he was still on duty.

This flurry of activity roused Kan-hi from his apparent reverie. He shook his head, as if to rid his mind of some clinging, unwelcome vision. "Forgive me, Commander. I have had too much wine. I forget myself." His voice regained its usual, lighthearted tone. "So tell me, how do the women of the Federation compare to our own?"

"Call me Will," he insisted. "If ever a question called for a diplomatic answer, that one's probably it. Let's just say that, throughout the many worlds that make up the Federation, I've always found much to admire with regard to the opposite sex."

Kan-hi laughed. "I suspected as much. After the treaty is signed, perhaps I will have to opportunity to meet many more of your women, and to see for myself just how diplomatic you're being."

"*If* the treaty is signed," the Heir said brusquely. It was impossible to ignore the scorn in his voice, so Riker didn't bother.

"I take it, sir," Riker said, "that you disapprove of your father's intention to link the Dragon Empire to the Federation?" Perhaps it was still possible, he thought, to allay the Heir's concerns over the treaty and win him over to the Federation's side. Certainly, it couldn't hurt to try; after all, Chuan-chi would someday be the Dragon himself, provided the G'kkau didn't annihilate the Empire first.

"I would not be so sure of the Emperor's intentions," Chuan-chi said. "My foolish young brother is doubtless eager to be corrupted by foreign women and other influences, but the Dragon is beyond such insidious temptations. He will see that the sacred destiny of the Dragon Empire is not snared in a web of outside entanglements."

"So instead we must hide behind our borders like a tortoise afraid to stick its head out from its shell?" Kan-hi challenged his brother. "There's an entire universe out there, full of new ideas and opportunities! Are we supposed to just pretend all those other worlds don't exist? Do you expect that they will always be content to pretend we're not here?"

*The G'kkau certainly won't,* Riker thought. It was ironic, and more than a little troubling, that the treaty depended on the marriage of the Pai noble who seemed most opposed to it. Too bad Kan-hi, who was obviously more open to the prospect, was only the Second Son. *I know how the Romulans would handle this,* he mused ruefully. They'd assassinate both the Dragon and the Heir and set up a puppet government under Kan-hi. That's not how the Federation operated, of course, but he wondered whether the G'kkau were capable of that kind of subtlety. Could Kan-hi be in cahoots with the G'kkau? He hoped not; he liked the roguish young prince much better than the Heir, who had a much more sour disposition.

"As you, my dear brother, pointed out mere minutes ago," Chuan-chi said with a smirk, "there is no treasure in the heavens that can compare with the

Green Pearl, so why should I wish to sample the unwholesome pleasures of the Federation? Then again, brother, under the circumstances, I suppose you have nothing better to do."

Murder flashed in Kan-hi's eyes. He clenched his fists against his sides. Riker noted that the Second Son's fingernails were shorter and of a more practical length than those of many of the other Pai nobles, including the Heir. He guessed that Kan-hi led a more active life than most of the palace's residents. Right now, however, he seemed on the verge of becoming too active. Kan-hi struck Riker as being only moments away from slamming his manicured fists into the Heir's face. "Why, you vile excuse for a Pai!" he fumed. "If you weren't my brother . . . !"

"Then I would be spared at least one embarrassing relation," Chuan-chi finished the sentence for him. "As well as a disgrace to the honor of our line." He crossed his arms over his chest, apparently unafraid of any violent reaction from his brother. His fingernails, Riker observed, were each over six centimeters long. Ten golden rings, each holding a different precious jewel, adorned his fingers. He held his chin up high, as if inviting an attack. Where Kan-hi seemed boiling over with red-hot fury, Chuan-chi's haughty manner and frozen posture were cold as ice.

Riker was not the only one to note the mounting tension between the two princes. All around the suite, the scattered guests turned their heads in the direction of the confrontation, the abundant wine and women temporarily forgotten. The mood of the chamber suddenly became hushed and expectant, poised to explode at any minute. Riker had been in enough barroom brawls, not to mention any number of Klingon get-togethers, to know that trouble was brewing. He had no idea which of the assembled warriors supported the Heir and which were sympathetic to Kan-hi, but he sensed that a potentially lethal free-for-all was only heartbeats away. His right hand drifted toward his phaser, then hesitated. Were any of the Pai carrying energy weapons? He didn't want to start a firefight in these close quarters, not if he didn't have to.

"How dare you to malign my honor!" Kan-hi roared.

"Honor? What honor?" Chuan-chi said. Cold disdain dripped from every syllable he uttered. "Your disobedience and disrespect dishonors our father, your emperor. And your fondness for foreign alliances smacks of treason to the very idea of the Dragon Empire."

"I'll show you treason!" Kan-hi said, lunging to his feet. Too much wine had impaired his balance, however, and the sudden movement left him swaying where he stood. "I'll kill you," he vowed while he tried to focus his eyes on his hated half-brother. Riker took advantage of his momentary disorientation to intervene. He stood up between Kan-hi and the Heir.

"Gentlemen, gentlemen," he said, raising his voice so that all present could hear him. "Let's not waste time debating politics. This is supposed to be a party, in honor of the Dragon-Heir and his coming marriage." To his right, he heard Kan-hi mutter something angrily beneath his breath. The young prince stepped toward his brother, only to be calmly but firmly blocked by Riker. *Interesting,* Riker thought. *Kan-hi is touchy about the wedding. I wonder why?*

"Anyway, why spoil a happy occasion? Especially with all these lovely ladies around? Where I come from, there's an ancient saying: 'Make love, not war.'" Riker's gaze swept the room. He had everyone's attention. The scene still felt tense, but at least no one was making any threatening moves just yet. There was still time to turn things around. Keeping one eye on Kan-hi, he bent long enough to lift his goblet from the floor. "More wine!" he cried, and, like a genie summoned from a lamp, a fetching young woman wearing only two strategically placed strings of beads appeared to replenish his cup. As soon as she was finished, he raised the goblet up high. "A toast," he declared, "to love."

*You can't get less political than that,* he thought. *Who is going to object to love?*

*Except maybe a Vulcan, that is.*

For a long, drawn-out moment, nobody joined his toast. Then, to Riker's relief and surprise, Kan-hi lifted his cup as well. "To love," the Second Son said glumly. The edge of his anger apparently dulled for the moment, he slowly lowered himself down to his waiting cushion, rubbing his forehead with his free hand. Riker turned his attention to Chuan-chi. The Dragon-Heir remained as stiff, and about as cheerful, as a marble statue at first. His face was a frozen mask of utter contempt directed at his brother. After it became obvious, however, that Kan-hi was not going to launch an attack upon his brother's person, Chuan-chi's posture gradually relaxed beneath his robes. *Is it just my imagination,* Riker thought, *or does he look slightly disappointed?* Perhaps the Heir was looking for an excuse to sic his men upon the Second Son?

Riker wasn't sure, even as he watched the Heir reach languidly for his own gold-encrusted goblet. "To love," he said, yawning conspicuously.

As unenthusiastic as the Heir's toast sounded, it served to signal the end of the current standoff. Throughout the prince's outer harem, voices and cups were raised in praise of love, even though the bellicose expressions of many faces belied the gentle sentiment. There was no question, Riker saw, that many of the hot-blooded warriors reclining in sybaritic comfort felt themselves cheated out of a good fight. He had delayed an explosion, not defused it. Even now, only a few yards away, the black-eyed victor of the previous skirmish was glaring at Riker with obvious animosity. His foot-long fingernails, now tipped with traces of drying blood, clacked together ominously. Riker deliberately avoided making eye contact with the warrior, suspecting that it might be considered a challenge. *We're here to win friends and influence people,* he reminded himself, *not to knock sense into anyone's head.*

With every appearance of casual ease, Riker sank down onto the plush, velvet divan. The soft cushion gave beneath his weight as he sat cross-legged between the princes. Beneath his red Starfleet dress uniform, his neck and shoulders ached slightly from maintaining—and concealing—his constant state of alertness. He reached back to massage his neck, only to be surprised by the gentle touch of hands already at work upon the sore muscles there. Strong fingers kneaded his flesh through his tunic, and Riker glimpsed turquoise nails at the periphery of his vision. "What—?" he exclaimed, startled but not all distressed by this sudden turn of events.

Looking over his shoulder, he saw that the lady of the turquoise fruit had returned, this time with no refreshment to offer aside from her own tender ministrations. Her body pressed gently against his back, and her blue-green lipstick glistened even more wetly than before. She kept her eyes downturned, declining to meet his gaze, but a smile lifted the corners of her mouth as he beamed welcomingly at her. *This is more like it,* he thought.

"Hah!" Kan-hi laughed, his good humor returning. "I think you have made a conquest, Commander . . . I mean, Will."

Chuan-chi merely sniffed disapprovingly. Perhaps, Riker thought, he considered the turquoise handmaiden a traitor to the cause of Pai isolationism. *Too bad. At least I'm making some friends here.*

Riker contemplated the woman's delicate features. She really was quite attractive and exotic. If, as Kan-hi had claimed earlier, this beauty was unremarkable by Pai standards, he had to wonder just how gorgeous the vaunted Green Pearl was. Could she really be beautiful enough to bring peace to this warring planet? Or to warm the dour heart of the Dragon-Heir? He grew steadily more curious to see the bride herself at tomorrow's wedding.

In the meantime, the woman's hands continued to work their soothing magic on his neck and shoulders, massaging away the stress and anxiety he felt. *Better be careful,* he thought, *or I'll be too relaxed to bodyguard the princes.* Still, he closed his eyes for just a second or two, letting his body indulge in the lovely young woman's accomplished pampering.

He nearly jumped out of his skin, though, when he felt *two more* hands sliding sensuously over his chest, working their way beneath the fold of his dress uniform. His eyes snapped open and his head twisted around to see another serving maid, the one clad solely in beads, kneeling before him, stroking his torso even as her sister servant ran her hands up and down his spine. Unlike the blue-eyed, ponytailed maiden behind him, this woman had waves of inky black hair flowing over shoulders and large purple eyes like amethysts. One string of tiny, silver beads dangled over the woman's generous breasts, while an identical string encircled her narrow waist, the beads rolling over her naked hips as she leaned closer to him. Staring wide-eyed at the new arrival, his beard only inches away from her pale white chest, her fragrant perfume filling his nostrils with the scent of fresh flowers, Riker found himself rendered briefly speechless. *Those are really small beads,* he thought.

Amused by Riker's predicament, Kan-hi had plenty to say. "My brother's servants appear quite taken with you, Will Riker. Apparently, one must never underestimate the effects of novelty on a female's delicate sensibilities, meaning no disrespect, of course, to your own individual magnetism, which I am sure is considerable." The Second Son chuckled as he watched the nubile serving maids wrap themselves around Riker, enveloping him in soft, warm, buxom, female flesh. "I trust you are enjoying yourself?"

Turquoise lips brushed his ear as the first woman nuzzled the left side of his neck. Beads rustled seductively as the other woman kissed the right side, purring as softly as a tribble. "I am, er, overwhelmed by their hospitality," he gasped. *This is getting out of hand.* He wondered how he was going to extricate himself, literally and figuratively, from the women's all-too-distracting attentions. It was a shame Data had not been able to come along; he definitely would have gotten an education.

Two extremely large men guarded the broad archway in front of Beverly Crusher. Huge, curved scimitars rested on the men's broad shoulders while some type of energy weapon hung on the sash about each guard's waist. Eyes fixed straight ahead, never deviating from their assigned task, the men stood at attention on opposite sides of the archway. The open doorway was framed by a breathtaking jade arch decorated with intricate engravings of men and horses. Beverly paused to inspect the engravings; as nearly as she could tell, the carvings illustrated the rise and fall of an ambitious warlord. The story, whether mythical or historical, reminded her of Lord Lu Tung's recently quelled rebellion against the Emperor. She glanced at the stolid, middle-aged man. In accordance with Pai tradition, he walked a few steps ahead of her.

"The Dragon, in his generosity, has provided me with quarters of my own within the Imperial Palace," Lu Tung explained. "This is the entrance to my harem, where my daughter resides until tomorrow."

"I look forward to meeting her, Lord Lu Tung," Beverly said. She wondered whether the Emperor had deliberately placed Lu Tung's quarters beyond this engraved saga of thwarted ambition. A not-so-subtle message, perhaps, and a permanent recrimination? They passed under the archway, leaving the armed guards behind.

Lu Tung's harem proved to be surprisingly spacious. Despite the cautionary carvings over the gate,

Beverly observed, the rebel lord had hardly been confined to the Tower of London. The hall they traversed seemed infinitely long, the combination of dim lighting and puffs of brightly colored incense making the farther end difficult to discern. Doorways, painted a dizzying variety of hues, opened onto a variety of chambers on either side of the hall. Beverly peeked through the open doors as she hurried by them, getting quick glimpses of opulent furnishings and gilded, luxurious decor. Women, all strikingly beautiful and clad in long, elegant gowns, drifted along the length of the hall, bowing to the floor as they recognized their lord. Although their garments superficially resembled Beverly's, she noted that the women's gowns were slit higher along the sides, and cut lower in the front. This was a harem after all, she recalled.

"What a lot of women there seem to be," Beverly said, intrigued. "Do they all reside here?"

"Of course," Lu Tung replied. Beverly contemplated the back of his head, wishing she could watch his facial expressions. She hoped she wasn't being too nosy. "These are just servants, really."

For servants, the women did not appear to be doing much besides gliding to and fro through the outer chambers of the harem. Indeed, their lavish, expensive-looking attire seemed quite ill suited to housework or other practical duties. Surely, though, the women's function couldn't be entirely decorative, could it? "Your servants are unusually attractive," she said.

"They're mostly there as insulation between my inner harem and the outside world," Lu Tung explained.

"I see," she said, understanding at last. "Just in case someone gets through the palace's defenses, and past the men with the swords."

"Quite right," he said. "This way intruders will be distracted and not get to my daughter or my concubines before I am able to intercede. I take excellent care of all my women."

Although Beverly could not see his face, Lu Tung's voice sounded sincere. As spoiled Pai males went, he struck Beverly as a decent sort; so far he had treated her with respect, and had not made any improper advances to her even though he now had her alone in his harem. (Beverly did not bother with false modesty. All decked out in her robes of peach and emerald, she *knew* she was stunning.) None of which, she reminded herself, meant that Lu Tung had not been responsible for the assassination attempt during the banquet. A man could be chivalrous and still plot to conquer a throne; Klingon legend held that even the fierce Kahless had shown mercy toward the women and children of his enemies. As the Dragon's longtime enemy, Lu Tung had to head the list of suspects.

"Is your daughter near, Lord Lu Tung?" Beverly asked.

"At my instruction, she sits in the Room of Prolonged Anticipation tonight."

"Not too prolonged, I hope," Beverly joked.

"Not at all," Lu Tung replied. "Here we are." Unlike the other doorways they had walked past, this one was closed and seemingly impenetrable. Aquamarine trimming outlined a rectangular metal gate wide enough to permit two people's passage if not for the dense, black door blocking their path. Beverly touched the dark-hued metal with her fingers; it felt like solid iron. An embossed dragon, at least six meters tall, guarded the door, beneath a string of unfamiliar Chinese characters painted above the upper edge of the door. Beverly could not read the turquoise calligraphy, but she assumed that the writing, along with the ferocious dragon, meant "Keep Out." Her fingers traced the outline of the dragon's sharp fangs. Two glittering rubies, embedded in the metal, formed the dragon's eyes.

"Excuse me, Doctor," Lu Tung said, stepping between her and the iron door. He held up his right hand before the dragon's eyes. "Lord Lu Tung and guest," he said loudly. "Provide admittance for two."

To Beverly's surprise, the dragon's jeweled eyes moved.

Two pairs of moist lips murmured in Riker's ears. Four graceful hands burrowed beneath the folds of his dress uniform.

"If you prefer," Kan-hi said solicitously, "I'm sure private chambers can be found for you and your new admirers. Isn't that so, brother?"

Chuan-chi acted merely bored by the sight of two of his own women crawling over Riker. "Naturally," he said. "It was the Emperor's wish that we extend you every courtesy." Clearly implied in his tone was the suggestion that the Heir's own wishes were quite different from his father's. Not that it mattered to Riker. He couldn't allow this amorous pair to separate him from the princes he was responsible for protecting. *I just hope Captain Picard appreciates my devotion to duty.*

"Maybe some other time," he said, trying to gently shove the beaded woman away from his face. "Not

that your . . . staff . . . isn't charming, but I would prefer the honor of your own company this evening."

Kan-hi was not convinced. "But what about making love, not war?"

"That's just an expression." The beaded maiden
slid off Riker's lap as he struggled to his feet. He felt
the other woman hanging from his shoulders, her
painted toenails barely grazing the floor behind him.
"Thank you very much, miss, but . . . I'm very flat-
tered, but . . . excuse me . . ." Using both hands, he
pried the women away from him as courteously as he
could until, abruptly, he found himself standing free
and clear—with a saffron ribbon dangling from one
hand and a string of beads wrapped around the other.
"Oops," he said weakly.

"Dog!" an angry voice cried out. "Defiler of Pai
womanhood!" The voice came from the warrior with
the blackened left eye, who lumbered toward Riker
with rage blazing in his one good eye and moral
indignation reverberating in his voice. Up until now,
Riker hadn't realized just how big the man was. His
skull looked roughly the size of a bull's and his fists
were as big as baby Hortas. He weighed easily three
hundred pounds, not counting his robes. Sumo wrestling, Riker recalled, was of Japanese origins, not
Chinese; but considering the sheer mass of incensed
warrior stomping this way, he couldn't help wondering if maybe the original Pai colonists hadn't im-
ported a sumo or two.

"This isn't as bad as it looks," he said, trying to
shake the incriminating garments from his hands.
The yellow gauze clung like static to his fingers. The
string of beads tangled itself into knots. *I can't believe
I actually said that,* Riker thought. He felt like he'd

transported into some bad bedroom farce, except that the homicidal behemoth charging him was not a figment of any playwright's imagination.

Was the Heir likely to intervene? Riker half expected Chuan-chi to halt his attacker with a single firm command, but heard nothing from either the Heir or Kan-hi. Reluctantly, he reached for his phaser, ready to stun the charging man into submission. There was no point trying to reason with the man; Riker knew berserker rage when he saw it. His fingers searched for the phaser, coming up empty. *What the hell?* he thought. *Where did my phaser go?*

The dragon's eyes sparkled.

Refracted light glinted off the polished surface of the rubies as they rolled in their sockets, inspecting first Lu Tung and then Beverly herself. She thought she heard a low, mechanical hum coming from the interior of the door. The rubies' gaze returned to Lu Tung. He held his upraised hand still, and Beverly noted, for the first time, a matching ruby on one of Lu Tung's many golden rings. Two thin red beams of coherent light jumped across the centimeters separating his hand from the door, linking the three rubies. Then the beams vanished, and a deep, guttural voice came from the mouth of the dragon: "Admittance is granted, Honored Lord. This humble guardian greets you and your honored guest."

Beverly expected the door to recede into floor or the adjoining walls. Instead, it simply blinked out of existence, leaving her wondering about the technology involved. Had the massive door and its watchful dragon been a hologram all along, or had some sort of transporter/replicator equipment dissolved the doorway? The trappings of the Dragon Empire were so archaic by Federation standards that it was easy to forget that they were not really a medieval society. Beverly considered herself duly reminded of the Pai's scientific capabilities. "Very impressive," she complimented Lu Tung.

"More than you know," he said proudly. "In the event of an unwelcome incursion, the Eyes of the Dragon are more than capable of disintegrating any unwanted caller."

"Oh," Beverly said. "It is reassuring to know that your daughter is so well protected."

"The Green Pearl is the treasure of my existence," he said, his voice growing even more solemn than usual, "and the price of ultimate peace."

Beverly thought she detected a note of reluctance in his tone. How did he really feel, she wondered, about marrying off his "treasure" to the Dragon-Heir? She had not had much of an opportunity to observe the prince back at the banquet, but what she had seen had hardly looked impressive. Certainly, both Will and Jean-Luc seemed to have formed a low opinion of Chuan-chi.

The dragon door reappeared mere seconds after she followed Lu Tung into the room. A momentary chill passed through her, as though a prison door had slammed shut behind her. There was no turning back now . . . or was there? She resisted the temptation to tap the comm badge concealed within the overlapping folds of her robes. Could she beam out if necessary, or was the harem shielded against transporter technology as well? She couldn't figure out a diplomatic way to ask Lu Tung.

The walls of the inner chamber were bright, inlaid

with many silvery pearls, as were the many overstuffed pillows that seemed to be the room's only furnishings. Beverly spotted a pile of stuffed dragons and unicorns resting in one corner; the chamber seemed to be very much the private lair of an adolescent girl. She doubted if Lu Tung spent much time here.

"Father?" A light voice rose from a heap of cushions in the room's center. Its possessor rose and bowed in a perfunctory fashion to Lord Lu Tung. "This one is honored and delighted that her honored ancestor has deigned to notice her existence." The words were delivered so rapidly that they almost blurred into one long continuous syllable. The greeting was obviously a formality that the young woman recited automatically and with great haste, eager to get it over with.

The girl lifted her head, and Beverly beheld the Green Pearl.

His phaser was gone, Riker realized.

No time to figure it out. The huge warrior was almost upon him, his massive legs scattering the trays and dishes laid out before Riker. Crystal and fine china shattered beneath the man's heavy tread. The man wore only a pair of sandals, but his lumbering steps shook the floor as if he was shod in gravity boots. "Spawn of a dung beetle!" he roared. "Prepare to be squashed like the insect you are!"

Riker was not intimidated by the warrior's invective or by his size; he'd faced larger monsters in Worf's calisthenics programs. *The bigger they are*, he thought, *et cetera, et cetera*. Clenching his fists, he drew back to deliver a knockout punch. The sooner he wrapped up this fight, the better. Riker smiled grimly. The big bruiser was probably so drunk he'd never know what hit him.

Riker aimed for the man's chin, and was caught by surprise when his opponent deftly blocked the blow by raising his right forearm in front of his face. "Hah, well done, Tu Fu, well done!" Kan-hi cheered Riker's adversary. The man lunged for Riker, who ducked beneath the giant's outstretched arms, then butted his head into the man's enormous stomach. Tu Fu staggered backward, smashing another porcelain plate beneath his feet. "Oh ho!" Kan-hi enthused cheerfully; he was clearly an equal-opportunity spectator. "Five hundred cycee on the outworlder!"

"I'll take that wager, brother," Chuan-chi said. "Five hundred cycee—and fifteen concubines—on the valiant Tu Fu."

Other male voices chimed in, betting for or against the Starfleet officer, but Riker was too busy to figure out which way the odds were running. He glanced about hastily for his missing phaser, but could spot no sign of the weapon. All of a sudden he remembered the two handmaiden's hands crawling over his body a few moments ago. Could one of them have lifted the phaser during the confusion? Suspicion wrinkled his brow. Maybe this was more than a drunken brawl. Tu Fu's sudden attack, immediately following the theft of his phaser, smacked of premeditation and conspiracy. Kicking his feet free of the surrounding pillows and cushions, Riker reevaluated his foe. Tu Fu was obviously more sober than he looked and a good deal faster.

The warrior came at Riker again, this time slashing out with an open palm. Riker yanked the upper half of his body backward, away from the blow, but the sharpened tips of Tu Fu's elongated fingernails grazed the front of Riker's dress uniform, tearing five long gashes in the sturdy red fabric. Riker's eyes widened in surprise. He hadn't realized the Pai's long nails were more than decorative. *I'll have to keep one eye on those nails,* he thought, *or risking losing both of my eyes.* He threw another punch at Tu Fu, but his fist once again collided with one of Tu Fu's meaty arms.

All around Riker and the giant warrior, wedding guests and serving women had drawn back, forming a circle of excited Pai around the two combatants. Scattered cups, dishes, and cushions remained strewn about the harem floor. Boisterous bachelors, clutching overflowing goblets of wine, cheered and booed the battlers, jostling each other to gain a better view, while the female servants scurried away toward safety or else hid behind the bodies of the men, peering at the fight over the bachelors' shoulders. Even the humorless Chuan-chi appeared to be caught up in the growing excitement, shouting words of encouragement to Tu Fu just as the enraged soldier took a second swipe at Riker. Lowering his head just in time, Riker felt Tu Fu's razor-sharp fingernails brush over his scalp. A lock of Riker's dark brown hair fell almost unnoticed to the floor. *I don't think this is what the captain had in mind,* he thought ruefully.

The fighters circled each other warily, with Riker taking care to remain at a safe distance from Tu Fu. The Pai was easily three times Riker's weight; if they started grappling up close it would be too easy for the other man to use his mass against Riker. He wasn't about to let that happen. "Coward!" Tu Fu taunted him. "Are you afraid to fight me?"

"Hah! Show him what you can do, Will!" Kan-hi yelled from the sidelines. *Easy for him to say,* Riker thought. At the corner of his eye he caught a glimpse of the Dragon's scapegrace younger son standing in the forefront of the mob watching the fight. He had one arm each around the shoulders of two nearly naked serving girls who looked like they were holding the inebriated prince upright. Riker only got a quick look at the two women, but he could have sworn they were the same seductive pair who had tag-teamed him less than ten minutes ago. Had one of them taken his phaser? And if so, was Kan-hi in on the plot?

Tu Fu gave Riker no leisure to consider the possibilities. A ferocious growl rumbled out of the warrior's wide chest and he raced at Riker with both clawed hands outstretched before him. Riker suddenly felt like a matador facing down an onrushing bull. *Worf would love this,* he mused at the exact moment that he tensed to dive out of the way. *Left or right?* he wondered, coolly considering his options. "Get him, Tu Fu!" a voice commanded from somewhere right behind him. "Destroy the foreigner for the honor of the Empire!"

That order could only have come from Chuan-chi, Riker realized, recognizing both the voice and contemptuous tone. *Some host,* he thought, scowling. Then the full implications of the situation hit him with the force of a disruptor blast. If he darted out of Tu Fu's path, then the huge warrior's headlong rush would carry him—and his deadly talons—straight into the Dragon-Heir himself. Would Tu Fu be able to halt his charge in time? Riker doubted it. A vivid image of the Heir impaled upon the big Pai's bloody claws flared to life in Riker's mind, as clear as anything he'd ever seen in a holodeck. In the flickering light of the painted paper lanterns Tu Fu's immense shadow speeded ahead of him, casting a pall over Riker and, behind him, Chuan-chi. Ten sharpened, foot-long fingernails zeroed in on Riker's face. He had only a heartbeat to react.

He met Tu Fu's charge with one of his own. Crouching low, he surged under the giant's arms, slamming his right shoulder into the Pai's midsection with all the force he could muster. The impact was not enough to fully overcome Tu Fu's accumulated momentum, but he slowed the other man down enough to give everyone else a chance to get out of the way. He heard gasps and squeals and wild laughter behind him, but, thankfully, no shouts of mortal anguish. The Heir had been spared an "accidental" demise. Riker was just paranoid enough, or properly suspicious enough, to wonder for a fleeting second whether or not Chuan-chi had been the actual target all along. After all, in the middle of an unplanned, uncontrolled scuffle, anything could happen. . . .

Sharp, burning pain brought an abrupt end to Riker's theorizing. Tu Fu's nails dug into his back, rending fabric and flesh. Only the fact that the warrior was still off-balance from his interrupted lunge kept Tu Fu from taking full advantage of his position and sinking his nails even deeper into Riker's body, perhaps all the way to fragile internal organs. Riker knew he couldn't let Tu Fu get a better grip. Before Tu Fu could strike again, he grabbed hold of the warrior's right leg just above the kneecap. Years of martial-arts training paid off when Riker flipped Tu Fu over his shoulders. The Pai grunted in surprise as he somersaulted over Riker, landing flat on his back where only moments before the Dragon-Heir had cheered him on.

"Excellent! No, truly sublime!" Kan-hi exulted, wedged between (and seemingly propped up by) his brother's women. He did not sound, Riker judged, like a man whose assassination plot has just been foiled. Perhaps he'd been totally oblivious of his brother's recent close call. Or maybe he was a very good actor.

Riker spun around on his heels, hoping to take the offensive before Tu Fu climbed back on his feet. Maybe he could still finish the man off before anybody really got hurt. To his dismay, though, he saw that some of Tu Fu's friends had already hauled him upright. He glared at Riker with sheer hatred and bloodlust in his good eye. "Damn," Riker muttered, contemplating the way Tu Fu's allies gathered in his wake. Once the bachelors really started taking sides, this one-on-one could easily escalate into a near-riot. There was no way he could guard both princes in that sort of bloody chaos.

"Another five hundred cycees on the Federation man," Kan-hi said boldly. His handsome face was flushed with wine.

"A thousand cycees and one hundred concubines on Tu Fu of the Dragon Empire," Chuan-chi responded. Raucous cheers greeted his challenge.

*Great,* Riker thought sarcastically. *Make this a matter of imperial honor.* He only hoped a thousand cycees (whatever a cycee was) wasn't worth killing over.

\* \* \*

Beverly could readily see why the warlord's daughter was known as the Green Pearl. The girl's most striking feature was her eyes, which were large, bright, and chartreuse, while her smooth, unblemished skin was pearly white. The contrast between the brilliance of her eyes and the paleness of her face was the like the flash of phaser fire against the void of interstellar space. The Green Pearl wore a simple, sea green gown, surprisingly unadorned by Pai standards. Apparently, even the design-crazy Pai realized that excess frills and ornamentation could only distract the eye from the future bride's natural beauty. The tips of tiny velvet slippers peeked out from the beneath the hem of her gown. The Green Pearl was substantially younger than the Dragon-Heir; Beverly guessed she was about seventeen.

"My daughter," Lu Tung addressed her, "this woman is a visitor from the United Federation of Planets. She has generously volunteered to look after you tonight. Dr. Crusher, please meet my daughter, Lady Yao Hu, called the Green Pearl of Lord Lu Tung."

The girl rolled her eyes at her title. The extravagant label clearly embarrassed her. "She came on the starship? They travel with their women?"

"She is a skilled healer," Lu Tung explained. "And a Starfleet officer, if you can imagine such a thing."

"Really?" Her eyebrows shot up and became lost beneath her bangs. "How fascinating!" The girl gazed at Beverly with open curiosity. Beverly assumed Yao Hu seldom encountered strangers in her father's harem.

"I am very happy to meet you, Lady Yao Hu," Beverly said warmly.

"Thank you." The girl nodded in Beverly's direction, then turned back toward Lu Tung. "But really, Father, I don't need a baby-sitter. I'm getting married tomorrow, which means I'm practically an adult!"

"Hah! That's what you think!" A second girl popped up from where she had been hidden in the depths of an overstuffed couch farther within the shadowy confines of the chamber. "Greetings, Exalted Lord, and Esteemed Sire of the Green Pearl," she said. "This one is honored and delighted and so forth. . . ."

"Hsiao!" the Pearl said indignantly. "That's hardly respectful."

The other girl looked a few years older than Yao Hu: shorter and tomboy-slim even in her scarlet robes, with dark hair cut short to the shoulders. "You're not my mother yet," she warned.

"I will be tomorrow, and then you're going to have to be a lot nicer to me," the Pearl said.

"I'll still be the elder, and *you* will have to be nicer to *me.*"

"Indeed?" said the Pearl in a dangerous tone.

"That is enough," Lu Tung commanded, silencing the bickering adolescents. "Dr. Crusher, this is Hsiao Har, the Heir's daughter from his first marriage. Since she is soon to be my Pearl's stepdaughter, she has been visiting for the past few weeks. After all, they must learn to live together . . . or so it is hoped."

The tomboy tossed her head defiantly. "This is absurd. She can't possibly be my mother. It's ridiculous."

"And I wouldn't want her as a daughter, anyway!" the Pearl retorted. "She is far too disobedient and horrid."

"You're the horrid one."

Lu Tung scowled, heavy furrows forming across his brow. He bowed in Beverly's direction. "Madam, I leave my daughter—and future granddaughter—to your care." Beverly suddenly felt like she was being left in command of the *Enterprise* during a Borg assault.

*What in the world have I got myself into?*

"Thrash him, Will!" Kan-hi urged. "For the Federation!"

A sneer twisted Tu Fu's blocklike visage. Dark purple swelling had spread over his injured eye like some sort of cancerous tumor. "Federation . . . hah! This is what I think of your Federation!" he spat, heaving a wad of sticky, green, foul-looking saliva at Riker's feet. "The Federation is *pi t'i*," he snarled, using an insult apparently beyond the vocabulary of Riker's Universal Translator. That was fine; Riker got the gist of it.

"Come now!" Kan-hi exhorted him. "You're not actually going to let him say that, are you?"

Riker didn't need a medical tricorder to know his blood pressure was rising. Ordinarily, he would have liked nothing better than to feed Tu Fu his own fingernails one finger at a time, but this wasn't merely another shore-leave brawl. He had a job to do, so he forced himself to keep cool. He glanced again at the Pai's blackened left eye; Tu Fu couldn't possibly see anything through all that swelling. An idea occurred to Riker. . . .

*"Pi t'i* yourself," Riker said, deliberately provoking his opponent. Tu Fu reacted exactly as planned. Bellowing like an incensed Klingon *targ,* he hurled his vast bulk across the empty floor at Riker. Riker

weaved to the left with malice aforethought, coming up squarely on the Pai's blind side. Now Tu Fu failed to block Riker's punch. His right fist connected with the warrior's exposed chin, sending a shock of vibration all the way down Riker's arm to his shoulder bone. The man's jaw felt like it was made out of duranium. *Uh-oh,* Riker thought. This didn't look good.

If Riker's blow hurt Tu Fu, he didn't show it. He slammed into Riker with all his weight, carrying Riker backward with the force of a stampede. The crowd of onlookers must have parted to make way for them, for the next thing Riker knew he and his enemy had smashed through one of the vertical paper screens dividing the outer harem into various compartments. Paper shredded and wooden supports snapped beneath an avalanche of thrashing, battling human bodies. Riker heard women screaming and a male voice cursing. He saw five or six young ladies, mostly nude, running away in panic. A Pai nobleman, similarly unclad, was rolling frantically out of the way, grabbing up his discarded garments as he scrambled to his feet only a few meters distant. *I guess someone isn't a fight fan,* Riker thought wryly—right before the back of his head came to rest against the floor of the harem. A surplus of overstuffed pillows cushioned his crash landing but failed to prevent the entire weight of the sumo-sized warrior from pounding him into the pillows. His battered rib cage shrieked in protest; he'd been on heavy-gravity worlds that hadn't crushed him this much. He could barely breathe.

Even Tu Fu seemed momentarily stunned by the impact of their fall, or perhaps he was merely disoriented by the torn remnants of a colorful silk hanging currently wrapped around his head. His silk-shrouded face was only centimeters away from Riker's. He sprawled on top of the Starfleet officer like a misplaced mountain. Riker briefly considered kneeing Tu Fu where it would hurt most, but figured that the Pai would probably judge that tactic dishonorable in the extreme. Instead he took a deep breath, straining to expand his lungs against the tremendous mass pressing down on him, then pried his arms out from beneath Tu Fu. Clasping both hands together, he drove his locked fists into the underside of the warrior's chin. Tu Fu's head snapped back, exposing his naked throat. Riker chopped him in the neck with the edge of his right hand. Tu Fu grunted in pain and tried to pull himself off Riker, who rocked back and forth on his spine until he had enough momentum to roll both himself and Tu Fu all the way over. Now Riker was on top, with Tu Fu's unwieldy bulk spread out beneath him. He jabbed his knee into Tu Fu's stomach, and heard shouts and laughter all around him. The circle of spectators had re-formed around the fighters, Kan-hi and the other bachelors whooping and hollering as Riker raised both fists high above his head, ready to bring them crashing down on Tu Fu and ending the show here and now. He wondered what Kan-hi would do with all the money and concubines he was about to win.

A splash of wine struck Riker in the face . . .

"Father, wait!" the Pearl objected as Lord Lu Tung prepared to depart. "You can't leave her here." Green eyes found Beverly's. "I mean no disrespect, Doctor, but, as I said, I truly have no need of a nurse or chaperone. Your kindness does me great honor, but you must not inconvenience yourself for this one's sake."

"It's no inconvenience," Beverly insisted. As long as Yao Hu remained a potential target for an assassin's deadly efforts, she could not afford to leave the young bride alone. Well, alone with Hsiao Har anyway. Not that she suspected the Heir's tomboy daughter of any evil designs, but she didn't think relying on one teenage girl to protect another was exactly what Jean-Luc had in mind.

"Indeed," Lu Tung said sternly. "It is not right that a bride go to her wedding without the comfort and guidance of an older, wiser woman. You should be grateful Dr. Crusher has agreed to accompany you tonight."

"I am, Father, truly I am," the Pearl said, "but . . . but . . ." She seemed at a loss for words, but quite stricken at the prospect of being left in Beverly's charge. *Why is that?* Beverly wondered. She was not offended, merely puzzled. *Why is this so important to the Pearl?*

"Don't worry, Lord Lu Tung," Hsiao Har spoke up. "I can look after your precious Pearl."

*"You?"* The young bride appeared offended by the very idea, even more so than by the notion of Beverly watching over her. *I guess I'm the lesser of two evils,* Beverly thought with some amusement.

"Well, I am both older and wiser," Hsiao Har said. She strode across the cushion-strewn floor until only a few meters separated her from the Pearl. Beverly noted that the Heir's daughter was slightly taller than the other girl, who glowered at Hsiao Har. Beverly hoped she wouldn't have to referee any actual wrestling matches between the two.

"Much older," the Pearl taunted Hsiao Har. "Much, *much* older. But wiser? I hardly think so."

Lu Tung sighed wearily, but did nothing to halt the verbal sparring between his daughter and Hsiao Har. Apparently, the disputes of mere females were beneath his dignity to notice or deal with. *That's women's work,* Beverly thought with a touch of resentment; her opinion of Lu Tung descended one notch. "Madam," he said, bowing his head, "I wish you good luck." He waved his hand before the heavy iron door and its guardian dragon. Lasers flashed briefly between the door and his ring, and Lord Lu Tung stepped through the now-open exit. Seconds later, door and dragon rematerialized, sealing Beverly in with her quarreling young charges.

"Brat," the Pearl hissed at Hsiao Har the instant her father was out of sight. "Crone!"

"Baby," returned Hsiao Har. "Fetus!" She dropped into what suspiciously resembled a martial-arts stance. Beverly suddenly suspected that the women of the harem might not be the fragile flowers she had assumed them to be.

"*Yao*-goblin!" the Pearl said, raising her hands before her, karate-style.

"*Nan hai tzu!*" Hsiao Har responded. She raised one foot, the tip of her slipper extended toward the Pearl. The situation looked to be rapidly escalating out of control. *Red alert.* Beverly thought automatically.

"Girls!" Beverly clapped her hands together. *I sound like the mother in a Victorian novel,* she thought ruefully, but it seemed to work. The girls backed away from each other, their tense bodies gradually lapsing back into less aggressive postures. With any luck, she thought, they'll be reluctant to misbehave too badly in front of a perfect stranger. Hsiao Har glared balefully at the Pearl, who, without much grace or warning, collapsed onto the nearest cushion. She crossed her arms sullenly in front her. Her lower lip formed a definite pout. *What's she most upset about,* Beverly wondered, *her fight with Hsiao Har, my presence here, or*—a thought suddenly occurred to Beverly—*her imminent wedding to the Heir?* Whichever it was, Beverly figured she was in for a long and awkward evening.

*All my years of Starfleet training,* she reflected, *and I end up playing den mother at a kung-fu slumber party.* She was definitely going to have to talk to Jean-Luc about her job description.

She just hoped the others were having an easier time of it.

The wine splashed against Riker's face, blinding him only seconds before his fists could complete their downward plunge. The harsh, stinging liquid caught him completely by surprise; he had no idea where it had come from or who had thrown it at him. He blinked and sputtered, shaking his head and flinging off tiny droplets of emerald-colored wine in every direction. The alcohol stung his eyes, its cloying, fruity flavor filling his mouth and nostrils. The luke-warm liquid ran down his cheeks and dripped from his beard. *Damn,* he cursed silently. *When I get my hands on the joker who tossed that wine . . . !*

Tu Fu stood up suddenly, sending Riker flying. He felt himself plummeting to the floor, then landed hard on his left side. His hip smacked against marble tiles, sending a jolt of agony shooting up his side. Still

blinded by the wine in his eyes, he tried to roll away
from Tu Fu but he didn't move fast enough. A heavy
foot stomped down on his back, driving his face into
the floor and pinning him beneath Tu Fu's elephan-
tine tread. Riker blinked again, shaking his head
violently in a vain attempt to rid himself of the last
drops of the sticky, clinging liquid that obscured his
vision, but still his eyes stung as if on fire, tearing up
faster than he could wipe them away with the back of
his hand. *Very well then,* he thought. He didn't need
his eyes to clobber this brute once and for all.

"You should have listened to me, outlander," Tu Fu
crowed. "I said I would grind you into the dirt like a
bug and so I will." He dug his heel into the base of
Riker's spine. "No foreign devil can stand against a
true warrior of the Empire."

Kan-hi disagreed. "Don't just lie there!" he yelled
at Riker. "Get up! Do something! Vanquish him this
minute!"

"Once again you have wagered unwisely, my brother," Chuan-chi said. Riker could readily imagine the
smirk on his face. "No wonder you have so many
gambling debts."

Riker had heard enough. Tu Fu twisted his heel
once more, but Riker did his best to ignore the
excruciating pain in his back. Mentally, he removed
himself from the harem, the palace, and Pai itself,
placing himself instead on a gray, padded mat in an
empty gymnasium somewhere in Alaska. He saw his
father standing a few meters away. A reinforced red
plastic helmet, its visor down, rendered Kyle Riker
completely sightless, but that didn't matter. *Anbo-
jyutsu* was not about eyes, but motion. Controlled,
efficient motion. "Trust your other senses, then let

them go," his father had told him over and over in countless training sessions just like this one. "Let your unconscious keep track of where you are in relation to your opponent. Concentrate on nothing except the moment and the motion. The moment *is* the motion." With an effortless flip, Kyle Riker dropped his son face-forward onto the mat. He held him down with one foot, standing like an old-time safari hunter posing astride a fallen lion. The younger Riker fought back tears of frustration and anger. There was no possible escape from this humiliating position . . . or was there? Kyle Riker would not let his son give up. "There is a defense to every attack," he repeated endlessly until Riker was sick of hearing it. "An escape to every trap." Riker squirmed helplessly underneath the constant pressure of his father's foot. *"Anbo-jyutsu."* Kyle said in his memory. "Don't think about it. Just move."

Riker moved.

His legs snapped up behind Tu Fu, striking like twin cobras. He hooked his feet around Tu Fu's legs, as wide around as small pillars, then straightened his own legs in one convulsive jerk. The huge Pai warrior was flung backward. Riker heard the man's skull crack against the marble floor, followed by the sound of heavy, regular breathing. Riker recognized the reassuring rhythm of unconsciousness.

Applause and some jeers greeted Riker's victory. Turning over and sitting up, he took a second or two to wipe his eyes thoroughly free of wine and tears. As his vision cleared, he saw Kan-hi standing nearby with a jubilant smile on his face. The two women who had been flanking him had vanished. Riker glanced around, looking for them, but was unable to locate either woman amid the assembled crowd of bachelors and serving maids. He still had his suspicions about his lost phaser, not to mention that sudden faceful of wine. "He okay?" he asked Kan-hi, nodding in the direction of Tu Fu's collapsed form.

"I suppose so," the Second Son said blithely. "I'm sure the women will summon a physician if there's anything serious . . . but enough about that enormous fool! That was most impressive, friend Will." He slapped Riker on the back. Riker winced. His back was still sore from where Tu Fu's nails had gouged him.

"I'd like to give that guy a manicure," he groused. *Preferably with a phaser set on maximum.*

Kan-hi inspected the lacerations on Riker's back and the gashes in his uniform. He shook his head thoughtfully. "No, this just won't do, Will. Your garment is quite ruined. Here, have one of my own robes." Kan-hi undid the ties on his outermost gown and casually shucked the flowing, yellow robe. Riker saw that the prince still had several more layers of clothing beneath his top robe. Kan-hi held out the robe, offering it to Riker.

"That's not at all necessary, sir," Riker said. He carefully stood up, feeling a short stab of pain in his lower back as he straightened himself out.

"But I insist," Kan-hi said. He laughed loudly. "With the money you just won for me, I will be able to afford a whole new wardrobe. Isn't that so, brother."

Standing not far away, his hands folded primly over his chest, Chuan-chi frowned at his younger sibling. "Have no fear. Unlike some others I might mention, I always repay my debts. *All* my debts," he emphasized with an openly venomous look at Riker. *I may have just saved your life, you stuck-up ass,* Riker thought angrily about the Dragon-Heir. The more he contemplated the matter, the more he became convinced that his scuffle with Tu Fu was not just a random act of unpremeditated violence. Someone wanted him or Chuan-chi taken out of the picture. Perhaps they had both been targets. He made a mental note to discuss the incident with Captain Picard at the first opportunity that presented itself. He wondered how Deanna and the others were faring and if they were safe.

At the moment, though, he simply accepted the yellow robe from Kan-hi. One of the ever-present serving maids lightly wiped the blood from his face and shoulders before helping him don the expensive silk robe. "Well, if you insist," he said amiably. "I guess my uniform has seen better days." He took a gander at the Dragon-Heir's lengthy fingernails and remembered the way Tu Fu's nails had sliced through his flesh. "Are everybody's nails that sharp?" he asked.

"Oh no," Kan-hi told him. "Tu Fu belongs to the Sacred Order of the Extended Digits. Their nails are dipped daily from birth in a special solution that hardens the nails and increases their tensile strength."

"Good Lord," Riker said, both impressed and appalled. "Is this, er, a large order?" He certainly hoped not.

Kan-hi shook his head. Riker noted that the Second Son swayed slightly as he spoke, but seemed to have sobered up enough to stand without assistance. Perhaps he was not really as drunk as he'd appeared before. "Many are chosen, but few survive to adulthood. Most cannot resist the temptation to scratch an itch."

Riker found himself rendered speechless for a moment. *Probably best not to think about it too much,* he decided. Instead he chose to conduct a quick survey of the party. His eyes scanned the chamber. Quickly and efficiently the remaining female servants were tidying up and restoring order to the outer harem. The perforated paper screen had already been dragged away and replaced with a new screen that served to hide the unconscious warrior from sight. A harp string was plucked somewhere in an adjoining compartment and the plaintive strains of soft music attempted to soothe the savage breasts of the hot-blooded young men. Fresh fruit and wine materialized in bountiful quantities, carried in on the slender arms of still more alluring young women.

Unfortunately, Riker observed, most of the men were paying little attention to the music, the refreshments, or the beautiful women. The bachelors milled about restlessly, some of them grouping around Kanhi while the rest lingered in the vicinity of the Heir. There was an air of expectancy in the chamber. Everyone seemed to be watching Riker and the two princes, and waiting for something to happen. Even the serving maids seemed on edge, despite their persistent smiles and demure behavior. Riker sensed that the potential for violence had not ended with his defeat of Tu Fu. If anything, his brief tussle with the Pai warrior might have actually whetted the party-goers' appetite for a real, knock-down-drag-them-out brawl, which was the last thing Riker wanted to get going, especially with an assassin or two lurking somewhere among the decorative screens and plush divans. *Think,* Riker ordered himself. There had to be some way he could channel the aggression and competitiveness of these men into a less dangerous pursuit. But how?

A broad grin spread over Will Riker's face as the solution presented itself to him.

"Tell me, gentlemen," he asked, "have you ever heard of a game called poker?"

# Chapter Seven

WORF LOOKED AROUND as he was led through the halls of the Imperial Palace. The servant who led him moved silently and very fast, so that even Worf's long stride was barely able to keep up.

So far, the Klingon warrior did not think much of Pai. The lavishly decorated halls, the gaudy attire of the people they passed, even the scented smoke hanging in the air, struck him as decadent, soft. Any race who so elaborately and painstakingly carved even the very hinges of every door was obviously lost to all sense of proper discipline. Up ahead, Worf spotted an artisan of some sort lying on his back atop an anti-gravity platform several meters above the floor. The craftsman peered through thick magnifying lenses as he employed a laser-stylus to etch in details far too minute to be seen from the floor below. *What a waste of time,* Worf thought. A low growl escaped his lips as he walked under the floating platform.

Finally, and none too soon as far as Worf was concerned, the servant stopped smoothly in front of an ornate door inlaid with pale blue and pink enamel. Worf growled again, as the door slid open and he found himself face-to-face with a scowling Pai noble.

In true Klingon fashion, Worf automatically assessed the stranger's potential as an adversary. The Pai was only a few centimeters shorter than Worf, and clad in armor from head to foot. The armor reminded Worf of illustrations he'd seen in his human step-father's history books, particularly the chapters concerning the old Asian empires on preindustrial Earth. The gold and silver beads covering the chestplate and helmet were a typically decadent touch, but otherwise the armor seemed sturdy enough. Only the Pai's face was exposed, revealing a broad face and two glaring eyes beneath heavy black brows that met above a nose that looked as though it had been flattened, and broken at least once, in past battles. A scar running down the man's right cheek also testified to its owner's violent past. Worf nodded approvingly. The man's battered-but-unbowed visage was the first thing he'd seen on this prettified jewelry box of a planet that he could identify with.

Most importantly, though, Worf noted the unsheathed swords the Pai warrior held in each of his hands.

"I am Chih-li, Imperial Grand Minister of Internal Security, First Rank," the man barked. "Your very presence insults my honor."

His words hit Worf like a slap across the face. "What do you know of honor?" he demanded.

Chih-li raised his chin proudly. "The safety of the Dragon, his family, his guests, and his property is my responsibility and mine alone. To suggest I require foreign assistance is to besmirch my honor in the most heinous manner imaginable."

Worf's steady gaze never left the blades in Chih-li's hands. "Honor demands I obey the commands of my captain. I cannot do otherwise."

"I see," Chih-li said. He fixed Worf with a penetrating stare. "Then our course is set." He raised both swords in front of him. Worf reached for his phaser. "Choose your weapon," Chih-li said solemnly.

Worf's hand came away from his phaser. Understanding dawned in his eyes and behind the ridges of his brow. "You challenge me?"

Chih-li nodded, thrusting the hilts of both blades toward Worf. "It is a matter of honor," he declared.

That was good enough for Worf. He suspected that Captain Picard would not approve of this duel, but failed to see any alternative. He could think of no greater way to offend the Pai, and sour relations between the Federation and the Dragon Empire, than by refusing to respect their standards of honor. Honor, to his mind, was the only universal verity strong enough to unite such disparate peoples as the Pai and the various component races of the Federation, not to mention the Federation and the Klingon Empire. Honor, mutually accorded, was the cornerstone of the Klingon-Federation alliance, just as it was their shameless lack of honor that made accommodation with either the Cardassians or the accursed Romulans unthinkable.

Worf accepted a sword from Chih-li's right hand. The long silver blade gleamed beneath the flickering light of the paper lanterns. He saw no nicks, scratches, or other defects upon its surface. Stepping back, he swung the sword experimentally, slicing through the foggy, incense-laden air. The sword was neither as heavy nor as versatile as a Klingon *bat'telh,* but it struck him as a good weapon nonetheless. "This will do," he grunted.

No other words were necessary. Chih-li shifted his remaining sword to his now-empty right hand and extended the point toward Worf, who assumed a defensive pose. His lack of armor put him at a disadvantage, Worf realized, but only a coward would refuse a challenge on those grounds. Besides, he did not intend to grant first blood to the Pai.

Chih-li attacked ferociously, driving Worf farther back into the hall. Behind the Dragon's Minister of Internal Security (First Rank), the enamel-covered door slid back into place, cutting off both combatants from the chamber beyond. Worf retreated only a few steps, however, before meeting the Pai's assault with an attack of his own. Steel clanged against naked steel as they tried to force each other back through sheer force of arms. Their faces, only centimeters apart, met above crossed blades. Chih-li clenched his teeth. Sweat dripped from beneath the brim of his helmet. Worf could see the effort—and the determination— written on Chih-li's face. His opinion of the Dragon Empire rose by the minute.

Back and forth, they tottered, neither warrior willing to yield one centimeter to the other. Worf would press forward for an instant, only to be pushed back a second later by Chih-li's unrelenting exertion. The Minister of Internal Security was strong for a human . . . or a Pai. Changing tactics, Worf stopped pressing against his adversary's sword and stepped abruptly to one side. Caught off guard, Chih-li stumbled forward, his own momentum carrying him onward into the space Worf had vacated. The flat of Worf's blade struck Chih-li right below his ribs. The blow knocked the wind out of the Pai, who gasped out loud. *Good,* Worf thought. He didn't want to kill Chih-li, and not just for the captain's sake. The Pai had proven an honorable opponent. Worf raised his free hand, forming it into a fist, and prepared to strike Chih-li at the back of his neck, just below the rear of his helmet. With luck, one good blow would render the Pai unconscious and bring the duel to an honorable, yet bloodless, conclusion.

But Chih-li was not as stunned as Worf hoped, and much more acrobatic. Before Worf's fist could lower the boom on him, Chih-li flipped headfirst over Worf's sword, spinning through the air and landing on his feet several meters behind Worf, who barely had time to turn around before Chih-li came charging at him once more, shouting an incomprehensible battle cry at the top of his lungs. Worf quickly raised his sword to meet the razor-sharp blade descending toward his head.

Blue sparks flashed as the swords smashed together. The ring of steel echoed down the wide expanse of corridor. Worf's sword searched for chinks in his opponent's armor, but Chih-li's skillful parries never let Worf's sword get that close. Out of the corner of his eye, Worf saw a bevy of servant girls coming down the hall, clad in flowing robes of peach and lavender. High-pitched screams rose from the young women as they came upon the fierce struggle being waged in the hall. "A demon!" one of them shrieked. "The minister is battling a demon from hell!" Worf felt mildly offended.

Yanking up the hems of their gowns, the women scurried away as fast as their lithe young legs could carry them. Worf barely noticed their departure; all his concentration was consumed by his unceasing duel with Chih-li. Their silver swords darted in and out of each other's defenses like a pair of fighting fishes. Chih-li's chestplate was scratched and dented around the abdomen, where moments earlier he had fallen headlong against Worf's sword, but his armor had protected the warrior underneath. A handful of gold and silver pearls had been dislodged by the blow; they rolled about on the white tile floor, aggravating Worf, who had to struggle not to slip and fall on them. Despite his best intentions, he felt the fire in his heart growing hotter by the moment. He wanted to spill blood, not pearls.

Feint. Thrust. Parry. The duel carried them down the long hallway. Chih-li was the more accomplished fencer, technically, but Worf, unencumbered by heavy metal armor, was faster and more agile. *This battle is taking too long,* he thought, fighting to keep his berserker rage under control. He must not forget his true mission: to protect the Dragon and his followers. In time, perhaps, his superior stamina would wear the Pai down, but Worf did not have time to wait that long. Every second he spent dueling with Chih-li kept him away from his duty. He had to bring the combat to an end as quickly as possible. *My mistake,* he thought. *I should have spent more time in Lieutenant Barclay's "Three Musketeers" holodeck scenario.*

Parrying Chih-li's sword once more, Worf attempted a sudden riposte. The unexpected thrust took the Pai unawares; he had to jump backward to avoid being skewered between the eyes. Worf did not let up, keeping Chih-li on the defensive. His sword crashed down again and again upon the other man's blade, forcing Chih-li to use his sword as a shield, not a weapon. Chih-li staggered backward until his back collided with a wall. Worf had him cornered now. A grim smile twisted the Klingon's lips. He seemed to tower above Chih-li as the Imperial Minister of Internal Security ducked, his head hunched below his shoulders, beneath Worf's savage blows. Worf wondered if disarming Chih-li would be enough, or would the Pai's honor only be satisfied by being rendered wounded or unconscious? However, it would not be long now. Worf raised his weapon, ready to chop Chih-li's sword in two with his very next blow.

Then his comm badge beeped, distracting him. "What?" he exclaimed, glancing down at his chest. Chih-li seized the opportunity, springing upward with the speed of a stampeding *targ*. The tip of his sword sliced between the pommel of Worf's weapon and the hand that held it. Worf grunted in pain as his sword went flying through the air, clattering to the ground several meters away from where he now stood.

"Lieutenant Worf?" Data's voice emerged from Worf's badge. "Ensign Craigie has detected some unusual signals from the Dragon Nebula. I thought you should be notified, although the readings are within the parameters of what might be expected from a trigol-type nebula under conditions of . . ."

"Tell me later," Worf barked, backing away from

the point of Chih-li's sword. "Worf out." Dark Kling-on blood dripped from his palm, staining the golden surface of his badge when he tapped it. Chih-li advanced toward Worf, a triumphant grin transforming his features. Worf felt the swordpoint against his chest, pricking him through his yellow Starfleet uniform. His hand drifted toward his phaser, then halted. *No,* he concluded, *that would not be honorable.*

"You fought well, outlander," Chih-li conceded. "If I required assistance, which I categorically do not, you would be a welcome ally." Beneath the rim of his helmet, his forehead wrinkled in puzzlement. "I confess, I am unfamiliar with your customs. Do you prefer death or surrender?"

Sitting in the captain's chair on the bridge of the *Enterprise,* Data found it odd that Worf cut off his transmission so abruptly. He hoped that he had not interrupted Worf at an inconvenient moment.

Although most of the senior officers had beamed down to Pai, the bridge was fully staffed. Lieutenant Tor remained stationed at the conn, while Lieutenant Melilli Mera, a tall Bajoran woman, sat at Data's usual post. Data could hear her silver earring chime whenever she moved her head; he suspected the sound was too soft to be detected by the ears of most humanoids. Ensign Cameron Craigie, a recent graduate of the Gibson Science Institute in Montreal, monitored the science station. It was Craigie who had detected the anomalous readings coming from the Dragon Nebula.

"Any further information, Ensign Craigie?" Data asked.

"No, sir, the concentration of ionized plasma in the nebula is higher than one would expect, but it's holding steady. It could indicate the presence of a sizable number of starships within the nebula, or it could just be a statistical glitch. The nebula itself makes obtaining reliable readings difficult."

"Understood," Data said. "Continue to monitor the nebula and alert me if the situation changes." Data assimilated the ensign's report, adding it to the list of variables operative at this time. He considered informing the captain, but swiftly decided to wait until more information was available. As he had attempted to explain to Worf, the current readings, while unexpected, did fall within the outer parameters established for a trigol-type nebula of this variety.

The turbolift doors opened behind Data, and Geordi La Forge stepped onto the bridge. "I hate dress uniforms," he said, tugging at the neat standing collar of the formal uniform. "And what's all this about a guided tour anyway? I have enough to do finalizing the wedding fireworks without this sort of thing."

"I am sorry, Geordi," Data said, rising from the command seat. "The Lord High Celestial Mechanic of the First Rank and the Grand Astronomical Savant have both expressed an interest in Federation starship technology. It seemed politic to offer them a firsthand look at the *Enterprise*'s engines."

"Isn't this a violation of the Prime Directive," La Forge said hopefully, "showing them Federation technology?"

"Apparently, the Dragon Empire already has star travel, although it seems a little cumbersome to us, being based on nebular-sail dynamics rather than warp and impulse drives. Besides, the Empire will shortly be a part of the Federation."

"That's not what I heard," La Forge said. "Rumor has it the Dragon is giving the captain a rough time about the treaty."

"That is correct," Data confirmed, "but I can assure you that the Dragon will almost certainly *not* sign the treaty if we treat his scientists with anything less than respect." Everything he had observed about the Pai supported the proposition that they placed great importance on matters of propriety and personal honor. In that manner, they resembled many of the 6,726 humanoid species Data had studied and committed to memory.

"Oh, I'll be perfectly charming," La Forge said grumpily. "I'll show them every bolt and fuse-scar on the fuselage if they want to see them. I just hope they're on time. I still have half the remote phaser programmables to charge."

A soft tone punctuated La Forge's complaints, coming from Lieutenant Melilli's console. She silenced the deadman's warning and was keying rapidly.

"Commander Data," she said. "We have intercepted a transmission sent from somewhere in the nebula."

"Thank you, Lieutenant." Data crossed to her station and looked over her shoulder as she continued running a computer check. "Can you pinpoint the source?"

"I'm working on it, sir," she said. "It won't be easy in this Prophet-cursed gas cloud."

"What about the content of the transmission?" Data inquired.

"It's encrypted," Melilli said. "The computer is attempting to break the code, but it may take a while."

"I see," Data said. "Please call up the digital breakdown of the transmission so I can see it for myself."

Melilli complied, and a stream of numerical information raced across her screen, faster than a human mind could absorb. "Thank you," Data said a few heartbeats later. He assigned 36.89% of his reasoning faculties the task of deciphering the coded transmission. Fortunately, he was more than capable of addressing several tasks at once.

Data stepped away from Melilli's station and joined La Forge by the command chair. "The G'kkau?" La Forge asked quietly.

"Most likely," Data affirmed. "In what quantities and to what purpose we can only speculate."

La Forge shook his head. "I sure hope the captain and the others are straightening everything out down there. I have a feeling our time is running out."

"I have no feelings to rely on," Data said, "but the probability of an imminent G'kkau invasion grows more likely. We must be prepared for any eventuality."

Ensign Kamis, a Benzite, looked up from the communications console. "Commander Data? Commander La Forge? The Imperial scientists are on board." Puffs of methane and ammonia rose from the breathing apparatus positioned under his mouth.

"Damn," La Forge swore. "I meant to be there when they arrived."

"Please inform the transporter room that Commander La Forge is on his way," Data informed

Ensign Kamis. "Geordi, please say nothing about the G'kkau to the our guests. There's no point in alarming them until the captain manages to bring Pai under Federation protection."

"Don't worry, Data," La Forge said as he hurried toward the turbolift. "I can be alarmed enough for all of us."

Data assumed Geordi was joking, but he could not be sure. Humor remained a difficult concept to grasp. He regained his seat in the captain's chair and consulted his internal chronometer. The Imperial wedding of the Dragon-Heir and the Green Pearl of Lu Tung was to be held at sunrise, approximately 10.5782 hours from now. He hoped that his fellow officers could keep the participants alive until then.

# Chapter Eight

*A KLINGON NEVER SURRENDERS,* Worf thought. Chih-li's sword dug into his chest. He retreated a few steps more, and a dark, rectangular shadow fell over him. *The shadow of death,* he thought fatalistically. He looked upward and saw the bottom of a man-sized, metal platform hovering about four meters above his head. A youthful Pai peered over the edge of the platform, gazing at Worf through thick plastic lenses. Of course, Worf recalled. The artist decorating the ceiling.

"Well?" Chih-li inquired. "Death or surrender? I'm afraid I don't have all day. The Dragon's security, you know."

Worf did not respond. Instead, without warning, he bent at the knees, then jumped straight up. Chih-li's jaw dropped, and the artisan gasped in fright, as

Worf's hands caught onto two sides of the floating rectangle. As he'd hoped, the platform did not buckle or totter under his weight but indeed held him aloft. Hanging on to the platform, he kicked out at Chih-li with both legs. The soles of his boots smashed into the Pai's jaw, sending his helmet soaring through the air. The gold-and-silver artifact tore through a paper lantern, ricocheted off the ceiling, then rattled noisily across the floor before finally coming to a halt not far from where Worf's sword had landed. Meanwhile, the force of Worf's kick upset the platform's equilibrium. Before the antigravity stabilizers could compensate, one end of the platform tipped toward the floor, spilling the young craftsman onto Chih-li himself. Sliding headfirst off the platform, the youth knocked the Imperial Minister of Internal Security to the ground, where the two Pai lay sprawled in a confused and angry tangle of limbs. By the time Chih-li, cursing loudly, managed to extricate himself from the panicked artist, Worf stood before him, holding both swords in his dark Klingon hands.

"Your choice, Minister," Worf said gruffly, offering Chih-li his sword back. "Do we continue, or do we halt this conflict in order to better serve my captain and your emperor?"

Eyes wide with surprise, Chih-li contemplated the Klingon facing him. Like Worf, the Pai's black hair was bound up in a ponytail at the back of his skull. Blood, red as a human's, flowed from his nose and lips where Worf's boots had kicked him. Chih-li wiped the blood away with the back of one armored glove while he rubbed his chin with his other hand. The Klingon warrior in Worf hoped the Pai would choose to resume battle, but the Starfleet officer longed for a more sensible decision.

"A most honorable gesture," Chih-li said, accepting his sword from Worf. "Perhaps you are correct. Our duty to our respective superiors must supersede our private dispute. I suggest we postpone this matter until we have seen to the security of the wedding gifts. For now, I will gladly value your assistance, although it must undoubtedly be considered superfluous."

"Agreed," Worf growled. His blood still burned with the fire of battle. He struggled to restrain his fury.

"You understand, of course," Chih-li insisted, "honor demands that we resolve this matter at the earliest possible convenience. After the wedding, that is."

"I look forward to it," Worf said.

"As do I," Chih-li replied.

The Green Pearl stood patiently among the scattered cushions of Lu Tung's harem while Beverly ran her medical tricorder up and down the girl's frame. This physical checkup had merely been an excuse to get Beverly into the harem, but she saw no reason not to genuinely treat the bride to a physical while she was here. Besides, it gave the Pearl something to do besides fight with Hsiao Har. So far, the readings were all in order; Yao Hu appeared in perfect health. That spoke well, Beverly thought, for Pai medicine. "Exactly how old are you?" she asked the Pearl.

"I was born in the Year of the Ascending Phoenix, seventeen summers ago."

"Baby," Hsiao Har taunted her. The Heir's daughter stood on her head a few meters away, her scarlet robe falling down around her waist, revealing a pair of violet silk trousers underneath. She insisted she was exercising, but Beverly suspected she just resented all the attention being paid to the bride-to-be. Beverly wondered if it bothered Hsiao Har that the younger girl was getting married first.

Frankly, Beverly thought that, by Federation standards, they were both far too young to be even thinking of marriage. *Seventeen years old . . . my God,* she mused. *They're mere children.* Beverly herself had married earlier than most of her colleagues on the *Enterprise;* even still, she'd been halfway through medical school, with a firm grasp of what she wanted to do with her life, when she wedded Jack Crusher. Sheltered behind harem walls, how could Yao Hu possibly know enough about herself to make any sort of lifelong commitment? *Different cultures, different standards,* Beverly reminded herself. Yet she knew how she'd react if Wesley suddenly announced that he wanted to get married: *"Not until you're much older, young man!"*

Granted, Wesley's first serious crush had been on a shapechanging alien princess who occasionally transformed into a furry, eight-feet-tall, bug-eyed monster. At least the Dragon-Heir belonged to the same species as the Pearl. *(Says the woman,* she chided herself, *who fell for an intelligent slug, not to mention the family ghost!)* Who said love had to make sense? She just hoped Yao Hu would be as happy in her marriage as she had been with Jack.

"Dr. Crusher?" the Pearl asked softly, interrupting Beverly's nostalgic musings.

"Call me Beverly," she insisted, putting away her tricorder. "You can sit down now."

"Thank you, Doc . . . Beverly." The Pearl knelt upon a plush, satin pillow embroidered with golden thread. The soles of her tiny slippers poked out from behind the back of her sea green gown. "My honorable father suggested that you were a woman of great wisdom and experience."

"Your father is most kind." Beverly shrugged casually. "I suppose I've learned a thing or two over the years." *Good Lord,* she thought, *I sound like my grandmother.* This particular mission was making her feel older by the minute.

The Pearl lowered her gaze, unable to meet Beverly's eyes. "Before my wedding," she began hesitantly, "there are matters I would discuss with you."

*Uh-oh,* Beverly thought. *Now what?* Something was obviously troubling Yao Hu, Beverly could tell that much. "What sort of matters?" she asked.

Still upside down, Hsiao Har snickered loudly.

"I would prefer to discuss them *in private,*" the Pearl said, casting a venomous glance in her future stepdaughter's direction.

"She wants to know about men and women," Hsiao Har called out. The Pearl flushed bright red, whether out of fury or embarrassment Beverly couldn't tell. "The baby wants you to tell her all the secrets of the marriage bed."

*Good Lord,* Beverly thought, comprehension blooming suddenly. *No one has told the bride the facts of life.* She wondered if this was what Lord Lu Tung had intended all along; no wonder he was so eager to accept her services. Her cheeks still burning, Yao Hu looked up at Beverly with desperate, pleading eyes of emerald, while Hsiao Har grinned maliciously not far away. Both girls watched her expectantly, waiting for her to speak.

*Oh, dear,* Beverly thought. *This is rather more than I bargained for.*

Six Starfleet security officers stood posted around the wedding gifts, accompanied by an equal complement of Pai warriors in full armor. Worf nodded in approval. Ideally, of course, a battalion of Klingon warriors would provide *real* security; unfortunately, there were not yet enough Klingons in Starfleet to fill out even one security roster. Thus far, Worf's example had not inspired many of his fellow Klingons to follow in his footsteps; this troubled him sometimes, although he would never admit it, not even to Deanna.

In any event, a dozen guards seemed more than enough to stand watch over the vast collection of treasures and trinkets assembled in the so-called High Hall of Ceremonial Grandeur. In truth, Worf found this ostentatious display of wealth and luxury rather distasteful—and further evidence of the Dragon Empire's misplaced priorities. All this pomp and circumstance for a mere wedding? Worf was unimpressed. A Klingon wedding, by contrast, was short, direct, and admirably uncomplicated, requiring little more than an exchange of vows between a warrior and his (or her) chosen mate. On the Homeworld, he thought, this wedding would have been concluded hours ago. Entire wars could be fought and won, however, in the time it took to marry off a pair of Pai. Worf shook his head in disbelief.

"Is something wrong?" Chih-li asked. The Imperial

Minister of Internal Security stood beside Worf, holding his gilded helmet against his chest.

"No," Worf said. His gaze swept over the guards standing attentively at their posts. "It is well."

"Indeed," Chih-li agreed. "Not that your people are in any way necessary."

"I have my orders," Worf reminded him.

"Yes, well. We do what we must, I suppose."

Chih-li talked too much, Worf thought, like all the rest of the Pai. Still, he had come to respect the stalwart Pai warrior, who clearly took his duty and his honor very seriously. But how did that honor apply when it came to the safety of Dragon himself? In a very real sense, Worf recalled, the security of the wedding gifts was just a blind; Captain Picard wanted him on hand to protect the Emperor and his guests. Could he now suggest as much to Chih-li without provoking another duel? Worf eyed his new ally very carefully.

"There is another matter," Worf said slowly, lowering his voice so he could not be overheard. "The captain has informed me that an attempt has been made on the Dragon's life."

"Yes," Chih-li conceded. He looked more mournful than offended. His voice held a note of resignation when he spoke. "The Dragon has refused to permit any measures to protect him. It is a matter of honor."

"Yet an assassin almost succeeded mere hours ago," Worf said.

The minister lowered his head. His chin sank onto his chest. "I should have protected him, despite his direct orders. He would have had me killed when he found out, but still—"

"If there is one attempt," Worf emphasized, "there may be others."

"I have already offered to kill myself in atonement for my failure at the banquet," Chih-li said, "and the Dragon denied me that privilege."

Worf sympathized. "It is understood among my people that such a thing could best be atoned for only by death."

"Really?" Chih-li cocked an eyebrow. "Are your people truly so similar to our own?"

"We have lived the way of honor for ten thousand years," Worf said diplomatically. He took a deep breath before fully confiding in Chih-li. "My captain has asked me to do everything possible to insure the safety of the Dragon between now and the wedding."

"We also have lived honorably for generations." Chih-li sighed wearily. "Yet there is little we can do when the Dragon allows nothing."

"What the Dragon does not know about his defender's actions will neither anger nor dishonor him."

"You interest me strangely, Lieutenant," Chih-li said. "Please clarify."

Worf was encouraged by the Pai's lack of ire. "I would suggest that we protect him without his knowledge, that we establish such forcefields and other barriers as we can without alerting him to their presence."

"Yes," the minister said thoughtfully, stroking his chin. His lip was still swollen where Worf had kicked him. "After all, it may be the honorable thing for the Dragon not to care about his life, but a man dedicated to the Dragon's welfare can honorably take what measures he deems necessary." Chih-li gave Worf a serious look. "We cannot inform the Dragon, of course. To do so would infringe upon his honor in an inexcusable fashion. I am curious: what would your people consider such an act?"

Worf gave the matter some thought before answering. "Treason, most likely, but it could also be seen as refusal to follow the orders of a dangerous commander."

"The Dragon is not dangerous!" Chih-li protested.

"He is dangerous to himself."

"A good point," the Pai said, apparently mollified. "And the punishment for such treason?"

"In the Federation there would be a court-martial, which, if the individual in question was convicted, could result in punishment ranging from expulsion from Starfleet to fines and imprisonment."

"Soft," the minister said.

"It seemed so to me when I first joined Starfleet."

"And where you come from?"

"In the Klingon Empire, an individual committing such an act would, if caught, be forced to run barefoot over *k'atha* blades."

"And if he saves his leader's life with such disobedience?"

"He would be permitted a pair of sandals."

Chih-li smiled warmly, clearly impressed by the finer nuances of Klingon justice. "On Pai," he said proudly, "the common punishment for such a thing is to induce the disobedient one to eat a live *huang lang shu.*"

Worf scowled. "That seems rather soft, merely eating something."

"The *huang lang shu* is a small animal capable of

living for short periods without air. Placed in a suddenly constricted environment, he will attempt to bite his way free."

"Eating his way out of the malfeasant," Worf said. "That is moderately creative."

"It has long been thought so," Chih-li stated. "It was my father's father's idea, when he was the Supreme Advisor for Exquisite Punishments to the previous Dragon."

"Your grandfather devised this method? Most ingenious."

Chih-li bowed as much as his armor permitted. "In my grandfather's name, I thank you."

"It seems rather complicated, though," Worf said. "You need to have the correct animal present."

"The ideal punishment is not always the most convenient," Chih-li explained. "Treason is an exceptional circumstance, of course. Most ordinary matters are less involved. For instance, if you and I were to attend a dinner together, and I were to accidentally spill your wine and fail to offer my own goblet and my outermost robe in atonement, you would be entitled to remove my second concubine from my harem, keeping her or selling her as befits your preferences."

Worf doubted that any Klingon female worthy of the name would allow herself to be bartered in such a transaction. Still, he was intrigued by the intricacy of the Pai's code of honor. "What form of misdemeanor," he asked, "would cause the removal of your first concubine?"

"Really," the Pai said, blushing beneath the bruises on his face, "I cannot say. It would be most improper to speak of such matters in front of an honored guest."

Worf was pleased to note that he had gone from an unwanted intruder to an honored guest in so short a time. Despite their eccentricities, he concluded, the Pai were an honorable people at heart, unlike the despicable G'kkau. More than ever, he recognized the importance of keeping the Dragon Empire safe from the voracious fangs of those treacherous reptiles.

"Are we agreed then," he asked, "to discreetly protect the Dragon from any further assassination attempts?"

Chih-li glanced around hastily to assure himself that no one was listening to their conversation. "We are agreed," he said in hushed tones, "provided our methods are unobtrusive and inconspicuous. I have the usual forcefields built into much of the palace's structure. It is a simple matter to bring them up to full power. Sensors for darts and other projectiles are in most of the major chambers, but I can do nothing about the Dragon's private rooms."

"That is unfortunate," Worf said, "but unavoidable." Captain Picard was accompanying the Dragon, he recalled; he would have to rely on the captain to guard the Emperor directly. "What of attacks from the air?" he asked.

"Protective shields are in place, along with long-range sensors and antiaircraft weaponry installed in the upper towers. Perhaps you would care to inspect their deployment?"

Worf bowed his head in the manner of the Pai. "I would be honored," he said.

"Excellent," Chih-li said genially. "Come. We can work out the details of our duel as we walk."

# Chapter Nine

"THESE ARE THE PALACE KITCHENS," the Dragon said. A pair of huge bronze doors slid apart, disappearing into hidden recesses in the adjoining walls. A gust of hot air emerged from the kitchen, carrying the aroma of exotic spices and flavors. Along with the ever-present incense, Picard found the odor slightly overwhelming.

"A privilege," he murmured, none too sincerely. His stomach was still recovering from the rich and unappetizing dishes he'd been subjected to during the wedding banquet. The gamy, greasy taste of the *rahgid* eyes lingered on his tongue. He heard Deanna, walking two paces behind Picard and the Dragon, smother a laugh. Mu, the Dragon's faithful chamberlain, had disappeared on some errand or another.

The doors opened into an enormous space. Even

here, everything was ornamented, although the materials employed were less overtly expensive—no gilt, no jewels, no bioluminescence. In the kitchen, the decorators had relied instead on pure color, and they had used it lavishly, in sweeping expanses of green, purple, and puce. The long tables all through the center of the room, and the open hearths, ovens, and stoves that lined the walls, were brightly colored, albeit dusted with white flour and fresh green salad leavings, and splattered with the sticky spills inevitable in any kitchen of whatever size. Small dogs, resembling a cross between a bulldog and a Pekingese, ambled freely through the kitchen, munching on table scraps.

Years ago, during a brief sabbatical on Earth, Picard had visited Hampton Court, the summer palace of King Henry VIII, and toured the enormous kitchens that had once provided for the British monarch's many lavish feasts. The Dragon's kitchens reminded him of those cavernous ancient kitchens, or at least a multicolored, phaser-bright replica of the same. *How can such an impressive kitchen produce such noxious food?* he wondered.

Most of the people in the room—the chefs and their assistants, Picard guessed—had clustered around one table near the center of the room, conversing in loud voices. "That is where we are going," the Dragon said, gesturing toward the site of the activity.

One of the chefs, an elderly man with a stringy white mustache, glanced up as they approached. "I am so sorry, masters, but no one is allowed—" He paused, jaw dropping. "Your Excellence!"

As he fell to his stomach on the flagged stone floor, he managed to jab his neighbor with his elbow. The neighbor went through the same motions—the gasp, the sagging jaw, the jab, the fall. In an instant, Picard, the Dragon, and Deanna found themselves the only upright people in a room suddenly filled with the slight haze of flour puffed from everyone's aprons.

The Dragon picked his way through the kowtowing chefs to the table they had been gathered around. "This is what I brought you down to see." He pointed a foot-long fingernail at a object resting on the table: it seemed to be some sort of tentacled rabbit with large horny growths springing from its forehead. The animal was still, lifeless, and partially skinned.

"Oh!" Deanna exclaimed, apparently taken aback by the grisly sight. The Dragon turned his face toward her. "I'm so sorry, Your Excellence. I forgot myself."

The old man's cherubic face beamed at her. "That is quite all right, my dear. It's good to see a little life in a young woman, not to mention such delicate sensibilities. Your captain must find you very refreshing, eh?" He poked Picard in the ribs.

Picard suppressed an urge to flinch. "I take it there is something exceptional about this animal?"

"Fresh *p'u tzu*," the Dragon declared proudly. "It has a gland about here—" He poked the rabbit-thing's abdomen. "—where it stores all the toxins it would ordinarily release into its urine. What we like to do is to remove the gland, and braise it lightly with peppers. It's very piquant; I think you'll appreciate the maturity of its flavor."

Picard swallowed. "I am sure it will be as delightful as everything you have offered." *How many Pai delicacies must I eat,* he wondered, *before I get an opportunity to discuss the treaty with the Dragon?* "Perhaps we might retire and let the cooks resume their work?"

"What?" the Dragon said, momentarily confused. Then he glanced down at prostrate kitchen staff. "Oh, yes. Up, up, everyone! We mustn't keep Captain Picard waiting." The Dragon took Picard by the arm and led him over to a long wooden bench next to a open fireplace full of smoldering coals. The various cooks jumped up the minute the Dragon's back was turned and hastily gathered around the *p'u tzu.* Picard noted that their formerly heated discussion was now much more subdued.

The Dragon sat astride the bench and gestured for Picard to do the same. Lifting one leg over the low bench, Picard sat down facing the Emperor. Deanna quietly placed herself on a stone ledge in front of the fireplace.

"It won't be long now," the Dragon promised. "They are extracting the gland even as we speak. It should be eaten *instantly* so we will dine on it here, in the kitchen like peasants. Amusing, no?"

"Yes, quite," Picard murmured. "While we wait, now might be a good time to discuss the treaty a bit further."

"Are you still on about that?" the Dragon exclaimed in amazement. "Take some time off, Picard! Treat yourself to a holiday."

"You are most generous, Excellence, but I fear I cannot fully relax until I have discharged my duty to both the Federation and the Dragon Empire."

"You are a persistent man, Picard," the Dragon

said. "I admire that—up to a point." Perhaps he would have said more, but Mu suddenly burst into the kitchen. The chamberlain was breathing heavily, as though he had run a long way, and beads of sweat dotted his brow. Picard noticed that Mu held on to a small black box as though his life depended on it.

"Ah, there you are, Most Excellent and Exalted One!" Mu gasped. "I have been looking everywhere for you." His wide eyes took in the messy, busy appearance of the kitchen, as well as the simple hardwood bench upon which the Dragon and Picard now sat. "Exalted One, you need not rest your sacred frame upon so humble a seat. I will summon the Imperial bearers to fetch a throne immediately."

"Never mind that," the Dragon said, dismissing the chamberlain's concerns with a wave of his pudgy hand. "Did you bring it as I commanded?"

"Yes, Exalted One," Mu said quickly. He proffered the black box to the Emperor, who snatched it out of his trembling hands.

"Excellent," the Dragon chortled. He turned his attention back to Picard. "Do you play *ch'i*, Captain?"

"*Ch'i*, Excellence?"

"A marvelous game, Picard, a most civilized game. You must learn it." The Dragon snapped open the polished wooden carrying case, revealing a design not unlike a chessboard, along with several sculpted figurines carved from ivory and obsidian. The Dragon laid the board flat upon the bench between him and Picard. The Starfleet captain did not recognize any of the playing pieces. "We shall play here," the Dragon proposed, "while my chefs exert themselves for the delight of our palates. Your young lady may stay and watch our match. Unless, that is, there is somewhere else you must be?"

"Not at all," Picard insisted. While the assassin remained at large, he did not dare leave the Emperor alone. He resigned himself to a long and possibly tedious evening. "Perhaps we might even touch upon the treaty as we play?"

"If you insist," the Dragon allowed, with a great show of tolerant bemusement. A pungent odor wafted through the kitchen; the scent was redolent of hot blacktop submerged in cod liver oil. Picard almost gagged at the smell alone. "Ah, grand, it is ready." The Dragon clapped his hands together. His fingernails clattered like chopsticks. "The first bite is all yours, my dear captain."

"You honor me too much," Picard said.

"A full house," the Heir said, and laid out a king, two queens, and a five and three of diamonds.

"Not exactly," Riker said, trying not to sigh. Good thing the *Enterprise* had been able to beam down a deck of cards so promptly. After all, one never knew when one would end up having to amuse a harem full of feuding warriors during a drunken bachelor party.

"It looks full to me," Chuan-chi protested. "A man, a woman, and some jewels."

"I'm sorry," Riker said. "I have two pair, and I'm afraid I win again."

Poker had not been an unmitigated success. True, the novelty of the game had intrigued the Pai nobles, and no one had tried to murder him recently, but cardplaying did not come easily to the Heir and his guests. Riker had explained three times now the combinations possible, and the odds of each, yet the Pai seemed no closer to understanding the game.

Pillows and cushions had been cleared away to provide a flat square of floor on which to play. Riker, the Heir, the Second Son, and a bookish-looking young man named Meng Chiao squatted around the square, cards in hand, while the rest of the bachelors leaned over their shoulders, watching the games with varying degrees of interest and befuddlement. Coins of gold, silver, and bronze were piled upon the floor. Riker's stake came from a replicator on board the *Enterprise;* Geordi had beamed them down to the party after Riker sent him a few sample coins. Serving girls continued to glide through the outer harem, refilling goblets and fetching refreshments.

"I do not see the sense of it," the Second Son complained as he handed over a pile of the golden coins they were using in the place of real poker chips. Riker hoped the coins were not too valuable; he had little sense of Pai currency or of the stakes they were playing for. "You give me cards on which I bet. And then you give me more cards, and then you win. There must be more to it than that."

"There is," Riker said. "It's all a matter of odds." This was a familiar speech by now; having given it three times, he felt he could recite it in his sleep or in any language throughout the galaxy. "Different combinations of cards have varying degrees of likelihood that they will show up."

"Oh, I understand *that,*" Chuan-chi said sourly. "The Admirable Tutor of Advanced Mathematics explained probability to me when my younger brother still required a nursemaid. No, what puzzles me is the notion that the odds will change anything."

"They will if you bear them in mind and bid thinking of the likelihood of drawing a specific card from the pack to fill out your hand."

There was shocked silence. "You mean," Kan-hi said, "cheat?"

"It is not considered cheating to compute odds in poker and use them to your advantage," Riker explained.

"It can hardly be honorable," the Heir said. "It would be taking unfair advantage of the other players."

"As the stars fall from the sky, so does the lilac entice the bee," Meng Chiao intoned. "Silver spurs outweigh the ostrich." Riker had learned that the scrawny youth's official title was Speaker of Aphorisms, and Meng Chiao seemed to be doing his best to live up to his title. So far, none of Meng Chiao's sayings had made a bit of sense to Riker, but the assembled warriors always nodded as though the Speaker had said something profound. *Must get lost in translation,* Riker guessed, *even the Universal kind.*

"Indeed," Kan-hi said, agreeing with his brother for the first time that evening. "No one else has seen my hand, so they don't know what my chances are. Should I be showing everyone my cards?"

"No!" Riker said. "I mean, that's not necessary, Excellence. You know your hands, which no one else does, but they know their hand, which you do not. It is fair because it is mutual."

"I suppose," Kan-hi said, "but it still doesn't seem honorable."

"I would think that would appeal to you, brother," the Heir said. "Certainly you have no talent for games of honor."

Kan-hi jumped angrily to his feet. He wobbled unsteadily, the victim of too much wine in too short a time. "Take that back!" he demanded.

*Damn,* Riker thought. Just when he thought he had calmed the party down. His muscles tensed, ready to throw his body between the Dragon's sons if necessary. He hoped Kan-hi would not try anything drastic.

"I think not," Chuan-chi responded. "Your gambling debts alone testify to your incompetence in matters of sport, along with your many other failures at war *and* love."

Kan-hi's eyes filled with open hatred. "I challenge you to a duel," he cried out. "Now, tonight, before the wedding!"

The Dragon-Heir calmly sipped his wine. "You are even drunker than you look. You are my brother. You cannot challenge me without our father's permission."

*Is that true?* Riker wondered. He couldn't make head or tail of the Pai's complex rules of honor.

Kan-hi's fists clenched at his sides. He looked like he was ready to explode. Riker remembered his own "brother," Thomas Riker, and some of their own bitter conflicts. Not to mention the malevolent jealousy of Data's brother, Lore. Brother against brother. Was the sorry saga of Cain and Abel some sort of universal constant? Kan-hi definitely seemed ready to kill his older brother, in the name of who knew what ancient slights and rivalries.

Instead, he spun around and staggered, reeling, toward the exit. "I don't have to stay here and be insulted," he called out, "especially by you!" The door slid open and Kan-hi disappeared into the hall.

Chuan-chi watched him go, a thin smile playing upon his lips.

"I fear my brother is not feeling well," the Heir said to Riker.

"Shouldn't someone go after him?" Riker suggested. *How am I supposed to guard both princes if one of them goes storming off like this?*

"No," Chuan-chi said. "He will undoubtedly be back shortly. He loves gambling too much to stay away for long."

"Perhaps we should not play—"

"Nonsense, Honorable Riker," the Heir said decisively. "It was your idea, so we shall stay where we are and continue our game. Let my idiotic brother wallow in his wounded, misbegotten pride."

Meng Chiao shook his head sadly. "The egg of the eaglet is the hammer of the woodsman."

"Huh?" Riker said. Lacking any other options, he dealt another hand.

"Ah," the Dragon said, rubbing his hands together. His fingers were sticky from the sauces and secretions of the last few hors d'oeuvres. "I'm afraid I have your Imperial Rat-Catcher cornered."

Picard eyed the playing board. "Which piece is that?"

The Dragon cackled to himself. "Really, Captain, you are most amusing."

Picard was losing badly, or so he gathered. Although *ch'i* looked not dissimilar to chess, he could barely keep up, not because he was not a good chess player but because he *was,* and kept expecting the piece that resembled a knight (if an incomprehensibly ornate knight) to move like one, only to learn that it did something else entirely. There was no apparent queen, only several sorts of nobles and other characters, each of whom appeared to move in different ways at different places in the game, which was turning out to be extremely long.

More important, he had made little progress in convincing the Dragon of the urgency of the Empire's situation. Nor had Counselor Troi managed to turn the Dragon's attention toward the as-yet-unsigned treaty. She remained sitting by the fireplace, watching the seemingly endless game, and making occasional light conversation, which, to her credit, the Dragon certainly seemed to appreciate. *If nothing else,* he thought, *perhaps Deanna will help the Dragon to see the women of the Federation in a more favorable light.*

"Sir," Picard began again, "the G'kkau are utterly ruthless. I know you have great—and doubtless well-earned—confidence in your own forces, but the G'kkau have hundreds of warships and you have rather fewer, or so I have been informed."

"I have forty-five interplanetary ships, and six nebular cruisers," the Dragon said calmly. "That should be ample."

"But the odds are overwhelmingly against you," Picard said.

"So much the better," the Dragon told him. "It will make for much honor for the victors."

"And if the victor is not the Dragon Empire?" Picard asked grimly. "We must consider that possibility. Is it worth risking the potential suffering of your women and children in the event of a G'kkau victory?" He regretted having to be so blunt, but perhaps he could use the Dragon's sense of chivalry to make the old man see reason.

"Of course not," the Dragon responded. "All the more reason, then, for the Empire to win." He winked mischievously at Troi. "Your move, Captain. I still hold your Overeducated Fool."

"So you do," Picard said, trying hard not to sigh.

"This is the matter-antimatter reaction chamber," La Forge explained. "In a very real sense, the MARC is the heart of the *Enterprise.*"

He stood before a large plane of transparent aluminum and pointed at the reaction chamber on the opposite side of the sheet. His guests, he knew, could observe only a complex assembly of carbonitrium and molyferrenite alloys. His VISOR let him see a lot more. Even through the thick, transparent sheet La Forge saw the radiance of the dilithium crystals cradled within the reaction chamber, and he watched the high-frequency EM field around the crystals crackle and vibrate, producing a rainbow of colors beyond the narrow range of ordinary human vision. He looked on, wonderstruck as ever, as a trickle of antihydrogen met its positive counterpart, igniting a transcendent, space-warping fire that seared itself upon the optical sensors in his brain.

"Most impressive," said the Celestial Mechanic of the Imperial Court.

*You have no idea,* La Forge thought.

"If we were to join the Federation," the Celestial Mechanic asked, "would this technology be made available to us?"

The Pai scientists were humanoids of ordinary size and body temperature. So far, their tour of the *Enterprise* had been placid and uneventful. As public-relations gigs went, La Forge had experienced a lot worse, the groups he had escorted ranging from arrogant Federation ambassadors who thought they knew everything there was to know about warp drives to throngs of hyperactive children on field trips from the ship's classes and day-care facilities. With any luck, La Forge thought, he could get back to his *real* work soon.

"That would be up to your leader, the Dragon," he said. "If he thought it would benefit your empire, it would be shared with you, along with engineers and technicians to train your people."

"It would unquestionably make nebular travel much easier," the Astronomical Savant said.

"At its top sustainable speed," La Forge estimated, "the *Enterprise* is able to cross the Dragon Nebula in four and a half days."

"Astounding," the Celestial Mechanic said. "I certainly hope the Dragon bears that in mind."

"Feel free to mention it to him," La Forge said. "Now, would you like a sneak preview of something I have planned for tomorrow?"

The two Pai scientists looked at each other for a second. "For the wedding?" the Astronomical Savant asked.

"Yes. We are to mount a light show for the festivities. It's scheduled for right after the ceremony, but as you two are fellow scientists, I thought you might appreciate the technical details. Also"—La Forge grinned—"I'm quite proud of what we whipped up, and I would love to show it off to you."

"We should be delighted," the Celestial Mechanic said. His colleague assented readily. La Forge had gotten the impression that the Celestial Mechanic outranked the Astronomical Savant, but he wouldn't have bet a warp field coil on it.

They took a turbolift to Holodeck Three, and La Forge led the Pai scientists into the empty holodeck. The scholars swiveled their heads about, uncertain what to make of the glowing yellow-on-black grid pattern. "Is this the light show you mentioned?" the Celestial Mechanic said uncertainly.

"It's very nice," the Astronomical Savant added in haste.

"No, no," La Forge chuckled. "This is just the empty stage. Computer, run Program Seven-D/La Forge/Fireworks. Freeze just after inception of program."

Instantly, a blue-and-green globe appeared in the center of the holodeck, floating serenely at eye level.

"Pai," La Forge explained. "The entire show will be staged from on board the *Enterprise*. Much of the remote equipment is already orbiting in space. The rest will go out first thing in the morning. We're using our defensive phasers to produce light and color instead of the usual destructive force. Additionally, I've added a few new twists, including a transformational hyperbolic extender which should interact with some of the colored phasers to generate some terrific effects."

"It sounds most . . . technical," the Astronomical Savant commented. La Forge guessed that he hadn't understood most of his explanation. He wondered what sort of engineering background an "astronomical savant" required.

"I suppose it does," he said. "Forgive me for running your ear off, but I am pleased with what we've managed to accomplish. Let me show you the mock-up. Computer? Run program at twelve times speed."

The globe lit up. Coruscating light flickered and rippled, sheathing the entire globe in a radiant display. Sheets of light shimmered, showing patterns half-hidden in the color.

"It's all based on the auroras of Earth, my home planet," La Forge said, unable to keep silent. While it might seem ironic to assign a blind man the job of designing a light show, La Forge had leaped to the challenge. *Hey,* he thought, *Beethoven was deaf, wasn't he?* Through his VISOR, he watched his artificial auroras unfold, until the last swirls of iridescent light wrapped around the globe and wisped away.

*Pretty good,* he thought smugly, *if I say so myself.*

"That was it?" the Celestial Mechanic asked. He sounded distinctly underwhelmed.

"Sure it is," La Forge replied, with a little more heat than he intended. "That was state-of-the-art Federation technology."

"Oh, that's all right," the Celestial Mechanic cooed soothingly. "It's really quite pretty. We just didn't realize there wasn't more to it. I mean, after your description—"

"Wait a minute," La Forge said. "Is there a problem with the light show?"

"No, not at all!" the Celestial Mechanic said.

"It's lovely, really," the Astronomical Savant added.

"There *is* something wrong with it."

"Not wrong, precisely," the Celestial Mechanic said. "Just rather ordinary."

*Ordinary!* La Forge bristled at the suggestion, then

took a deep breath to calm himself. There was more at stake here than his own ruffled ego. "I think you'd better explain this to me," he said. "I want my light show to reflect well on the *Enterprise*—and the Federation."

"I'm sure it will. It looks as though you had worked very hard on it," the Celestial Mechanic reassured him. "The only problem—"

"—and it's just a little one, a tiny little thing," interjected the Astronomical Savant.

"—is that it wasn't five years ago that we went through the Dragon's Tail, so almost everyone remembers it."

"Since you *what?*" La Forge asked.

"Went through the Dragon's Tail," the Celestial Mechanic repeated. "Rather poetic, really, calling it that. But what it means is that, every century or so, Pai and the rest of the Empire's core system passed through one of the nebula's trailing clouds of gas. The gas interacts with the solar and atmospheric gases to produce a display of lights a little like yours."

"Well, very like yours," the Astronomical Savant said. "It lasts about a year."

"I was just an Underscientist of the Fifth Rank," the Celestial Mechanic recalled, "but I managed to do some work on it. It was breathtaking." He looked dreamily at the miniature globe, quiescent again. "The gases develop rippling effects, like scales in green and pink, and flat planes of color that beat against each other—"

"The little pops of certain compounds interacting—"

"The shimmering and the iridescence—"

La Forge looked from one scientist to the other. "So

what you're telling me is that the Dragon Nebula naturally produces a light show like this every so often."

"Well, not quite like this. It's a lot more active."

"More colors," the Astronomical Savant agreed. "And it did it just five years ago. Almost everyone will remember it. It is truly unforgettable."

*So how come I've never heard of this spectacular natural wonder before?* La Forge thought angrily. Then he remembered that the Dragon Empire had been cut off from the rest of the galaxy for generations. "All that work," he muttered. *Right down the wormhole.*

"Oh, I'm sure your little show will be charming," the Celestial Mechanic said. "Doubtless it's more impressive at full size." He glanced around nervously. "Can we inspect your warp nacelles now?"

"Lieutenant Kesel can explain the workings of the nacelles to you. Barbara?" he called to an assistant engineer from the Dark Horse system. "Can you explain to these gentlemen how the warp nacelles work? I have to get back to work."

*Do I ever,* he thought.

"It's my turn," the Dragon said gently. "If you recall, I have two turns in a row when my Peasant Farmer surprises your Homely Maiden."

Dozens of black and white figurines were deployed across the varnished surface of the playing board. The sights, sounds, and smells of the busy kitchen faded into the background as Picard tried to focus on the game. They had been playing *ch'i* for at least an hour now, but he could not begin to make sense of the strategies involved. The Dragon's technique for teaching him the game seemed to be to explain nothing until Picard made a move, and then to explain to him how he had forgotten some esoteric and eccentric rule. He hoped his growing frustration was not weighing too heavily on Deanna's empathic senses.

"Excellence," he said, determined to keep working toward the only victory that counted. "Please understand that the Federation is not in any way interested in lessening your honor or your autonomy as an Empire. In fact, Federation membership would offer you greater opportunities for honor, as you enter into new relationships of mutual respect with peoples and societies you might otherwise never encounter."

"Yes, yes," the Dragon concurred without much interest. His gaze remained glued to the gameboard. "It looks as though you have forgotten your Drunken Guard, Captain."

"I think perhaps I must have," Picard sighed. "Which piece is the Drunken Guard?"

"The one I am about to take," the Dragon said, reaching down for one of Picard's obsidian pieces and adding it to his growing pile of tiny statues. Picard began to fear that his entire "kingdom" would be depopulated before he convinced the Dragon to sign the treaty.

"You have an extraordinary variety of pieces in this game," he said. "Just as the Federation nurtures an infinite variety of cultures."

"That's because we actually play a number of games with them," the Dragon said, blithely ignoring Picard's editorial commentary. "For instance, this is the simplest variety: straight *ch'i*. In Married Bliss, however, all the pieces are 'wed' in pairs, who then fight one another, as well as uniting to fight outsiders." One of the pug-faced dogs bumped the Dragon's elbow, jumping up on its hind legs to beg for food.

"The simplest version," Picard said, incredulous.

The Dragon tossed the last, uneaten morsel of *p'u tzu* to the hungry dog. Picard was glad to see it go. "Oh, yes," the Dragon said. He clapped and the chief chef rushed to his Emperor's side. "Nan Hai, the captain looks hungry. Bring us a plate of the Thousand-Year Eyes."

Picard heard an amused chuckle from Troi, one quickly stifled into a fit of coughing. "Oh," she said, wiping the tears from her eyes. "I am so sorry, Your Excellence, Captain. This one seems to have inhaled a bit of dust or flour."

The Dragon smiled at Troi. "Here, have a sip of my wine, from my own glass." The Emperor's eyes twinkled as he spoke, and Picard experienced a sense of foreboding. The Dragon appeared to be taking too much of a liking to Deanna; Picard hoped the Emperor was not expecting the counselor as a wedding gift as well.

"Sir," he said, hoping to distract the Dragon from Troi's abundant charms. "Perhaps you can explain your move to me. . . ."

"Sir, I have intercepted another of those communications," Lieutenant Melilli announced.

Seated in the captain's chair, Data kept his gaze on the viewscreen ahead of him. The Dragon Nebula filled the screen, its swirling vapors concealing a myriad of mysteries. "I assume you are not using the word 'communications' unadvisedly."

"Naturally not, sir," Melilli replied with a certain

asperity. "The computer clearly identifies it as some sort of communication."

Data nodded. He had not yet broken what he assumed to be the G'kkau's code. Their encryption techniques had proven unusually challenging, perhaps because of their distinctly nonhumanoid thought processes. Under other circumstances, and with less at stake, the puzzle might have provided him with a stimulating source of recreation. "Can you locate the origin of the transmission?" he asked.

The Bajoran's earring jingled as she bent her head to inspect the readings displayed on her console. "Still hard to peg down," she said, "but the message has just been repeated. I may be able to triangulate from our respective positions at the first and second iterations of the message." She tapped a number of pressure-sensitive pads. "Yes, there we are. The message is being transmitted from a source in the Epsilon-Tertius sector of the nebula, one moving toward Pai at approximately warp six."

"That would put them at Pai at roughly four in the morning, Imperial Palace Time," Data calculated instantly, "at least two hours before the wedding. That is unfortunate. Because the treaty will not yet be in effect, there will be nothing we can do to obstruct the G'kkau." He felt safe in assuming the intercepted messages came from the G'kkau; there was a 98.7445 percent probability that he was correct. Furthermore, judging from the rising plasma concentrations in the nebula, more than one ship was approaching Pai.

Lieutenant Melilli appeared to share his conclusions. "Could we engage the G'kkau fleet before they get there?"

"I am afraid not," he said. "By the time we intercept the fleet, they will be well within the boundaries of the Dragon Empire. To take action against the G'kkau would violate the autonomy of the Empire."

"Isn't there anything we can do, sir?" Melilli exclaimed passionately. Data suspected that memories of Bajor's own trials during the Cardassian Occupation were coloring the lieutenant's emotional responses. In his experience, Bajorans placed little emphasis on the Prime Directive when confronted with political oppression. He, however, was not Bajoran, and neither was Captain Picard.

"We will do what we can," he stated. He tapped his comm badge, opening a line to the planet below. *"Enterprise* to Captain Picard."

"Have another glazed cornea," the Dragon said. "Captain, you are far too thin."

"Thank you," Picard said. "I would be delighted."

He was not, in fact, delighted in any way whatsoever. For several hours now, he had been consuming dishes composed almost entirely of various sorts of animal effluvia. He had always prided himself on his strong stomach, trained by decades of Starfleet service to accept the exotic cuisines of dozens of starfaring races, but on Pai he had finally met his match. There had been so much of it, and so much of it foul, that he felt more than a little queasy. An avid historian, he could not help remembering a twentieth-century American president who once disgorged the contents of a sick stomach at a conference with his Asian counterpart. Picard prayed that history would not repeat itself on Pai.

Additionally, the game of *ch'i* was not over yet. He had thought the Dragon had won when all of Picard's pieces were taken, and he'd congratulated him on his victory with a genuine enthusiasm that had nothing to do with the quality of his playing; but the Dragon assured him that this was only the first phase of the game, that now Picard was obligated to attempt to free all the warrior-pieces and marry off the dishonored women-pieces.

Troi brought him a goblet containing some clear liquid. "Have a sip," she whispered.

"What is it?" he asked warily, looking into its transparent depths. Nothing vile was floating in it, but he would not be surprised to find out it was some loathsome insect's saliva. He contemplated his reflection in the fluid, and hoped he didn't really look that green.

"Water," she said. "You could use some. If Beverly were here, I'm sure this is what she'd prescribe." Grinning weakly, she stepped back toward the fireplace. By now, only a few glowing red coals remained in the oven. Picard wondered if Deanna's empathic senses had forced her to share his nausea. If so, she deserved a commendation.

Picard started to sip the water. Then Mu arrived once more to whisper something into the Emperor's ear. A huge smile broke over the Dragon's jovial features. He gestured expansively toward the servants now converging from every corner of the kitchen. Picard observed the servants murmuring among themselves in an excited, possibly even agitated manner. *Something is definitely up,* he concluded. *What now?*

"At last," the Dragon chortled. "The final triumph of our culinary odyssey: *ma erh tsai mao tan ch'ing!*"

A half-dozen servants approached the bench in a solemn procession, headed by the master chef himself (identifiable by his vast bulk), holding a single tiny dish high over his head.

"This seems a lot to servants to serve one dish," Picard observed.

"This delicacy has not been prepared in a thousand years," the Dragon informed him. "Each of these peasants had some small part in its production, so they're eager to see it consumed; it will be something to tell their children and grandchildren. I have chosen to indulge them in this matter, provided you have no objections?"

"No, of course not." Picard found himself torn between relief and apprehension. If this was indeed to be the *final* item on tonight's menu, then it was truly a consumption devoutly to be wished. On the other hand, the earlier repasts had been so dreadful that he shuddered to contemplate what the Dragon might consider the pièce de résistance.

The chef awkwardly lowered his meaty frame until he was lying facedown on the floor before his Emperor. One hand still held the dish up high; Picard could spy only a covered serving tray seemingly sculpted from solid gold. Emeralds and rubies studded the gleaming lid, each one larger and more radiant than the one before it. Picard had not seen such shameless ostentation since the last time he dined with a successful Ferengi.

The chamberlain himself took the dish from the chef's hand. He gulped and swallowed nervously, clearly terrified that he might spill a drop of the precious comestible. Mu placed it carefully on the playing board between the Dragon and Picard, then slowly removed the intricately filigreed top. Picard eyed the contents of the dish for the first time.

Even by Pai standards, it looked sickening and smelled even worse. Gnarled objects that might have been talons floated in a murky fluid that showed oily swirls of dark clotted red and a viscous pale green. The concoction boiled and bubbled like a witch's cauldron; Picard spotted a speckled worm of some sort writhing within one of the bubbles seconds before it popped, dropping the wriggling creature back into the gangrenous depths of the broth. The acrid fumes rising from the frothing liquid made Picard's eyes water, and the noxious aroma—like a Klingon locker room right after a particularly frenzied battle—caused his gorge to rise.

"I am sorry," Picard said, choosing the lesser of two evils. "But I'm afraid it will be quite impossible to taste this."

"Why?" the Dragon said with a frown. His cherubic face grew petulant. "Do you mean it isn't satisfactory?"

"I mean it would be quite impossible," Picard repeated. Better to decline the meal, he decided, than to be rendered physically ill by it.

Scowling, the Dragon peered at the noisome mess in the gilded tray. He plucked free a talon from the stew; it came loose with a sticky, sucking sound. Filmy strands of semidissolved fiber clung to the talon; they might have been spiderwebs. The smell that rose from the talon was strong enough to tarnish the golden tray. The Dragon sniffed the claw. "Perhaps you are right," he said at last. "This is an old recipe; the cooks may have prepared it incorrectly."

A whimpering noise arose from the prostrate chef. The Dragon ignored it. He called out to one of the squat, pug-faced dogs prowling the kitchen. The animal trotted over eagerly. It gobbled the rancid talon in the Dragon's outstretched hand. The Emperor watched the dog warily. At first it seemed delighted by the snack. Within seconds, however, the dog was gripped by convulsions. It shuddered, coughed once, than collapsed onto its side. Mu hastily examined the dog. "I fear it is dead, Exalted One," he announced. Picard's back stiffened in alarm.

"Definitely prepared incorrectly," the Dragon said blandly. "Mu, have all who touched this dish incarcerated."

"Your Excellence . . . no!" the terrified chef protested. All over the kitchen cries of distress arose from the cooks and servers.

"Wait," Picard said, speaking loudly to be heard over the din. "Excellence, this may be more than a simple error in preparation. Consider: an attempt has been made to poison you once already."

"And you think this is another?" the Dragon said. The thought had obviously not occurred to him. "What a bother. And I was so looking forward to sharing this culinary treat with you."

Frustrated by the Dragon's apparent lack of concern for his own well-being, Picard struggled to maintain his composure. "Counselor?" he asked Troi. "What's your reading on the room? Anything incriminating?"

Troi shook her head. "I'm not detecting any sense of guilt or deception. If this was another assassination attempt, then the assassin is no longer present. That, or the assassin feels no guilt whatsoever."

*A chilling thought,* Picard reflected. He needed to get to the bottom of this latest incident as soon as possible. "Excellence," he said, "with your permission, I would like this dish and the dog examined by my people."

"You want a dead dog?" the Dragon said, somewhat taken aback.

"To examine for signs of poison," Picard explained.

The Dragon shrugged. "My palace is yours, although surely there must be better prizes we can grant you than a dead animal and a poorly cooked meal?"

"The dog will do, Excellence," Picard insisted. Poison or no poison, he was glad he'd been spared a taste of the foul concoction. *Saved by a failed assassination attempt,* he mused. His hand hovered above his comm badge; he was ready to contact the *Enterprise* and request that both specimens be beamed directly to sickbay for analysis.

To his surprise, Data contacted him first.

"I regret that I have some bad news, Captain," the android's voice came over the comm. "We have reason to believe that a G'kkau fleet is heading for Pai—and should be there within twelve hours."

# Chapter Ten

"YOU MEAN HE DOES WHAT?" the Green Pearl exclaimed. "It sounds dreadful!"

The future bride sat face-to-face with Beverly within the sealed harem chamber. Plush velvet cushions were strewn around them. At the far end of the room, Hsiao Har practiced somersaults and did her best to pretend she had no interest in Beverly and Yao Hu's conversation. Beverly suspected she was hanging on every word.

Knowing little about the sexual mores of the Pai had placed Beverly in a delicate position. If she told the Pearl too little, the poor girl would go to her marriage bed ill prepared for what was expected of her; yet if she told her too much, the girl might end up seeming far more worldly than a sheltered virgin should be, resulting in heaven knows what sort of scandal or repercussions. Beverly could just imagine the Pearl being stoned or exiled because Beverly revealed some forbidden Federation love secret. Faced with this thorny dilemma, Beverly had chosen to stick to the basics; fortunately, her exam of Yao Hu had proved the Pai to be just as humanoid as they appeared.

"It can be quite pleasant," Beverly said, hoping to reassure the girl.

The Pearl still looked aghast. "Surely you have never done this?"

"A number of times, my dear." Surely, Beverly thought, there could be no harm in alleviating the girl's fears. A happy honeymoon was in everyone's best interests.

"But you have no children," the Pearl protested, possibly because Beverly was not at home caring for them.

"I do have a son. He's about your age now." She wondered where Wesley was now. Off exploring the universe with the Traveler, presumably. She hoped she had prepared Wesley better for his journeys than Lord Lu Tung had coached the Pearl.

"And you *still* permitted this . . . act? Even though you had already done your duty to his father?"

"Well, yes, I did."

"Why?"

"It can be very enjoyable," Beverly said slowly, not wanting to say any more.

"How can it be?" the Pearl said, looking more distressed by the minute. "It all sounds so . . . undignified."

Off in the corner, Hsiao Har snickered loudly, but

Yao Hu was too anxious to even give her future stepdaughter another dirty look.

Beverly's heart went out to the Pearl. *This is no way for her to go to her wedding night.* "I assure you, it sounds more intimidating than it is. One's body has a say in this, and one's body often likes it quite a lot." Judging from the wary expression on Pearl's face, she remained unconvinced. Beverly took a deep breath and tried again. "Besides," she said, "then there is love."

"Love?" Yao Hu suddenly looked utterly crestfallen, as though the word itself had driven a dagger through her heart. Beverly hoped she hadn't made a terrible mistake. *Remember,* she told herself, *this is an arranged marriage. Love probably has very little to do with it.*

Still, she was in too deep to get out now. "Yes," she said softly. "Do your people speak of love?"

The Pearl nodded, biting her lower lip.

"When a man and a woman love each other," Beverly continued, "the act of making love becomes a very beautiful, tender experience. It's about sharing, really." She watched the Pearl's face avidly, worried about the effect of her words. "Do you understand what I mean, Yao Hu?"

Instead of replying, the Green Pearl burst into tears. Water streamed from her large emerald eyes. Her breaths turned into wet, rasping sobs that shook her entire body. Letting out a cry of anguish, she buried her face in her hands.

*What have I done?* Beverly thought, horrified. Even Hsiao Har seemed stunned by the depth of the Pearl's despair. The young tomboy stopped tumbling and hurried to Yao Hu's side. Kneeling beside the stricken girl, Hsiao Har appeared, for the first time that evening, at a loss for words. Her eyes accused Beverly at the same time that they silently beseeched the Federation doctor to do something about the other girl's unhappiness. But Beverly didn't need Hsiao Har's demanding stare to feel guilty. *This is all my fault,* she thought. *Now what do I do?*

"Now, now," she cooed reassuringly, patting the crying girl's back. "I'm sure that in time you and the Heir will come to love each other."

"No," Yao Hu moaned. She raised her head from her hands. Her once-pale face was now flushed and red. Tears streaked her cheeks. "That is impossible!" she howled so loudly that Beverly prayed the room was soundproofed. What would Lu Tung think if he found his daughter like this? What would Jean-Luc say?

"No it isn't," she said. *Unlikely perhaps,* she thought, recalling the sour-faced older man she'd glimpsed during the banquet, *but not impossible.* "I'm sure the Heir is a wonderful man. Isn't that so, Hsiao Har? Tell the Pearl what a fine and caring man your father is."

The other girl shrugged. "I'm not sure I'd go that far," she said hesitantly. *Thanks a lot,* Beverly thought angrily, glaring at Hsiao Har as another burst of sobs rattled the Pearl's delicate frame. Beverly held on to the Pearl tightly, and felt Yao Hu leaning against her for support. *Never mind the treaty and the politics,* she thought. *I have to do something for this poor, heartbroken girl.* "The Heir will have to fall in love with you," she promised. "How could he not? You're the Green Pearl, after all."

"No, no," Yao Hu cried, shaking her head violently. "You don't understand. I *can't* love Chuan-chi. It's impossible!"

"But why not, dear?" Beverly asked. She stroked the Pearl's long, ebony hair.

"Because I love another!" the Pearl confessed. She buried her face against Beverly's robes.

Beverly's jaw dropped. So did Hsiao Har's. The doctor and the Heir's daughter stared at each other. Neither of them had any idea what to say now.


"Are you quite positive, Data?" Picard asked. He had removed himself to a quiet corner of the imperial kitchen in order to have a private conference with the *Enterprise*. From where he now stood, in the shadow of an enormous oak cupboard, he could see Troi busily entertaining the Dragon with what was no doubt sparkling conversation. The Emperor seemed to be having rather too good a time, in fact; Picard did not approve of the way the Dragon's hand kept finding Deanna's knee. Still, the counselor would have to fend for herself for the time being. Judging from what Data had just reported, more than Deanna's virtue was at stake.

"I am afraid so, Captain," the android said via Picard's comm badge. "Our sensors now confirm that a fleet of nearly one hundred G'kkau warships are en route for Pai, with an estimated time of arrival of two point seven-six hours before the wedding. We are unable to take aggressive action against the fleet, since they are largely concealed within the nebula; and we would be unable to do so in any case, since such action would be seen as an affront to the Dragon Empire."

"I am aware of the issues involved, Data."

"I did not doubt that, sir. What are your recommendations, Captain?"

"You will need to find a means of stalling the fleet or preventing their approach to Pai without actively engaging them."

"Understood, sir. If there were a single ship, I would interpose the *Enterprise* between the G'kkau vessel and the planet. Sadly, that is not feasible in this case."

"You will need to find something that is feasible," Picard instructed. A chef passed by him, carrying a pot of boiling water. A thought occurred to Picard. "By the way, Data, have you managed to test the food that was beamed up a few minutes ago, along with the dead animal?"

"Yes, Captain," Data replied. "Dr. Selar examined the specimens immediately. She reports that the toxin looked to be natural, possibly derived from some native snake or reptile."

"I see," Picard said grimly. Then the fatal dish was no accident after all. He felt a chill when realized how close the unknown assassin came to killing both the Dragon *and* himself. *Thank goodness,* he thought, *the stuff was too vile to eat.* His queasy stomach had saved both their lives. "Thank you, Data. Please keep me informed. Picard out."

He glanced over at the Dragon, who was moving steadily closer to Troi, a lecherous grin upon his face. *Time to go rescue Deanna,* he thought, striding across the kitchen. *If only it were so easy to save the Dragon Empire. . . .*

* * *

Worf and Chih-li strolled through the opulent corridors of the Imperial Palace. Worf had found the palace's external defenses more than adequate, if hardly sufficient to repel a full-scale G'kkau invasion. Now, as they headed back toward the High Hall of Ceremonial Grandeur to check once more on the safety of the wedding gifts, they continued their discussion of Pai, Klingon, and Federation codes of honor.

"Here is another question," the Minister of Internal Security said. The metal links of his armor made chinking noises as he marched beside Worf. "What would happen if your *fu t'ou* was gored by your neighbor's *fu t'ou?*"

"That would depend," Worf said gruffly, "on what a *fu t'ou* was."

"A sort of herbivore," Chih-li explained, "good for pulling wagons."

"Ah," Worf said. "A *sark*. In the Federation, it would depend on whether the beast had been goaded, and whether the goading had been consciously effected, at which point the individual responsible would be fined and sent into therapy for treatment of the instability that would cause one to deliberately hurt an animal. If convicted of the accusation, that is."

Chih-li scowled. "Not a very interesting penalty."

"In the Klingon Empire," Worf said proudly, "such an event would require the death of the offending *sark,* and a payment of five thousand *Huch.*"

"Only five thousand?" the minister asked. *"We* would cut off the offending neighbor's hand as well."

Worf shook his head slowly. "According to Klingon law, we would cut off the hand of an offender only if they appeared too cowardly to discipline their own *sark*."

The minister gave the matter some thought. "What crime," he asked eventually, "would require the amputation of a hand under Federation law?"

"There would be nothing to merit it," Worf admitted. "Federation justice emphasizes rehabilitation over punishment."

Chih-li sighed disapprovingly. "I hope you will forgive me for again saying that the Federation seems rather soft."

"They are anything but soft in their dealings with their enemies," he said.

"Really?" the minister asked. He appeared skeptical.

"I am proud to have fought several battles as a member of Starfleet," Worf declared sincerely.

Chih-li gave Worf a serious look. "If you say so, then it must be so," he said gravely, displaying the genuine respect of one honorable warrior for another. "In that case, I suppose the Federation must be forgiven a certain, shall we say, gentleness in their internal dealings. Still, such slack justice would never work in the Dragon Empire."

"Nor among Klingons," Worf admitted.

They came upon the massive golden doors of the High Hall of Ceremonial Grandeur. The huge doors loomed before them. Worf was pleased to see that the doors remained locked and secure. He decided to notify the security team within of their arrival; he did not wish to be fired upon by a trigger-happy guard. "Worf to Lieutenant Atherton," he hailed the leader of his security team. "Worf to Lieutenant Atherton, please report."

No one responded to his hail. He tried another frequency, but still there was no reply. A low growl escaped his lips. "Something is wrong," he told Chih-li. "Open the door."

The minister pressed a silver-plated button on his armor, and the great doors began to swing open. Somewhere in the distance a gong sounded. Worf drew his phaser, setting it on stun.

The colored flames of many hanging paper lanterns bloomed to life as they cautiously entered the Grand Hall. Worf swung his phaser from left to right, ready to immobilize any foes who might be lurking behind the doors. Instead he was greeted by silence—and emptiness.

"The gifts!" gasped Chih-li.

"The guards!" Worf exclaimed.

The gifts, including the massive jade elephant, were gone. Only empty tables remained, bare of the trinkets and treasures that had previously adorned them. A dozen guards, from both the Dragon Empire and Starfleet, were sprawled upon the floor, unconscious or worse. After determining that the chamber contained no apparent threats, Worf knelt beside Lieutenant Atherton, a tall blond woman in a yellow-and-black uniform, and checked her pulse. It seemed steady.

Convincing Chih-li to accept a female security officer had been a challenge in its own right, Worf remembered. Now he hoped his persistence had not condemned Atherton to serious injury.

He tapped his comm. "Worf to *Enterprise*. I require medical assistance."

A calm female voice answered promptly. "This is

Dr. Selar," she said. Worf recalled that Dr. Crusher was currently elsewhere in the palace, tending to the Green Pearl of Lu Tung. "How can I assist you?" the Vulcan physician asked.

"The security team has been rendered unconscious in some fashion. They may require medical care."

"I will be beam down momentarily," she said. "Selar out."

While Worf contacted the *Enterprise,* Chih-li inspected his own guards. "My warriors appear to be unharmed, although sleeping," he stated. "Perhaps some gas or airborne anesthetic? I trust your people are similarly situated?"

Lieutenant Atherton stirred slightly, but did not wake up. "I believe they are well," Worf said, "but I will know more after our doctor has examined them."

"What puzzles me," the minister said, looking around at the vast empty space that surrounded them, "is how anyone could have removed so many objects, and objects of such size and comparative cumbruousness, in what was such a limited amount of time."

"A transporter?" Worf suggested.

The minister shook his head. "This chamber is shielded against transporter theft . . . which reminds me, I will have to lift the shields in order for your medical officer to beam down." He tapped a few commands into a miniature computer concealed in his gauntlet. "No, whoever performed this task had something less than two hours in which to complete it, which suggests an impressive access to manpower —discreet, efficient manpower."

Worf recalled the staggeringly wasteful display of wealth that had earlier filled this chamber. The minister's deductions sounded reasonable. "Every noble in this palace has a large retinue, do they not?"

"They have a not inconsiderable quantity of followers," Chih-li conceded.

"How many would have enough men to do this?"

The minister thought for a moment before answering. "Anyone in the Dragon's immediate family. Lord Lu Tung. Perhaps a handful of others. Anyone else would have had to bring in too many followers to maintain the deception that they were here for his comfort alone."

Energy crackled in the center of the chamber. Worf recognized the familiar sparkle of the *Enterprise*'s transporter. Dr. Selar materialized before their eyes, then walked briskly over to one of the fallen Starfleet officers. She ran her medical tricorder over the man's unconscious body. Chih-li's eyes widened perceptibly at the sight of Selar; evidently, he was not used to female doctors, let alone Vulcan ones.

"They appear to have been drugged, Doctor," Worf informed her.

"Yes," she confirmed. "This one was, at least; I assume the others were affected by the same agent. The symptoms suggest verapnerharmon or a local variant of that substance: largely harmless, but guaranteed to knock out most humanoids for three or four hours if admitted into the air supply in sufficient quantities. I imagine this chamber has a closed ventilation system?" she added, looking around.

"Yes, they all do," the minister said, "to prevent someone from poisoning the entire palace. Not, I hasten to add, that any Pai would ever stoop to so dishonorable a ploy."

"Indeed?" Selar said. She raised a quizzical eyebrow. "In any event, a strong stimulant should rouse the victims, although I recommend continued medical observation for the next forty-eight point five hours." She looked at Worf. "I will arrange to have the Starfleet personnel beamed directly to sickbay." She turned toward Chih-li. "I assume you can secure appropriate accommodations for the incapacitated Pai."

"Yes, yes, of course," the minister said, more flustered than Worf had ever seen him before. "Thank you for your assistance, er, Doctor."

Selar's expression did not change in the face of the security minister's discomfort. She walked away and began administering stimulant infusions to both Pai and Starfleet victims. Chih-li waited until she was several meters away before addressing Worf. "Quite astonishing," he said at last. "I have never seen a woman behave with such *forwardness.*"

"Vulcans require some getting used to," Worf replied diplomatically. Confident that his team was now in good hands, he turned his attention to the larger issue of the theft. "I'm afraid I must notify my captain of the disappearance of the gifts."

Chih-li nodded glumly. "And I must inform the Dragon." He looked as though he would have much rather fought another duel to the death.

*"What* is missing?" Picard said sharply.

Worf's deep baritone came clearly through the comm. "The display of gifts, sir."

"I heard you clearly, Lieutenant. I simply could not believe what I heard."

Picard rubbed his right temple. Thanks to modern

medical science, headaches were a fairly rare phenomenon, but he thought he felt one coming on. The situation on Pai was growing more complicated by the moment. He had barely signed off with Data, and was in fact standing between the oak cupboard and the bench the Dragon had occupied, when Worf hailed him to reveal the latest disaster. He listened carefully to Worf's report, then shook his head wearily. Worf had explained to him about the verapnerharmon, but he still found it hard to accept that six Starfleet security officers, not to mention a squad of armored Pai guardsmen, could allow several tons of gifts—including a life-size jade elephant!—to be stolen from under their noses.

Could the G'kkau be involved in this theft, he speculated, or the mysterious assassin? How did this tie in with the treaty, the wedding, and the imminent G'kkau invasion? The assembled gifts would be a tempting target for any thief, he thought. It might well be that the disappearance of the wedding gifts had nothing to do with the rest of the intrigue surrounding the royal wedding, but how could he be sure? "Mr. Worf," he said, "I want you to investigate this robbery thoroughly. It may have little bearing on our mission here, but we can't take that chance."

"Understood, Captain," Worf said. "Chih-li and I fully intend to apprehend the thief and recover the gifts."

"Chih-li?" Picard asked. He couldn't place the name immediately.

"The Minister of Internal Security," Worf reminded him. "We are conducting the investigation together."

"Very good, Mr. Worf. Make it so." He paused,

then spoke again. "And, Worf, I apologize if I sounded cross just now. This wedding is proving more stressful than we anticipated."

"Most human weddings do," Worf commented, "in my experience."

Worf signed off, and Picard wandered back toward Troi and the Dragon. Mu, he observed, had interrupted the Dragon's conversation with Deanna to whisper something into his emperor's ear. The nervous Chamberlain now looked absolutely stricken; his face was as pale as one of the ivory playing pieces on the *h'i* board. The Dragon himself seem taken aback by Mu's news. "What?" he said loudly. "All of the gifts? Even the elephant?"

Picard quickly explained to Troi what had occurred. "My condolences, Excellence," he said. "I share your surprise—and concern."

"Stealing the gifts from a wedding, and an Imperial wedding at that!" The Dragon was clearly appalled at the very idea. "I cannot comprehend it. What has become of honor that anyone could even think of such a thing?"

Picard found it odd, and more than a little annoying, that the Dragon should be more distressed by the prospect of a thief among his people than by the certainty of an imminent attack by the G'kkau. He found himself hoping that Worf would uncover a link between the robbery and the G'kkau; maybe *that* would finally focus the Emperor's attention on the alien menace. "I am sure," he said, "that the combined efforts of both of our security forces will quickly locate the thief and the missing gifts."

"Yes," Troi added. "Lieutenant Worf can be very resourceful. And persistent."

"I hope you are right, my dear," the Dragon said. Raising his goblet, he downed a large quantity of wine. The strong brew appeared to calm him. His smile returned, as well as the gleam in his eyes whenever he looked upon Troi. "It is good that you are here," the Emperor said to Deanna. "A beautiful woman can be such a comfort in times of trouble."

*Not necessarily,* Picard thought. Watching the Dragon watch Deanna was anything but a comfort; instead, he foresaw still more trouble ahead.

"What do you mean the Dragon is not yet dead?" Kakkh hissed angrily at his agent on Pai. "You promised he would die tonight!"

"It was that captain, Picard," the traitor whined. "If not for him, the Dragon would be dead by now, and I would be the new Emperor!"

*Not for long,* Kakkh thought silently. It was fortunate that his pawn was only an image on a viewer and not actually on board the *Fang;* otherwise, Kakkh doubted if he could resist the temptation to devour the foolish Pai noble in one satisfying gulp. *Two failed assassination attempts in one night! How hard could it be to kill one old mammal?*

"My method was exquisite," the Pai continued to protest. Kakkh did not need to smell his fear to know that the nervous-looking human on the screen was no longer as arrogant as once he had been. The Pai babbled as much to reassure himself as to allay Kakkh's doubts. "It was a flawless scheme, of classical design. I mean, poisoned *ma erh tsai mao tan ch'ing* no less! Why, do you know that no one has been murdered by poisoned *ma erh tsai mao tan ch'ing* for close to two millennia?"

"Perhaps," Kakkh snarled, "that's because it doesn't work!" He fixed cold, reptilian eyes on the worthless mammal whose pallid face appeared on the screen between his forelimbs. His inner eyelids winked malevolently. A forked tongue flicked between his fangs. "Be sure you understand me, Pai who would be Dragon. Tomorrow I will conquer Pai, one way or another. If you fulfill your promise before we arrive, you will be rewarded. *But* if we must lay claim to Pai without your assistance, then you will be merely one of many to fall beneath our claws. Do you comprehend what I am saying?"

"Yes," the Pai gulped. "Your words are must clear. The Dragon will die before dawn!"

*I'll believe it when I smell it,* Kakkh thought skeptically. He cut off the communication abruptly. *Stupid humanoid!* His jaws ground against each other in irritation. Dealing with these unreliable mammals made his scales itch.

Gar slithered up beside him. "Master Kakkh?"

"Yes?" Kakkh hissed.

"I have reason to believe that the *Enterprise* has intercepted some of our transmissions to Pai. They have also been scanning the nebula with a variety of sensor sweeps. They may have detected the presence of the fleet."

Kakkh snarled, then sank lower into his command pit. His tail whipped back and forth a few times. "No matter," he said finally. "The end of the game draws near, and there is little the Federation can do to stop us. We shall strike *before* the wedding and before the wretched treaty can be signed. Pai cannot join the Federation if Pai no longer exists!"

* * *

The more wine the Dragon drank, the more he appreciated Troi. He was openly flirting with her now, much to Picard's irritation. The Emperor's growing infatuation with Deanna did not make it any easier to convince him of the desperate urgency of the G'kkau situation.

At the moment, for instance, the Dragon had moved over to a seat by the fireplace next to Troi and was showing her each of the different *ch'i* pieces. The counselor had the slightly uncomfortable look of a woman cornered at a party. "This one is the Lascivious Wife," the Dragon said, winking at Troi. "In most versions of the game she moves every direction but forward, in leaps of two. You see how she holds the Intemperate Staff so tenderly?"

"Excellence," Picard broke in, hoping to rescue Troi and salvage his mission at the same time. "I must remind you that we have definite confirmation now that the G'kkau will be attacking Pai within hours. We face a crisis of interplanetary proportions."

"Must we deal with that now?" the Dragon sighed. "I was just about to explain to your lovely woman the romantic inclinations that brought my great-grandfather the title of the Patient One."

Troi rolled her eyes. "Please, Captain, tell us more about the dreaded G'kkau."

"You shouldn't trouble yourself with such matters," the Dragon said soothingly. "Here, have some more of this wine."

"But I find the subject fascinating," Troi said, batting her eyelashes. "How frightening *are* the G'kkau, Captain?"

Deanna was definitely performing above and beyond the call of duty this mission, Picard thought.

Certainly, she was making greater progress with the Dragon than he was, as proven by the resigned look that came over the Emperor's ruddy face as he reluctantly turned his attention back to Picard. "I can deny you nothing, fair maiden," he declaimed dramatically. "Now then, Picard, these creatures are reptiles, correct? Lizards?"

"In some ways, yes," Picard told him, "but sentient and undeniably aggressive."

"But still lizards nonetheless," the Dragon insisted, "so they can hardly be the terrifying warriors you describe. Lizards are soft and useless creatures, scarcely even edible, although there is one delicious little recipe . . ." His voice trailed off as his bleary eyes searched through the kitchen around them before abandoning the quest. "Anyway, surely the mighty Dragon Empire is capable of scaring off a few lizards in spaceships?"

"They have more than a few ships," Picard argued. "Close to a hundred in fact. And the G'kkau are far more fearsome than you imply. To our certain knowledge, they have razed dozens of planets already."

"Danger or no danger," the Dragon said loudly, "honor demands that we remove them ourselves. Indeed, if they are as ferocious as you say, it is all the more important that we comport ourselves fearlessly."

Picard felt as if he were slamming into a brick wall at warp speed. Was there no way to convince the Dragon to accept the Federation's aid before tragedy struck? "Your commitment to honor is more than admirable," he tried again, "and Starfleet has no intention of impugning your courage. We—"

"Enough!" the Dragon said sharply, his patience

clearly exhausted. "If you have nothing new to say, I do not care to continue this discussion any further." A scowl marred the Emperor's usually jovial expression as he glared sullenly at the gameboard. Picard feared that he had worn out his welcome, a fear confirmed by the Dragon's very next words. "The hour is late," he declared, yawning theatrically. "Perhaps we should continue our game another time?"

Under other circumstances, Picard would have liked nothing better than to abandon the pointless game and retire for the evening. Unfortunately, the treaty remained in doubt and the assassin was still at large. *How can I continue to guard the Dragon,* he thought, *when I am so obviously about to be dismissed?* "Are you sure, Excellence? I feel I still have so much to learn about the proper playing of *ch'i.*"

"Perhaps another time," the Dragon replied. "I fear I am keeping you away from your duties, Captain, not to mention your rest. No doubt your many concubines await you." Picard began to protest, but the Dragon had stopped listening to him. "Ah, woe is me," he said, his words clearly directed toward Troi. "A poor old man, all alone in this world of thieves and scoundrels, with no one to keep him warm at night. . . ."

"I find that very hard to believe," Troi said. "You are the Dragon, after all."

"Well, nobody *new* anyway," he said shamelessly, unfazed by the stern and disapproving expression that came over Picard's face. "Perhaps, if your captain would be so generous as to do without your company tonight, you would care to inspect the Imperial Bedchamber, also known as the Nocturnal

Temple of One Thousand Concupiscent Delights?" He rubbed his hands together eagerly.

*That's it,* Picard thought angrily. "Excellence," he said firmly, rising to his feet. "I must object to—"

To his surprise, Troi interrupted him. "I would be happy to accompany you, Most Excellent and Exalted One, provided that is acceptable to my lord and master Captain Picard." She winked at Picard, who found himself momentarily speechless. He thought he knew what Troi had in mind, but still . . .

"Deanna," he said quietly, too low for the Dragon to hear, "you don't have to do this."

"Don't worry about me, Captain. I can take care of myself—and the Dragon."

Troi was volunteering, he realized, to watch over the Dragon for the night and keep him safe from lurking assassins, but Picard couldn't see how she would be able to do that without exposing herself to a compromising situation. "Is there anything I can do to help make your mission . . . well, less eventful?"

"Actually, there is," Troi said brightly. "Perhaps you can arrange to have a bottle of Romulan ale beamed directly to the Dragon's quarters?" She treated the Dragon to a captivating smile. "It's a wonderful potion, Exalted One, perfect for romantic evenings."

*And likely to knock the Dragon off his feet,* Picard deduced, *on top of all the wine the Emperor has already consumed.* He had to admire Deanna's ingenuity, even though he still felt distinctly uncomfortable about allowing her to pursue this plan. *I should probably not mention this turn of events,* he thought, *to either Worf or Riker.*

ical factors limiting our responses." Data recalled his most recent conversation with the captain. The current prognosis for the treaty was not encouraging.

"Which way could it be?" Melilli wondered aloud. The distinctive creases on the bridge of her nose seemed to wrinkle together as she pondered the possibilities.

"There is one possible way of finding out," Data stated calmly. "Ensign Kamis, hail the G'kkau fleet."

Melilli looked quizzical. Data was not surprised that Melilli appeared puzzled by his command. As a former Bajoran freedom fighter, her first instincts were usually to shoot first and talk later. *Much* later.

"They know we are here," he explained. "Perhaps we can convince them not to proceed further." Data maintained a serene, inscrutable expression. "It is what is known in poker, Lieutenant, as a bluff."

"A color-blind unicorn finds the left-handed virgin," commented the Speaker of Aphorisms, "as the crescent moon dips twice in the same soup."

"Er, exactly," Riker said. Meng Chiao seemed to have a million ancient sayings lodged in his head, and none of them made a bit of sense. Riker shuffled the cards while glancing around the crowded harem for the Dragon-Heir. Chuan-chi had stepped away from the game momentarily to "rearrange my robes," which Riker had discovered to be a common euphemism for answering the call of nature. Riker would feel better when he had the Heir in sight; bad enough that Kan-hi had remained missing ever since storming out a short time before. He wondered what had become of the Dragon's younger and more wayward son.

Then, to his relief, the mob of bachelors parted to let Chuan-chi back to the historic site of Pai's first genuine poker game. "My apologies," he said curtly as, with much show of dignity, he slowly lowered himself onto a waiting cushion. "You may resume," he instructed Riker.

A few more players, all young lords of the Empire, had taken the Second Son's place in the game. The rest of the bachelors huddled around them in a circle, watching the game idly—and betting on the outcome—when they weren't pawing the serving girls or passing out from drinking too much wine. So far, there had been no further violence, which made the poker game something of a success, even though the Pai still seemed to be having trouble with some of the fundamentals of the game. "Okay," he said. "Ante up, gentlemen."

The various nobles drew forth tiny embroidered purses from the interior of their robes. Each removed a heavy golden coin from his purse and tossed it into the center of the playing area. Riker contributed a golden piece from his own supply, dealt the cards, then checked his hand. He had three jacks. Not great, but not too bad either. He might even win this hand. Not that he wanted to win necessarily. He just wanted to keep the Heir and the other bachelors amused and intact until the wedding. This was hardly the usual cutthroat Friday game on the *Enterprise*. *No,* he thought, *we'll just strive for enjoyable mediocrity.*

The betting proved unexpectedly daring, going two entire rounds with nobody folding. The kitty had grown from splashes of gold on the white tile floor to a small pile of gold coins. When his turn came around again, Riker considered his hand. His three jacks were good, but not so strong that he wanted to throw any more gold at it. He started to fold, and then an idea occurred to him. He looked at the grim, determined faces of other players. "Gentlemen, I'm sorry, but I have to ask: You don't all believe you're going to win this hand, do you?"

"Oh, no," the Heir said. "I have very little here, and will almost certainly lose what I am putting in."

"Then why don't you fold?" Riker asked.

"Fold?" Chuan-chi said. "I don't believe you explained this."

*I thought I had,* Riker mused. "Perhaps I did not make myself clear. Depending on how good your hand is, you must all make a judgment as to whether it is strong enough to merit throwing more money after the money you have already bet."

"We *must?*" the Heir said with hauteur.

"It is not required, no," Riker said hastily. "But it is a part of poker. When a hand is no longer worth investing in, one folds."

A long, tense silence greeted Riker's explanation. "What?" Riker asked finally.

"There is no honor in folding," the Heir said.

"The higher the mountain, the wetter the avalanche," Meng Chiao added.

Riker sighed. "I'm afraid I don't understand."

Another bachelor, one Lord Li Po, spoke up. "It is to admit one's inferiority to others. While I am willing to admit this to the Dragon-Heir, or even as a courtesy to yourself—" He bowed to both of them as gracefully as his voluminous robes and cross-legged posture permitted. "—it would be a dishonor to fold to any of my other noble compatriots, although I say this with no intention of offending anyone." He bowed to the rest of the players.

"That is quite understood," Chuan-chi said. "Indeed, I cannot imagine folding to anyone at this table." He spoke as though he was simply stating a matter of fact, comparable to the law of gravity or the half-life of dilithium crystals.

"But you need to fold in poker!" Riker protested.

"Then it is hardly an honorable game," the Heir said, "and I am unsure why you wished us to play this."

Riker suddenly saw his brilliant plan backfiring on him. "Certainly not to offend or cast doubts on the honor of anyone present," he insisted. "Wait, let me explain it this way. You say there is no honor in folding, correct?"

The other men murmured and nodded. "The light dims when the oyster swallows its pearl," Meng Chiao intoned.

"Whatever," Riker said. "If no one folds, the bidding will go on and on until each of you runs out of coins."

"Then we will also wager our properties, slaves, serfs, and women," one of the younger nobles said. Riker thought his name was Li Shang-yin, or was it Li Yin-shang?

"But at some point," Riker persisted, "each of you will run out of possessions, which means he who started with the most assets will win everything else."

Everyone turned to look at Chuan-chi, who was contemplating his cards with a typically sour expression on his face. "The Dragon-Heir owns Pai itself,"

Lord Li Po explained, "so the Heir would win, as indeed he should."

Chuan-chi shook his head. "There is nothing honorable about this. I might as well buy them outright."

"That is where chance and skill come in," Riker said, hoping he wasn't digging himself in deeper. "Folding is entirely honorable. It is like retreating in war, to fight again another day."

"But we don't do that," Lord Li Po said. "It is a warrior's duty to fight on until he is stopped by death."

Riker began to wonder if the Pai could possibly be related to the Klingons. Too bad they weren't more like the Ferengi, he thought. Then the only problem would be stopping them from cheating each other. "Look, it is a general's duty to determine the best use of his warriors, right?"

"That is true," the Heir conceded.

"So your cards are your warriors, and you are their general. You alone determine whether they are simply to be sacrifices, or whether they can turn the tide of battle."

There was another long pause while the Heir and his fellow nobles mulled over Riker's words. Riker tugged at the collar of his recently acquired silk robe. The harem seemed much warmer and stuffier all of a sudden. He prayed that he had not completely soured relations between the Federation and the Dragon Empire.

Suddenly, Meng Chiao's eyes lit up. He slapped his knee loudly. "Of course," he said. "I see it now. *The purple peacock crowns the hill of the scarlet ants!*"

"Ah," the Heir said knowingly. All the other Pai were nodding now, comprehension dawning for everyone except Riker. "You were right, Commander. That does make sense." Chuan-chi threw down his cards. "I fold."

"And I."

"And I."

One by one, the nobles folded, leaving a befuddled Will Riker to claim his winnings. Riker shook his head as he pulled the gleaming, golden pile toward him. *This may be tricker than I thought. . . .*

"One minute we were standing guard, glaring at the Pai soldiers, who were glaring at us. The next thing I remember was waking up on the floor while Dr. Selar asked me if I could recall what my name was." Lieutenant Nanci Atherton shrugged her broad, muscular shoulders. "I'm sorry I can't be more helpful, sir."

"This attack caught us all off guard, Lieutenant," Worf growled. "You're dismissed. Report to sickbay for a full examination."

Atherton walked away toward the transport site, leaving Worf and Chih-li alone in the now-spacious emptiness of the High Hall of Ceremonial Grandeur. Her footsteps echoed throughout the vacant chamber. Worf remained amazed at the sheer audacity of the unknown thieves. How had they managed to steal a roomful of treasures from the very heart of the Imperial Palace?

"We must search every room in the palace," he said. "The thieves cannot have gone far." It was not the first time he had reached this conclusion in the last half hour.

"That is impossible," Chih-li said for probably the twentieth time. "The Dragon's guests are men of great honor. It would be an enormous insult to even suggest that one of them might be a thief."

"But one of them most certainly is!" Worf snarled.

"Sadly, that appears to be the case," Chih-li admitted. The Minister of Internal Security paced unhappily across the bare marble floor. "And yet, we cannot dishonor the rest of our guests by searching their quarters. Each and every one of them would feel obliged to challenge us to a duel for even contemplating such a search."

Ordinarily, that prospect would have appealed to Worf, but time was running out. The wedding was now only hours away. Worf gave the problem serious thought. Upon reflection, it seemed to him that there were subtle differences between Klingon and Pai codes of honor. The Pai apparently placed great stock in *appearances,* while a Klingon's honor was based on his *deeds,* or so it seemed to him. He wondered if there was any way to turn that distinction to his advantage.

"We *must* search every room," Worf repeated. Chih-li began to object on principle, but the Klingon shushed him with a wave of his hand. "It should be possible, however, to ask in such a way as not to impugn the honor of any of your guests, perhaps by asking if someone else might have basely planted the stolen items in their quarters?"

The minister stopped pacing. A crafty smile appeared on his face. "You are both honorable *and* cunning, friend Worf. It may be that what you suggest is possible indeed. All we required was a polite fiction to allow all concerned to maintain the vestige of honor."

"Including the guilty party?" Worf asked.

"We shall deal with that problem after we have recovered the gifts. It is my sincere hope that an honorable suicide can be arranged . . . one way or another." The bloodthirsty gleam in the warrior's eyes faded as yet another thought occurred to Chih-li. "Our task is still a formidable one. There are over five hundred chambers in the main palace alone. A proper search could take days, if not weeks."

"Then we had best begin promptly," Worf said.

The Green Pearl's hysterical tears had given way to softer, more subdued sobbing, but that didn't make Beverly feel any better. Yao Hu's unexpected revelation had left Beverly feeling more than a little conflicted. Every maternal instinct in her body resisted the idea of forcing a young woman to marry a man she did not love; on the other hand, the future of the entire Dragon Empire depended on the wedding going off as planned. Beverly didn't know what to do—or think.

Currently, the bride-to-be was wrapped in the solicitous embrace of her future daughter-in-law, who appeared genuinely distressed by the other girl's plight. To Beverly's surprise, and considerable relief, Hsiao Har had proven both helpful and sympathetic during the ongoing crisis; apparently, there was a good heart beneath the girl's bratty mannerisms. Neither Beverly's gentle questioning nor Hsiao Har's heartfelt entreaties, however, had succeeded in persuading the Green Pearl to divulge the name of her true love. In fact, the Pearl had not really said anything at all since confessing her true feelings about the wedding; she had simply curled herself up into a tight little ball amid one of the many piles of pillows spread about the chamber. She looked like a tiny green figure lost amid a sea of pink. Her quiet sobs broke Beverly's heart.

To be honest, Beverly wasn't sure she really wanted to know the name of the girl's secret sweetheart. There had to be terrible penalties involved no matter how innocent their relationship had been—and, judging from the Pearl's obvious sexual naïveté, their romance had to have been pretty darn innocent. Even still, Beverly had enough on her mind already without having to worry about getting some foolhardy young man exiled or worse. But how was she going to get to the bottom of this without exposing the man's identity? And *should* she be probing this issue? Hadn't she done enough harm already?

It was all too much for her. She couldn't divorce the big picture—the treaty and the G'kkau—from the heartrending spectacle of the anguished girl among the pink pillows. She knew what Jean-Luc would say: The Prime Directive prevents us from imposing our own views of love and romance on another culture's marital customs. Besides, the greater good of the entire Dragon Empire depended on the Green Pearl's marriage to the Dragon-Heir; even discounting the all-too-real threat of the G'kkau, the marriage would also bring peace to the Empire after decades of civil war. How did the heartbreak of one young woman stack up against all of that?

Still, she was a doctor first and a Starfleet diplomat second; was she supposed to just ignore Yao Hu's suffering? "Damnit, Jean-Luc," she muttered angrily. "This is more than I bargained for." She needed advice from someone she trusted, someone who would be sure to take the girl's feelings into consideration, someone who could counsel her through this tangled emotional mess.

She needed Deanna.

"Hsiao Har?" Beverly crossed over to where the two girls sat hugging each other. Yao Hu was still lost in her grief, but the Heir's daughter looked up in response to Beverly's voice. "I need to have a private conversation with someone. Do you think you can manage on your own for a few minutes?"

Confusion marked the older girl's features. "But you cannot leave the harem," she said. "The Eyes of the Dragon guard the only exit."

"No, no," Beverly explained. "I'm not going anywhere. I just need to talk to somebody via my communicator. Do you understand?"

Hsiao Har nodded. The Green Pearl appeared completely oblivious of the rest of the world. Content that the situation had at least stabilized for the time being, Beverly left the girls and located the entrance to a private bathroom adjacent to the larger chamber. Like all of the Green Pearl's domain, the walls and furnishings were bright, pink, and generously decorated with her pearly namesakes. Beverly leaned against a counter of rose-colored marble and tapped her comm badge urgently. "Deanna? Hailing Deanna Troi?"

The comm established a link immediately; the harem was not as shielded as Lu Tung probably believed. "Beverly?" Deanna's voice came over the comm clearly. "Wha—what is it?" She sounded rushed and out of breath, almost as though she was being chased. Beverly wondered exactly where Deanna was at the moment.

"I've run into a little problem," Beverly said hesitantly. Could the Pai be monitoring their communications? Could the G'kkau? "I was hoping I could talk to you about it."

"Now is not a good time, Beverly," Troi gasped. Beverly heard snatches of conversation—and ribald laughter—in the background. "Exalted One, please! Not now! . . . I'm sorry, Beverly, did you say something?"

It sounded to Beverly like Deanna had problems of her own. "Are you okay?" she asked. "Is anything wrong?"

"The Emperor," Deanna said breathlessly, "has an enormous capacity for Romulan ale—among other things."

"What's that?" Beverly didn't understand. "Do you want me to notify Security?"

"No!" Deanna practically shouted through the comm; the vibration literally rattled the badge pinned beneath her Oriental robes. "I mean, thank you, Beverly, but that's not necessary. I can manage . . . I think."

Beverly still couldn't tell exactly what going on at the other end of the line, but she decided that Deanna sounded more embarrassed than endangered. If Deanna was really in serious trouble, she would have said so. Obviously, though, the Betazoid counselor was in no position to help Beverly wrestle with her own moral dilemmas. "Sorry to bother you. We'll talk later."

"Okay," Troi's voice answered. "Exalted One, wait! . . . That is, Troi out!"

*So much for that,* Beverly thought ruefully. Deanna would have a lot to explain the next time they shared an exercise session on the *Enterprise,* although it sure sounded like Deanna was getting plenty of exercise, of one sort or another, on Pai. That still left Beverly to face the reluctant bride on her own, something she wasn't looking forward to. Stalling for time, she contemplated her reflection in the full-length mirror mounted on one of the bright pink walls of the Green Pearl's private bathroom. Scores of gleaming pearls, uniform in their sheer lustrousness, framed the mirror; Lord Lu Tung must have raided every oyster in the Dragon Empire to decorate his daughter's chambers. Beverly thought she looked tired; it had been a long night, with only a few more hours to go before the (she hoped) inevitable wedding. Her elaborate green gown, that had once seemed so elegant, now hung on her weary body like last week's laundry strung out to dry. This mission was a hard one—and much more grueling than it looked.

In the end, she realized, there was no decision to make here. The Green Pearl *had* to marry the Dragon-Heir; there was no other way to bind the Dragon Empire together and save it from the untender mercies of the savage G'kkau. Foolishly, she had hoped that Deanna would somehow manage to pull another alternative out of the ether, but the fate of Yao Hu was locked in stone long before the *Enterprise* came within transporter range of Pai. Beverly just prayed that the Pearl would come to find peace in the life that had been chosen for her—and that future histories of the Dragon Empire would never forget the sacrifice this one young girl made for her people.

Beverly dabbed a tear from the corner of her eye, straightened her shoulders, and walked back into the plush, lush pinkness of the harem chamber. She stepped past a menagerie of discarded stuffed ani-

# *Chapter Twelve*

"THE SLOVENLY GARDENER grows more fruit than two hundred vegetarians," Meng Chiao recited. "Energetic is the goblin that fears the turquoise wallpaper."

"If you say so," Riker said. He threw his cards facedown onto the floor, then leaned forward to rake a large stack of gold coins toward him, adding them to an already impressive pile of Pai currency. He had been doing well tonight, perhaps too well; it was starting to get awkward and a bit embarrassing. "Thank you, gentlemen."

His hand brushed against his cards, flipping them over. Lord Li Po, whose deal it was, picked up the cards, then paused. "Hold!" he said indignantly.

"What is it?" Riker asked.

"These cards were no good," Li Po declared. He

spread them faceup on the floor, revealing nothing more than a paltry pair of threes.

"They weren't, were they?" Riker grinned. "But you bought it."

"You *lied?*" the Heir said. "You took our gold on a falsity?"

"Ah," Riker said, abruptly catching on to the mood of the party. The other players no longer looked amused; in fact, he became acutely conscious of the fact that he was currently surrounded by over a dozen Pai warriors who had each had too much to drink. For the first time in hours, he wondered what had happened to his phaser. "It's not a lie in poker," he insisted. "It's called bluffing."

"It looks like a lie to me," Li Po said. He had seemed like an amiable sort before, but now Riker saw the cold steel beneath the man's pleasant exterior. Li Po was, after all, undoubtedly a veteran and survivor of the recent civil wars, as were all the other men in the Heir's outer harem.

"A pickled skunk is not so black as the cat of a dissolute scribe," Meng Chiao added grimly. Riker still didn't know what he meant, but he got the tone easily enough. Meng Chiao was ticked off.

"I said nothing to you about the value of my hand," Riker explained. "I only continued to bid until each of you folded. You drew the conclusion that my hand was worthwhile."

"But," Chuan-chi said, fixing an icy gaze upon Riker, "you made no effort to disabuse us of the notion you knew we would be forming."

Riker shrugged in what he hoped was a disarming manner. "It is one of the tools of the game."

"It is hardly honorable," Li Po said. "Only a landless peasant would bluff."

"Trapped in a tunnel, a copper bell never rings," Meng Chiao agreed.

Riker was starting to wish he'd left with the Second Son. "That is not precisely the case," he said, thinking furiously. "To bluff is to permit the other person's errors to defeat them, just as you would not inform an opposing general of his mistakes when setting out his forces for battle—"

"That has happened several times!" Li Po protested. "Two thousand years ago, Lord Shen Fu did precisely that, preferring to win against his opponent's best attempt."

*I don't believe this,* Riker thought. "Did the general take his opponent's advice?"

"Certainly not," the Heir informed him. "It would have been dishonorable to go back on his battle plans at that late date, merely because of an adverse opinion. He was quite utterly destroyed."

"Seven thousand perished," Lord Li Po added.

"A nightingale's footprints are deeper than the ghost of a star," Meng Chiao explained.

Despite the anti-intoxicating effects of Dr. Crusher's infusion, Riker felt his head spinning. A man could go crazy, he decided, trying to sort out the Pai's confusing codes of honor. They seemed to take honor as seriously as a Vulcan regarded logic, and to just as absurd an extreme. "Look," he said. "What about this then? If you have an inferior force, would you wish to announce it to your opponent?"

"That would be quite unnecessary," Chuan-chi said. "There is no dishonor in not flaunting one's disadvantages. Indeed, one is obliged to put up a respectable appearance no matter how deficient one's forces."

"That is what a bluff is all about!" Riker said. "You have an inferior force—your cards—and you conceal it so that your opponent may commit himself to battle. Once he has done so, you are merely allowing him to continue to a greater or lesser extent."

"Hmmm," the Heir said dubiously. "It still smacks of deception."

"It is deception," Riker said. "But you allow your opponent no honor if you don't provide him with the opportunity to discern it." *I hope that makes sense,* he thought, *at least according to Pai standards.*

"True," Li Po said at last. "The commander is quite right. I myself must win honor by piercing the challenging illusion of a bluff. Deal the cards!"

Riker congratulated himself silently. *Either I'm finally learning to think like a Pai, or I'm just getting better at faking it.* As the other players anted up, he glanced down at his conspicuously large pile of winnings. *The captain won't thank me if I take everyone's money. Better to avoid another potential blowup.* "Tell you what, why don't I sit the next couple of hands out."

"You can't!" Lord Li Po said. "Not without offering us the chance to win back our gold."

*Uh-oh,* Riker thought. He looked at the other players' dwindling stacks of coins. At the rate they were mastering the game, he could probably empty their entire treasury before any of them really developed the skills to beat him. There was only one way he could manage *not* to clean them out.

*Lose.*

\* \* \*

*"Enterprise* to G'kkau flagship. Repeat: *Enterprise* to G'kkau flagship."

"Any luck, Lieutenant Melilli?" Data asked. Hailing the oncoming fleet had proven more difficult than anticipated, yet Data had discovered that persistence was often rewarded by positive results.

The Bajoran officer grimaced at the sound of static coming through the communications channels. "It's hard getting through the nebular cloud, but I think we've finally punched our way through." She listened carefully to the harsh buzz of the static. "Yes, we're receiving a response."

The viewscreen at the front of the bridge flickered. A dark, murky, roiling image began to seethe across it. "Sorry that's so unclear, sir," she said. "Let me—"

"There is no need for further adjustments, Lieutenant," Data said, recalling Captain Picard's earlier confrontation with the commander of the *Fang.* "That is an accurate representation of the interior of a G'kkau ship."

Thick clouds of inky smoke billowed upon the viewer, and Data discerned a dim, reptilian shape half lost in the gloom. "This is the *Fang,"* a voice hissed across the subspace radio. "I am Gar; you are not deemed worthy of speaking with the leader of our glorious fleet, Master Kakkh. Speak."

*Interesting,* Data thought. During their earlier encounter with the G'kkau, Master Kakkh had responded directly to the captain's hails. This change in behavior suggested that the G'kkau knew that Captain Picard and the other senior officers were currently on Pai and not aboard the *Enterprise.* He speculated about how the G'kkau had acquired this information even as he addressed Gar. "I am Lieutenant Commander Data of the *Starship Enterprise,*" he began.

"Why do you bother us with your hails? We will speak only to your commanding officer." Gar's voice rose to a squeaky hiss, like an old-fashioned teakettle coming to a boil.

"I am currently the officer in command of the *Enterprise,*" Data stated calmly. He did not consider this a dangerous admission, since logic suggested that the G'kkau were already in possession of this information. "I might also point out that I am not speaking with your commanding officer."

"That is completely different," Gar said. "We are inherently superior; you are scum."

"Webster's defines 'scum' as a thin layer of impurities which forms on the top of liquids or bodies of water," Data replied. "Clearly, this term does not apply to me. In any event, I have contacted you on behalf of the Dragon Empire and the United Federation of Planets to insist that you cease your approach to Pai."

"Scum," Gar said again. "You are a fool to warn us thus, and honorless."

Data ignored the insult. "Please clarify your remark."

"Your own Federation law," Gar sneered, "insures our safety once we are in Imperial space."

Data judged that this was the correct moment at which to attempt his bluff; he hoped Lieutenant Melilli was paying close attention. "The Federation and the Dragon Empire have entered into a treaty which permits us to defend Imperial territories from hostile approaches."

"Hah," Gar snorted. Steam rose from his nostrils, joining the other murky fumes suffusing the bridge of the *Fang*. "We know all about this treaty, and we know that it has not yet been ratified."

"It shall be," Data said. "Do you wish to take the chance, knowing that Captain Picard and the Dragon might be signing the agreement even as we speak?"

"Even so," Gar gloated, "you can do nothing until the wedding is complete. Pai will be a smoking ruin by then, and your precious treaty with it."

"I must again insist that you do not approach Pai," Data said.

"And how will you prevent us?" The reptile laughed, producing a wet, sloppy sound like a soaked carpet slapped against a stone floor. Then he cut off the transmission before Data could even begin to reply. The android found himself staring at a view of Pai itself. The blue-green sphere, filigreed with intricate patterns of swirling clouds, reminded him of the ornate decoration of the Imperial Palace. He resolved to conduct a comparative analysis of astronomical scenery versus humanoid interior decoration at the next convenient opportunity.

"He called your bluff," Lieutenant Melilli said.

"Perhaps," Data stated. "Still, we have succeeded in ascertaining the extent of G'kkau intelligence regarding activities upon Pai itself, which is apparently considerable. This strongly implies that the G'kkau have a humanoid confederate at the palace itself, establishing a probable link between the approaching G'kkau invasion force and the attempted assassination of the Dragon."

"So there is a traitor on Pai," Melilli said. "But, sir, the fleet is still going to reach Pai before we can do anything at all."

"Your analysis is correct," Data conceded. "Therefore, we must delay the fleet's arrival."

"But how?" she asked. Like most Bajorans, he noted, Lieutenant Melilli was quick to question authority.

"I have an idea," he said. "Please ask Lieutenant La Forge to report to the bridge."

The search for the wedding gifts was going slowly. Even though many of the Pai nobles were away at the Heir's bachelor party, their servants remained to guard their respective quarters, and, without exception, these servants required considerable persuasion before they would permit a search party to inspect their masters' accommodations. It was necessary for Chih-li to explain each time, in painstaking detail, why the search was not a violation of anyone's honor. Worf found himself growing more frustrated by the moment. Honor was a matter of vital importance, true, but so was the necessity for direct action, something the Pai seemed to make little allowance for.

"Tell me again," a frail, gray-bearded Pai manservant inquired of the Minister of Internal Security. "Why does your base invasion of these premises in pursuit of stolen goods not reflect badly on the honor of the distinguished gentleman whom I have the honor to serve?"

The aged Pai, whom Worf could have blown aside with one breath, stood between the search party and the entrance to a large suite of rooms currently being occupied by one Lord Li Po, who was apparently attending the Heir's bachelor party and so could not (or so the old man insisted) be disturbed until the morning of the wedding itself. Worf growled impatiently; time was slipping away and they had searched less than one-quarter of the Imperial Palace. Not for the first time, he wished they could simply scan the entire palace from on board the *Enterprise* and locate the missing gifts that way; unfortunately, the same shields that protected the palace from unauthorized transporter beams also blocked the *Enterprise*'s sensors. They would have to conduct the search the old-fashioned way, door by door.

Chih-li bowed his head toward the elderly servant. His dark hair hung down his back, since he had left his helmet behind in the High Hall of Ceremonial Grandeur. "Your laudable concern for your master's honor does you great honor as well," he said. "And yet, if a dishonorable scoundrel conceals his ill-gotten goods within your honorable master's rooms, then your master is dishonored if the goods go undiscovered."

The old man scratched his head, visibly puzzled. "But if they are undiscovered, how can my master be dishonored?" he asked. "And what honor is derived by defending the honor of a master whose honor is not in question?"

Worf's sharpened canines ground together in exasperation. He clenched his fists so tightly that his nails dug into his palms. His forehead throbbed beneath his bony ridges. *This is ridiculous,* he thought angrily. At this rate, they would not uncover the location of the stolen gifts until after the wedding of the Green Pearl's great-grandchildren. "I must go," he stated gruffly, stalking away from the old man and Chih-li. *If I remain another minute, I will eviscerate them all.*

"Honorable Worf," the minister called out. "Where are you going?"

"To investigate the scene of the crime!" he snapped, making his decision even as he announced it. *Why not?* he thought. Searching the palace, and debating the finer nuances of Pai honor with every lowly menial they met, was not getting him anywhere. Perhaps he had missed some vital clue at the High Hall of Ceremonial Grandeur. The more he thought about it, in fact, the more convinced he became that there was something not quite right about this entire scenario. Even allowing for a huge retinue of servants to handle the heavy lifting, how could anyone remove such a staggering accumulation of physical artifacts from the chamber without attracting attention?

As Worf strode down the wide, capacious corridors of the Dragon's palace, he passed clusters of male and female Pai going about their business. The palace never slept, apparently; despite the lateness of the hour, he could see servants and attendants scurrying down the long halls, carrying laundry, mops, wash-rags, sonic polishers, and last-minute decorations for the coming wedding. Worf's presence, as he marched determinedly along, his dark eyes glowering, his clenched fists pumping at his sides, never failed to alarm the timid Pai servants. They went out of their way to avoid him, often cowering against the nearest wall until he passed, then whispering excitedly in his wake. Worf was not offended by their reactions; rather, he expected just such a response, and would have been disappointed with himself had the Pai behaved otherwise. They did well, he thought, to fear an angry Klingon.

The constant stream of busy passersby tugged at the back of his mind, however. There was something about all this nocturnal activity that bothered him, but it took him a moment or two to put his finger on the problem: How had the thieves managed to transport their booty through these well-populated hallways without being spotted? It made no sense. After all, they had not gassed the entire palace into unconsciousness, so someone should have noticed a huge parade of thieves carrying all manner of extravagant gifts through the corridors of the palace, and yet, apparently, no one had. The furrows on Worf's brow grew even deeper as he examined the problem. *Never mind where the gifts are now,* he thought. *How did they get there?*

He quickened his pace, the sooner to reach the High Hall of Ceremonial Grandeur. If only there was a turbolift to rush him to the scene . . . ! He was on to something, he knew it. He would recover the gifts before the dawn, and demonstrate once and for all the efficacy of Klingon forthrightness as opposed to the endless verbal circumlocutions that the Pai seemed to have mistakenly confused with honor. *The Pai talk about honor,* he concluded, *but the Klingon achieves it.* A savage grin lifted the corners of his lips. Victory was within his grasp. He could taste it on the air, despite the sickly-sweet perfumes with which the Pai polluted their very atmosphere. He looked forward eagerly to searching the empty crime site once more, and indeed he was almost there. . . .

His comm badge beeped urgently. He stopped

abruptly, less than fifty meters from the soaring double doors of the High Hall of Ceremonial Grandeur. "Worf here," he barked.

"Mr. Worf," Captain Picard's voice said. "We have an emergency. The Green Pearl has disappeared."

The harem was in an uproar. Nubile serving girls and scantily clad concubines shrieked in alarm as Picard, accompanied by Lord Lu Tung himself, hiked past the massive armed guards, down the incense-laden hallways, past a multitude of doorways offering glimpses of dozens of luxurious boudoirs, to the very heart of Lu Tung's harem. Picard barely noticed the voluptuous pulchritude on display; his mind was filled with the dreadful implications of this shocking new development. He paid enough attention to his surroundings, though, to note that his presence alone was not responsible for the obvious consternation and excitement spreading through the harem. News of the Pearl's disappearance was traveling quickly. He just hoped the G'kkau had not learned of the bride's absence already—provided, that is, that they were not directly responsible for it.

Picard had barely left the Dragon's kitchens when Beverly informed him that the Pearl was missing; in fact, he had been searching for the palace infirmary in hopes of finding something to settle his upset stomach. All hope of intestinal relief disappeared entirely when he learned that the bride—the very linchpin of the Pai peace settlement—had vanished mysteriously. Acid had churned in his gut as he'd raced through the palace, encountering Lu Tung along the way. Picard couldn't help wondering what Lu Tung had been doing away from his own quarters, especially this late in the evening, but there seemed no tactful way to interrogate a father whose only daughter might have been abducted.

Lu Tung paused before a forbidding iron door embossed with the image of a ferocious dragon. Picard looked on as the former rebel commander used some sort of laser concealed in a ring to activate the lock. Ruby eyes sparkled in the skull of the dragon, shortly before the entire door dematerialized. Lu Tung stared at the now-open doorway with a bewildered expression on his face.

"This is impossible," he declared. "The Eyes of the Dragon have guarded this portal since the hour I departed. No one could have entered or departed this chamber. No one!"

Picard was inclined to believe him. Lu Tung appeared genuinely shocked by his daughter's disappearance. His formerly implacable visage betrayed signs of grief and anger; his broad face had flushed nearly as pink as the walls beyond the doorway. His hands trembled as he spoke, although whether he shook from fear or fury Picard could not tell.

He briefly wondered if Q could be responsible for the Green Pearl's inexplicable vanishing act. This seemed like one of his pranks; hiding a bride the night before a pivotal wedding might appeal to his cosmic sense of the perverse. But no, Picard chided himself, he could hardly get into the habit of blaming Q for every bizarre mystery he encountered. Q, as annoying as he could be, was hardly the only source of chaos in the universe. *Would that my life could be that simple,* Picard thought.

He found Beverly standing in the middle of a chamber of overpowering pinkness. A sulky-looking adolescent girl squatted nearby on top of a stack of rosy, brocaded cushions. For a second, Picard permitted himself the hope that the Green Pearl had turned up alive and well, but the apprehensive look on Beverly's face quickly dispelled that notion. "Hsiao Har," Beverly explained, nodding toward the girl. "The Heir's daughter by his first wife. She was keeping Yao Hu company."

"Yao Hu?"

"The Green Pearl," Beverly said. She took a deep breath as the missing girl's father approached them. She surely wasn't looking forward to this confrontation, but she turned to face the man directly. "Lord Lu Tung, I am so sorry. I only left her alone for a minute."

Picard half expected Lu Tung to shout at Beverly, to hurl curses and invective at her, blaming the foreign woman for disaster that had befallen them all. Instead, he dismissed her apologies with a wave of his hand. "I regret that you have become entangled in our private sorrows," he said. Emotion warred with sober dignity in Lu Tung's solemn mien. Picard had to wonder how sincere the warlord's grief was; had Lu Tung himself arranged the Pearl's disappearance in order to sabotage the peace? Only Lu Tung appeared to have access to the harem. Who else could have bypassed the dragon in the door?

Lu Tung cast a heavy gaze toward the young girl on the pillows. "Has she said anything?"

"Not a word," Beverly said. "I've tried to convince her to tell me what happened, but she's keeping mum. I think she's protecting Yao Hu, or thinks she is."

*That bodes well for the Pearl,* Picard thought, *since*

*it suggests that the girl fled of her own free will.* A surprise elopement complicated matters, but at least it was better than an abduction. With luck, the Green Pearl was still unharmed, although he wondered how long she could remain safe with assassins and alien invaders threatening all of Pai. Runaways often found more trouble than they anticipated.

Lord Lu Tung loomed over Hsiao Har. His deep voice rumbled from somewhere deep within him. "Hsiao Har, daughter of Chuan-chi, granddaughter of the Imperial Dragon, I charge you upon your honor to tell me everything you know about what has become of my daughter."

Hsiao Har looked up at him, open defiance written all over her face. "Go to any one of the Twenty-Five Hells," she said. "Perhaps the Frozen Hell of Overambitious Fathers. That would be fitting."

Lu Tung's face darkened. "This is no joke, girl!" he said, raising his hand as if to strike Hsiao Har.

"Sir!" Picard protested, stepping forward. Before either man could make another move, the Dragon charged into the room. Troi followed quickly behind him. The Emperor wore only a single saffron robe that strained to cover his Buddha-like proportions. His bare feet kicked the pillows out of his way; Picard noted that the Dragon's toenails were nowhere near as lengthy as his flamboyantly extended fingernails. He was surprised to see the Emperor up and about; he would have thought the Romulan ale would have put the Dragon out for the night.

"What vile trickery is this?" he bellowed. "Where have you hidden your daughter, Lu Tung?"

"Hidden?" Lord Lu Tung turned on the Dragon,

forgetting Hsiao Har for the moment. "How dare you suggest this is my doing! I bring my only daughter here in good faith, trusting her to the protection of your palace, and look what has become of her. My own flesh and blood stolen away under cover of night! Don't speak to me of trickery, Nan Er."

The Dragon looked as though he had been slapped across the face with something particularly slimy and disgusting. "Traitor!" he cried. "You have no right to call me by my given name. I am the Dragon—*your* Dragon—and I should have known better than to trust your two-faced protestations of peace. But I never thought you would sacrifice your own daughter to sabotage our alliance."

"Sacrifice?" Lu Tung shot back. "What greater sacrifice could there be than to let my daughter marry that cold-blooded excuse for an Heir?"

"Gentlemen!" Picard said loudly, stepping between the two men before they could come to blows. "This is getting us nowhere."

"But he is a liar and a traitor!" the Dragon shouted. "Why, if I had my sacred sword . . . !"

"And you are a fool, Nan Er," Lu Tung said. "You have always been a fool." He looked on the Dragon with outright contempt. Picard saw a hard-won peace falling to pieces before his eyes.

"Excellence, please!" he said. "Lord Lu Tung, we have no time for these futile recriminations. We must think of the Pearl!"

His argument struck home. Lu Tung backed away from Picard, turning away from the Starfleet captain and his longtime emperor and adversary. Picard saw Lu Tung's shoulders shake from the exertion required to control his emotions. When he turned to face Picard once more, the rebel general had regained most of his dignity and poise. *Now,* Picard thought, *if only I can calm the Dragon as well.*

But Troi was way ahead of him. "Exalted One," she said, holding on to his arm. "You must contain your mighty fury until we can discover the truth. Restrain yourself, for the sake of the poor, unworthy girl whose safety we are all so concerned about."

"Well," the Dragon said grudgingly, "perhaps I can delay my wrath a little longer. Still, I will not tolerate deception beneath my own roof."

"Nor is there any reason you should," Picard said. *Well done, Deanna,* he thought. He noted that her blue gown, although still intact, looked rather more disheveled than before. Shoving the matter aside for the moment, he addressed the Emperor in a firm tone. "First we must determine the precise nature of that deception."

"Well, I had nothing to do with the girl's disappearance," the Dragon insisted.

"Nor did I," Lu Tung said glumly, "although that should go without saying."

The two powerful Pai lords eyed each other suspiciously, but they no longer looked like they were ready to declare bloody war, at least not right away. *Thank heaven for small favors,* Picard thought. He took advantage of the lull in hostilities to sidle closer to Troi. The Betazoid counselor fell back from her close proximity to the Dragon. "We came as soon as we heard about the Pearl, Captain," she whispered. "The Dragon insisted."

He inspected her carefully. She appeared none the

worse for her sojourn in the Dragon's chambers. "I hope you were not too inconvenienced. Earlier, I mean."

"The Emperor is a remarkable man," she said, a coy smile playing upon her lips. "And full of surprises."

Her reply was curiously vague, Picard thought, but now was not the time to pursue the matter.

"So?" the Dragon said petulantly. "Now what are we to do?"

"Perhaps," Picard suggested, hoping to reinforce the sense of common purpose, "someone should notify the Heir?"

"Why?" the Dragon asked, looking quite surprised by the notion. "He scarcely knows the girl. Let him enjoy his party."

"Let me see if I got this straight," Geordi La Forge said. "We can't attack the G'kkau directly, and we can't even lay a string of photon mines along the Empire's borders without violating the Prime Directive. Is that right?"

"You have summarized our predicament quite concisely," Data said, "which is why we require another option, preferably one that will incapacitate the G'kkau ships rather than destroying them."

*Easy for you to say,* La Forge thought. He still hadn't figured out how to put on a fireworks display that would impress the jaded Pai. Now Data needed a deliberately roundabout way to immobilize an entire alien fleet. The life of a Starfleet engineer was never an easy one. . . . He examined the bridge's main viewscreen through his VISOR. The viewer now charted the progress of the G'kkau invasion force through the nebula, each approaching warship indicated by a small yellow triangle silhouetted against a swirling violet background—or at least that was how they appeared to La Forge; sometimes, he knew, his color perceptions were more vivid than those received by ordinary humanoid eyes. On the graphic display, the G'kkau fleet resembled a swarm of buzzing yellow-jackets en route to Pai. There had to be some way to slow them down, he thought. Some sort of interstellar fly trap. "What kind of drive do they have?" he asked.

Lieutenant Melilli answered him. "It's a primitive form of hammer drive, sir. A beta-neutrino drive capable of speeds in excess of—"

"I know the drive," La Forge said impatiently. The last thing he needed now was a lecture on alternative warp sources, not unless they could provide him with some snazzy fireworks by the time the sun rose on the Imperial Palace. "I did some of my Academy work on one."

The Bajoran officer gave La Forge an icy look.

*Ouch,* La Forge thought. He mentally added Melilli Mera to the long list of women he'd managed to get on the wrong side of. "Anyway, the trouble with beta-neutrino drives, and the reason Starfleet largely abandoned them, is that they tend to interact in nasty ways with high-energy plasma and positively charged particulates." His eyes widened behind his VISOR. "Exactly the sort of thing you find in a good-sized nebula!"

"The G'kkau don't seem to be having any problem," Melilli pointed out.

"They must be using a low-frequency EM emitter as a buffer," La Forge said. "Yeah, that would do it, as long as they managed to modulate the EM so that it stifled the beta emissions, which are what react to the nebular material."

"Interesting," Data said. He rose from the captain's chair and walked over to where La Forge was standing. "Geordi, would it be possible to render their neutrino drive vulnerable to the influence of the nebula?"

La Forge scratched his chin thoughtfully. "I suppose so. It wouldn't be too hard to adapt the photon mines so that they neutralized the buffer effect. Then their own beta emissions might trigger a chain reaction which could shut down their engines entirely." He considered the possibilities. "They'd have to be pretty close to the mines, though."

"That can be arranged," Data said. La Forge admired Data's confidence; his positronic brain seldom seemed bothered by indecision, maybe because he could run through all his options more quickly than could La Forge or anyone else. "How soon can the mines be readied?"

La Forge sighed. What he wanted to do was get back to his fireworks problem; once he tackled a challenge, he liked to see it through to the end without any distractions. Still, stopping the G'kkau obviously took priority. "An hour. Maybe ninety minutes tops."

"Sir," Lieutenant Melilli said. "I'm obliged to point out that even this passive approach might be seen as a violation of the Dragon Empire's autonomy."

"That is correct, Lieutenant," Data acknowledged. "Therefore, we will be planting the mines well away from Imperial space."

"But, sir—" She paused as if realizing she was about to overstep her authority. At Data's nod, however, she continued. "But then we'll be far from the G'kkau's approach to Pai!" Melilli objected. "Why do you suppose they will go out of their way, delaying the certain annihilation of the Dragon Empire, just to chase a Federation starship around a minefield?"

*I was kind of wondering that myself,* La Forge thought.

"We must give them an incentive, Lieutenant." Data turned to face the conn. "Lieutenant Tor, please set a course for the epsilon sector. Computer, access what is known of G'kkau vocabulary and usage."

La Forge couldn't wait to see what Data had in mind. *This is going to be good,* he thought.

Two muscular Pai warriors stood between Worf and the entrance to the harem of Lord Lu Tung. Each man brandished a scimitar and a surly expression. They were also armed with hand weapons, Worf observed, although they hadn't drawn them yet. He wondered briefly if he could draw his own phaser before the guards could fire their weapons; it would be intriguing to match Klingon reflexes against the Pai variety. If the Green Pearl was truly missing, however, there was no time to fight another duel, no matter how appealing the prospect.

*What a shame,* Worf thought. *Two against one . . . honorable odds indeed.*

"Stand clear," he barked to the guards. "My captain requires my presence."

"Neither man nor beast," one of the guards replied, as if uncertain as to which category Worf fell into, "may enter the Forbidden Sanctum of Lord Lu Tung."

The Pai warrior sneered at the Klingon in a manner

Worf found most insulting. Worf was tempted to make the Pai eat his own scimitar, but concluded that a phaser blast would be quicker. On stun, of course, with a wide-angle dispersal. His hand drifted toward his weapon. . . .

His comm badge chirped. "Lieutenant Worf?" said the captain's voice.

"Yes, Captain," Worf said, giving Picard his full attention. Stunning the guards would have to wait for a minute or two.

"Where are you now?" Picard asked.

"Outside the harem," Worf said, glowering at the guards. "Lu Tung's men appear reluctant to admit me to the women's quarters, but I expect to have the matter resolved shortly."

"You needn't bother," the captain said. "Chih-li is taking charge of the investigation here. I'm afraid your presence would only provoke the Dragon; he would surely consider it an affront to the honor of his own security forces. The Pai are quite sensitive regarding such matters."

"So I have discovered," Worf confirmed. "The Minister of Internal Security has already challenged me to a duel, but we have agreed to postpone our battle until after the wedding."

*"What?!"* The captain sounded alarmed at this new development.

"There is no reason to be concerned, Captain," Worf said. "The minister and I are most evenly matched. It will be an honorable and glorious battle."

There was a long, uneasy silence before Picard spoke again. "Mr. Worf, I have neither the time nor the inclination to deal with this now. For the present,

I suggest you confine your activities to finding the missing gifts."

"The gifts?" Worf said. "Surely the Green Pearl takes priority."

"I would not be at all surprised," Picard said, "if the two matters are related. Find the gifts and you may find the girl as well."

"Very well, Captain," Worf said. He inspected the two burly Pai guards who were even now watching him with what looked like bloodthirsty anticipation. It appeared it would no longer be necessary to fight his way past them. *Too bad,* he thought, *but duty calls. . . .*

Turning his back on the harem and its guardians, he marched briskly back toward the scene of the crime.

# Chapter Thirteen

"DAMN," RIKER SAID. "I lose again."

"What a pity," Chuan-chi said. "Such a shame to see your luck turning to this degree. For a time it seemed you might have bankrupted us all utterly."

"The seeds of fortune seldom bloom in hydroponics," Meng Chiao agreed.

Riker shrugged. He'd given up trying to translate Meng Chiao's aphorisms into sense, as well as giving up the last several hands. His once-impressive pile of winnings had diminished to merely a handful of golden coins. "Oh, I doubt my luck could have lasted," he laughed. "You are all fine players."

Lord Li Po reached for Riker's discarded hand. "Wait!" Riker said, but before Riker could stop him, Li Po flipped the cards over.

"You folded with a straight flush?" the noble said. "That was a winning hand!"

"It was a flush?" Riker said, feigning surprise. "Oh, so it was."

Chuan-chi's eyes narrowed as he peered at Riker suspiciously. "I think we must prevent such accidents in the future. From now on, any folded hands will be exposed at the end of the hand, to prevent any further errors."

"That's not necessary, sir," Riker said. "It was a simple oversight on my part. The hour is late, I was tired, and I missed the full value of my cards."

"Nevertheless," the Heir insisted, "we would not wish you to lose money you would have won had you not been tired."

*This isn't about money,* Riker thought, *it's about diplomacy.* This "friendly" game was turning out to be anything but relaxing. His neck ached and one of his legs had fallen asleep after his having squatted on cushions for hours. He shifted his weight awkwardly. "Making mistakes is just part of the game, gentlemen."

Lord Li Po coughed gently. "I believe the Heir's concern is that such mistakes might happen so consistently as to warrant a certain, shall we say, dubiety."

"It is a matter of honor," Chuan-chi said. Riker suspected he was enjoying the Starfleet officer's discomfort.

"A frosted mirror reflects only grapefruit," Meng Chiao contributed.

"I see," Riker said. *Losing is going to be harder than I thought.* "In that case."

"Shall we play another hand?" the Heir said.

* * *

235

Step by step, centimeter by centimeter, Worf scanned the High Hall of Ceremonial Grandeur. His tricorder probed the walls and floor; fortunately, no one had shielded the chamber against a scan from within. So far, he hadn't found what he was looking for, but he did not feel discouraged just yet. The High Hall was a large one. There were still many more cubic meters to scan.

The matter of the missing bride weighed heavily on his mind. Still, as instructed by Captain Picard, he continued his search for the stolen wedding gifts.

His fierce gaze never left the readout on his tricorder as he prowled the perimeter of the hall. His footsteps echoed eerily in the vast, empty chamber. He came to a halt a few meters ahead of the northeast corner of the room. The tricorder registered a sudden drop-off in the molecular density of the adjoining wall. Worf smiled, the thin, knowing smile of a hunter who has finally cornered his prey. *This is it,* he thought.

No doubt there was some mechanism concealed nearby: a lock activated by a signal of unknown nature. Worf searched for the lock for several minutes, but with no success. Whoever had installed the lock had hid it well. *This is taking too long,* he thought. If the captain was correct, and those who stole the wedding gifts had also taken the Green Pearl, then every second he delayed the bride's life remained at risk. There was no time to waste. He drew his phaser, raised its setting several notches, and fired upon the suspicious stretch of wall. Reinforced wood and tile disintegrated in the red glare of the phaser beam, revealing a hidden stairway descending into the lower depths of the palace.

Worf switched off his phaser. He grunted in satisfaction. The staircase before him was cloaked in shadows, but seemed wide enough to accommodate even a life-sized jade pachyderm. *No wonder no one spotted the thieves in the corridors,* he thought. *They took another route.* The discovery of the secret passageway lowered his opinion of the Pai even further. No self-respecting Klingon fortress would come complete with hidden escape routes; a true monarch would rather die than retreat from his own palace. He was aware, however, that other cultures did not share the Klingon's profound contempt for self-preservation, which was why he had come to suspect just such a covert tunnel to and from the High Hall of Ceremonial Grandeur.

Commander Data often invoked a fictional Terran hero who specialized in untangling complicated webs of deception. For himself, Worf had found the stories of this hero, frequently enacted within the *Enterprise*'s holodecks, to be overly cerebral and disappointingly bloodless. At this moment, however, he found himself sharing the sentiments of Data's favorite fictional role model. *The game is afoot,* he thought.

Phaser in hand, his eyes quickly adjusting to the gloom, Worf descended the staircase.

Geordi's voice sounded tired over the ship's intercom. "The last of the mines has been launched, Data, and should be in place in fifteen minutes. They're outlining a large sphere, just as you requested."

"Thank you, Commander La Forge," Data said. "You may return to your light show now."

"If I have the time," the engineer grumbled. "La Forge out."

"Unfortunately, the only fireworks we may see will be the flames rising from Pai as it burns," Melilli Mera said grimly.

Data looked at her from the captain's chair. "You have doubts, Lieutenant?"

"Yes, I do." She lifted her chin. "Sir. I still see no reason why the G'kkau should delay their mission to pursue us."

Data raised his voice. "Ensign Kamis, please open communications with the *Fang.*"

"Yes, sir." The Benzite manipulated the touchpads on his console. Murky, shifting forms showed on the forward viewscreen.

"Master Kakkh of the *Fang,*" Data began. "This is—"

"Hold on, sir," Kamis said. "That's just static." The image gelled slightly, and an emerald, reptilian shape seemed to swim into view. "Now, sir."

"Master Kakkh," Data said again. "This is Lieutenant Commander Data of the Federation *Starship Enterprise.*"

"This is Kakkh," the lizard replied. "Your leader is still not there."

"He is not," Data admitted.

The screen went blank.

"The G'kkau have broken the connection, sir," Kamis reported.

"Please raise them again," Data said.

This time the reptile actually snapped in their direction, showing large teeth that gleamed ominously even in the smoke and dim light permeating the bridge of the *Fang*. "You waste my time. We have no interest in your idiotic and transparent bluffs."

Data wondered briefly if the G'kkau played poker. "I did not contact you to bluff," he said.

"Do you then wish to surrender?" Kakkh hissed with what may have been amusement.

"Not at all," Data said.

"I see you have left Pai and retreated to the nebula. Very wise, in light of the slaughter to come."

"Permit me to point out," Data replied, "that the *Enterprise* is not currently in the range of your fleet's weaponry."

"We weep with disappointment," Kakkh said, reminding Data of an old Earth idiom concerning crocodile tears. "We are comforted only by the knowledge that most of your chief officers remain on Pai, and so will die hideously in the destruction."

"If you wish to destroy the *Enterprise*," Data continued, "you must change course to do so. The fastest approach vector, should you so desire, would be along oh-four-six prime."

"Sir—" Melilli said, her voice too low to be picked up by the communications channel. Data saw no opportunity, nor any compelling reason, to explain his strategy now.

"Do you intend to sacrifice yourself, you artificial mammal?" Kakkh taunted him. "Would you throw away your pseudoexistence merely to distract me from my inevitable victory?"

"No, Master Kakkh, I have merely called to tell you that you are the second cousin to a throkmelkk."

There was a moment of stunned silence, then Kakkh recovered his voice. *"What!?"*

"A throkmelkk, Kakkh. Also, your spawnmates are the product of a level-three mutation involving their farandolae. If they even have farandolae, as I have reason to doubt."

Kakkh's jaws snapped spasmodically. His tail whipped the inky fumes roiling behind him. "You must die! Die! Die!" he ranted. "Change course at once! Destroy the *Enterprise!*"

Another large lizard crowded into view on the screen. "Master Kakkh!" Gar protested. "What about Pai?"

"The rest of your crew," Data added, "are kebbs with irregular V-chromosomes."

The hisses and howls of rage, along with the sounds of sharp claws scratching against metal, coming over the communications channel threatened to deafen everyone stationed on the bridge. Ensign Kamis lowered the volume automatically. "That should suffice, I believe," Data remarked. "Lieutenant Tor, prepare to take evasive action if necessary."

"Yes, sir!" said the Andorian at the conn.

The turbolift doors breezed open behind Data. La Forge bounded onto the bridge. "How's it going?" he asked.

"Within expected parameters," Data informed him. As predicted by Starfleet files, the G'kkau had proved extraordinarily sensitive to epithets of an evolutionary nature. "Onscreen."

An empty starfield was replaced by a schematic of the G'kkau fleet's proximity to the *Enterprise*. The hostile warships were again represented by yellow triangles. Red disks marked the location of the photon mines, which formed a perfect sphere with the *Enterprise,* indicated by a blue circle, at the exact center of the sphere. The entire G'kkau fleet, led by the *Fang*, arrowed in on the *Enterprise*.

La Forge took his place at the Security position, where Worf usually stood. "I can detonate the mines at any time," he reported.

"Wait for my command," Data said, watching the screen. The first few yellow triangle crossed over into the sphere defined by the red disks. He waited patiently as more triangles followed them. "Red alert," he said. "Shields up."

"The first ships have entered the mined area," Melilli announced. "Twenty-five percent within range of the mines ... fifty percent ... Sir, it's hard to tell exactly how many ships are in range."

"Please do your best," Data said.

"It's about seventy percent ... eighty ... ninety ..."

Data examined the visual display on the screen. The lead ships were microseconds away from firing on the *Enterprise*. He could not risk losing the ability to communicate with the mines. "Fire," he said.

Concentric circles radiated from red disks, which immediately blipped out of sight. As the expanding circles overlapped with the edges of the yellow triangles, the triangles instantly ceased their relentless motion toward the *Enterprise*.

"That's most of them," Melilli declared. "But it looks like a few managed to get out of range of the mines before their drives seized up."

Without warning, Kakkh appeared on the screen. Smoke no longer filled his cabin, presumably a symptom of mechanical distress. Seen clearly, the skin beneath Kakkh's scales appeared rough and leathery. The pendulous dewlaps hanging from his throat had inflated dramatically; they looked ready to burst. "You—defective kung, you mutated glar—!"

"Yes, Master Kakkh," Data said, unmoved. "May I say in return that you are the segmented portion of an underdeveloped tadpole."

"We will listen no more to you!" Kakkh screeched. "You are too base to be heard. But know this: There are five G'kkau warships still functioning. We turn immediately to raze Pai—and ready it for the second wave of G'kkau conquerors! Despite your unforgivable trickery, you have not defeated us. Pai will fall, and the Dragon Empire with it."

The screen blanked momentarily, then reverted to a view of the surrounding nebula.

"Warp five back to Pai," Data ordered.

"What about what our scaly friend said?" La Forge asked. "Think we did any good?"

"We have significantly reduced the odds against us," Data said. "Furthermore, we have delayed the remaining ships so that there is a possibility that the wedding will be completed before the G'kkau reach Pai. Fortunately, our speed exceeds the G'kkau's, so we will have the opportunity to defend Pai, provided that the treaty is ratified in time."

"That's a big if," La Forge said. "By the way, I was monitoring your conversation with Kakkh, and I have to ask you something."

"Which is?"

"What's a throkmelkk?"

"I must fold," the Heir said.

"Which leaves me winning again," Riker groaned. With something like despair, he raked the gold coins toward himself. His pile of gold pieces was now large enough that it kept collapsing of its own weight, spreading out over the floor. He had tried stacking them neatly, but he was winning so frequently he barely had the time.

Chuan-chi was doing well, too; but everyone else was losing drastically. Meng Chiao, he of the inexhaustible (and incomprehensible) aphorisms, had only a handful of coins left, and several of the others weren't much better. *At least we'll be able to stop soon*, Riker thought. He glanced around the outer harem. He'd lost track of the time hours ago, but everyone looked too tired and worn-down to start another brawl, let alone try to assassinate the Dragon-Heir. Some of the bachelors, those less intrigued by the foreign novelty of poker, had already passed out on the various cushions and divans scattered throughout the suite. Snoring, Riker had discovered, was one of those universal phenomena that required no translation. Empty goblets and plates of half-eaten snacks littered the floor, along with the rumpled remains of the silk tapestries that had once hung from the walls. Even the ubiquitous serving girls seemed to be running out of steam. They wore dark shadows under their eyes, if little else, and barely had the energy to dodge the groggy gropings of the remaining bachelors. Only the poker game was still going strong.

*All those Friday nights when I couldn't get a pair*, he thought ruefully, *and now I can't lose.*

Lord Li Po dealt a new hand. None of the Pai nobles were fast at it, having little experience with playing cards, but they getting the hang of it. Riker's cards flew into his hand as if they were sentient. He picked them up and saw a natural three of a kind. *Not great*, he thought, *but not bad enough*. He wondered if he could get away with discarding one of his three jacks.

As the hand progressed, it became clear that a couple of the others had good hands. He noted that Meng Chiao appeared confident enough to bid highly; with luck, he'd lose and go out this hand. The bidding was high and fast. A pile of gold grew in the center of the exposed floor space. Meng Chiao laid down his last coin. "The weeds of a humid summer have slippery roots," he said philosophically. "I have an additional fifty cycee to raise you."

*Wait a second,* Riker thought, alarmed. *If we start accepting credit, who knows how high the stakes could get?* "I would prefer not to take money that isn't on the floor."

"But we always permit this!" Lord Li Po said indignantly. "One seldom carries enough gold to play for long."

"You gamble like this all the time?" Riker asked. As far as he knew, this was the first poker game in the history of the Dragon Empire.

"We wager on horses, dice, the favors of unattached courtesans," Li Po explained. "Naturally, we accept each other's credit. It is the only honorable thing to do."

"Even my dissolute brother is allowed to tender notes of obligation," Chuan-chi said, "although it is doubtful that he will ever be able to repay what he already owes." The Heir fixed Riker with an icy stare. "Do you mean to imply that we would not honor our debts?"

"No, of course not!" Riker said.

"Then we will proceed," the Heir declared. "The

honorable Meng Chiao has pledged a further fifty cycee to this hand. Will you raise or call?"

Riker stared gloomily at his hand. Over the course of play, he had drawn yet another jack, leaving him with an even stronger hand. *Now what am I going to do?* he thought. *I can't take everything they own. The captain would never forgive me.* He called Meng Chiao's bet. *Please,* he prayed desperately, *don't be bluffing.*

Meng Chiao's face fell as he laid down his cards. A pair of aces. "The eagle flies over the wayward shark, the shark swims under the forbidden grotto."

*You can say that again,* Riker thought glumly. He reached out to claim his winnings.

The hidden stairway led to a maze of subterranean tunnels running beneath the Imperial Palace. Worf navigated through the tunnels by the sickly green glow of bioluminescent tiles embedded along the center of the walkways, much like the emergency lights on most Starfleet spacecraft. The tunnels smelled musty and old, and looked as though they had not been used for decades, if not centuries. Cobwebs hung like sticky gray curtains across every archway, while a thick layer of dust covered every exposed surface. Worf heard water falling slowly, drop by drop, somewhere in the distance. Rats squeaked and insects chittered behind the walls and beneath his path; sometimes small creatures scurried out of sight moments before he caught a glimpse of them. *Vermin,* he thought disdainfully. He was tracking bigger prey.

If not for the years of neglect and disrepair, it might have been easy to get lost in this byzantine underground labyrinth, but Worf easily discerned the route the thieves had taken. They had left a trail even a human could follow: torn webbing, footprints in the dust, and scratches alongside the walls of the tunnels where the outlaws must have scraped some of the larger items they were carrying. Worf suspected the jade elephant must have smashed against the tunnel walls a few times. A little while later, he discovered fragments of broken porcelain lying on the floor of the tunnel, where a clumsy thief must have dropped one of his prizes.

At an intersection where two tunnels met, he came upon a more provocative clues. Two pairs of footsteps, one pair small and delicate, came down the left-hand tunnel, eventually merging with the route taken by the caravan of thieves. Worf could not know for certain, but he would have been willing to bet a hundred *Huch* in Klingon currency that the left-hand tunnel eventually led to the harem of Lord Lu Tung, the last known location of the coveted Green Pearl. Judging from the footprints in the dust, before they disappeared entirely in the disorderly trail of the thieves, the Pearl appeared to be traveling of her own free will. Worf grunted. The tracks supported Dr. Crusher's theories regarding a secret lover and possible assignation. Worf did not know whether to condemn the girl for her disobedience or applaud her for her spirit. In the end, it didn't matter; his own duty compelled Worf to return her to her father in time for the wedding.

Candlelight flickered up ahead. Worf's eyes, accustomed to the faint green glow of the tunnels, blinked against the sudden brightness, which seemed to be coming from just around the next corner. Worf's grip tightened on his phaser. Crouched over to form a smaller target, he stalked forward as quietly and stealthily as he could. A small white mouse scampered out of his way, squeaking loudly. Worf could have gladly bit its head off.

A shadow of roughly humanoid proportions fell across the light on the wall, then vanished in a flash. All of Worf's senses went on alert. He crept to a point mere centimeters away from where the tunnel took a sharp turn to the left. Straining his ears to their limit, he thought he heard the sound of controlled breathing. He sniffed the musty air; above the omnipresent reek of decay, he scented the unmistakable tang of fear. Someone was waiting in ambush just around the corner, someone who desperately did not want to be found.

Worf dived around the corner, feeling something whoosh through the air where his head should have been. He hit the ground rolling and was halfway up, one knee resting on the dusty floor, before another heartbeat had passed. "Freeze!" he barked, drawing his phaser on a young male Pai standing by the curve in the tunnel. A woman screamed behind him, followed by the sound of soft footsteps charging toward his back. The woman, whoever she was, was no warrior; without even turning his head, he grabbed hold of her outstretched arm and flipped her over his shoulder onto the floor. His phaser, held tight in his other hand, never wavered; it remained pointed at the Pai youth, who held on tightly to what looked like a solid gold statuette in shape of a monkey. That was what the youth tried to hit him with? Worf felt embarrassed that he had actually bothered to duck such a ludicrous weapon.

Rising to his feet, Worf quickly surveyed his surroundings. He was in a cavernous basement approximately the size of the High Hall of Ceremonial Grandeur. A number of lighted candles, resting upon ancient casks and crates, illuminated the chamber; the smoke from the candles rose and disappeared in the shadows concealing a high, vaulted ceiling. Looking around, Worf was not surprised to find the missing wedding gifts.

They made an impressive pile. Instead of being neatly laid out as they had been when Worf first viewed them, they were jumbled together, with smaller objects tucked into or teetering atop larger objects. The elephant had an entire range of thick golden cables hung across its back. Worf wondered whether they had managed to move all the gifts at the same time or if the theft had required multiple trips. How long had Atherton and the rest of the security team been knocked out?

He kept one eye on his prisoners. The young man still stood by the entrance to this underground vault. His golden robes, although wrinkled and smudged with dirt, looked as though they had been expensive once. Surprise gave way to anger on the boy's face. He was handsome by human standards, Worf judged, although somewhat lacking in character. The Green Pearl's secret lover? Worf suspected as much. "Drop the monkey," he said. It fell from the Pai's hands, striking the rough brick floor with a metallic clank.

Her breath knocked out of her, the girl lay motionless for a moment or so, then stirred and sat up. The minute she opened her brilliant chartreuse eyes, Worf knew he had found the Green Pearl of Lu Tung. Her tiny slippers matched the footprints he'd found earlier in the tunnels. "Who are you?" she asked, staring wide-eyed at Worf's inhuman visage. *"What* are you?"

Worf ignored her query, his gaze searching the dimly lit corners of the vault. "Where are the others?" he asked. These two alone could not have possibly carried all the gifts through the tunnels, not in a dozen nights.

"Dismissed," the youth said. "That is, I allowed them to return to their quarters."

"And who are you?" Worf demanded. He had never seen this particular Pai before.

Despite the phaser aimed at him by a ferocious-looking Klingon, the boy put up a brave front. His hands on his hips, his chest thrust out proudly, he declared, "I am Kan-hi, Second Son of the Dragon."

The Green Pearl, kneeling upon the floor, sighed in adoration. Worf felt like sighing, too, albeit for a far different reason. Their mission, he realized, had just become much more complicated.

He tapped his comm badge. "Captain, Worf here. I have news for you. . . ."

# Chapter Fourteen

THE GAME HAD TURNED into a rout. The men started gambling away their concubines, their wives, their interplanetary yachts, even their estates. Several were down to the plain cotton undergarments they wore under their elaborate robes. Their fine clothing, along with everything else they had brought to the party, was stacked beside Riker. All of their estates and other possessions were neatly listed on a scroll laid by his elbow. Riker kept expecting his lost phaser to turn up in the ante. It never showed, but it was about the only thing on the planet he hadn't won yet.

Moaning out loud, he laid down his third straight in a row.

"That cleans me out," Lord Li Po said, rising slowly to his feet. "I will have my wives, concubines, and servants delivered to you following the wedding." He bowed deeply.

Meng Chiao had also reached the limit of his resources. He teetered upon wobbly legs. "A wealthy fool soon parts with his fortune."

"Hey!" Riker said, startled. "That actually makes sense!"

"Pay him no heed," Li Po said. "He is too drunk to recite it properly." Even as they spoke, the Speaker of Aphorisms slumped, then slid down onto the floor. His mouth hung open as his eyes fell shut. "See what I mean," Li Po said.

Only the Dragon-Heir himself remained in the game. Riker faced his last remaining opponent, who just happened to be the Heir to the entire Dragon Empire. Those bachelors still remaining conscious, stripped nearly as bare as the exhausted serving girls, crowded around the game, watching every move. Under such close observation, Riker realized, there was no way to lose on purpose. He had no resort except to pray that his winning streak ended right now.

"Perhaps we should stop," Riker suggested for about the fiftieth time. The last time he tried to leave the game, assassin or no assassin, Chuan-chi had posted guards by the door to prevent him from departing.

"Oh, no," said the Heir. "You must stay. It is—"

"—a matter of honor," Riker finished for him. "I know, I know." Pai had a bad case of gambling fever, Riker decided. He felt like an old-time explorer, introducing smallpox to unsuspecting populations.

"Deal," the Heir said tersely.

Chuan-chi had a good poker face, not showing much beside a sort of focused dyspepsia, but now his eyes flickered as he inspected his cards, the rapid eye movements suggesting that he was checking his hand again and again, as if not believing them.

They were playing Rigellian Hold'em. Each of them had three cards remaining facedown on the floor, their identity unknown until the conclusion of the betting. Riker consulted his own hand, and breathed a sigh of relief. He didn't have so much as a pair. *Good,* he thought.

Chuan-chi raised his gaze from his cards, and stared evenly at Riker. "Although I shall not inherit the whole Empire until that far-off day when my father goes to greet his ancestors," he explained, "Pai belongs by tradition to the Dragon-Heir. I will wager this planet itself against everything you have managed to win."

*He can't be bluffing,* Riker decided, *unless he's also the finest actor on Pai.* This was looking better and better. He could lose it all on this hand. No doubt the Heir would eventually end up redistributing his winnings among his friends and allies. "Agreed," Riker said.

He flipped over the cards on the floor.

The Dragon-Heir laid down four aces, but it was a full minute before Riker could put down his royal flush.

"Excuse me," he said numbly. "I *really* have to stop now."

"Entering Pai orbit in approximately five minutes, sir," Lieutenant Tor announced. The Andorian turned her antennae toward Data.

"Onscreen," Data said. Pai—a blue-green sphere frosted with cloud cover—appeared on the main viewer. Data identified the various continents in view. By his calculations, the sun would be rising over the Imperial Palace in less than half an hour. "Location of the surviving G'kkau warships?"

"They're hot on our heels, Data," La Forge stated. "They should be here any time now."

"Orders, sir?" Lieutenant Melilli asked.

"We will hold our fire," Data said, "until we receive word from Captain Picard that the wedding is concluded and the treaty is in force. Then, and only then, will we be free to defend Pai from G'kkau aggression." Data briefly glanced over the faces of the officers now stationed on the bridge: Tor, Craigie, Kamis, Melilli, and Geordi. Could they be apprehensive about the coming confrontation with the G'kkau ships? A good commanding officer was responsible for the morale of all personnel under his command; that was a recognized Starfleet principle. Data judged that this was an appropriate moment to say something inspirational. "In the meantime, there is no harm in raising our own shields. In fact, there is a sixty-seven-point-eight-six-four-three-percent probability that the *Enterprise* will survive this mission."

"What about Pai?" La Forge asked. "And our people down on the planet?"

Data did not think it advisable to announce the appropriate probabilities out loud. "It is now nearly dawn at the Imperial Palace. We must suppose that Captain Picard has used his inestimable diplomatic talents to resolve all of the outstanding difficulties surrounding the treaty."

"I sure hope so," La Forge said, "because I don't

think the G'kkau are going to wait for the wedding reception, let alone the honeymoon."

That was unlikely, Data thought.

The Sacred Temple of Perpetual Harmony was anything but. Beyond a filigreed archway looking out onto a garden full of fragrant cherry blossoms and beneath an open skylight designed to capture the first rays of the rising sun, utter turmoil raged among what was supposed to have been the wedding party.

"Betrayed by my own son!" the Dragon wailed.

"With my only daughter!" Lord Lu Tung lamented.

*Well,* Picard thought, *at least they've finally found something in common.*

Kan-hi, his hands in shackles provided by Chih-li's guards, stood defiantly off to one side, flanked by both Worf and the Minister of Internal Security. A doddering old priest, who looked to be about two hundred years old, appeared completely baffled by the confusion. The Green Pearl knelt weeping by the altar, occasionally casting longing glances at her captive suitor; someone had managed to get a wedding gown of emerald and olive onto her, but the veil was already soaked through with tears and the bride near the point of collapse. Beverly hovered near Yao Hu, unable to offer much in the way of consolation, and holding hands with Hsiao Har, who seemed to share the heartbreak of the other girl. In time, Picard guessed, the Heir's daughter would have to answer for her part in the Pearl's escape from the harem, but presently everyone was too upset over the illicit couple to worry much about any accomplice. Troi waited near the entrance to the temple, keeping an eye out for Riker and the groom, who were due to arrive at any moment. Thankfully, the bulk of the wedding guests were still sleeping off last night's celebrations; the actual wedding ceremony, Picard had learned, was a small private affair usually limited to the bride and groom's immediate family. Under the circumstances, the crew of the *Enterprise* had been allowed within the temple, but the several dozen Pai nobles visiting the palace were here for the feasts and receptions after the religious ceremony. *More small favors,* Picard thought, *although what I could really use is a miracle or two.*

His comm badge chirped, and Data identified himself. "The *Enterprise* is prepared to defend Pai," he stated. "I trust the wedding is about to commence."

"Your trust is gravely misplaced," Picard informed him. "What is the status of the G'kkau fleet?"

"Our plan was largely successful, but not completely. The vast majority of their ships are now drifting without engines in a comparatively benign sector of the nebula. Judging from the transmissions we have monitored, I understand that it will be days before even the nearest G'kkau ships can arrive to rescue them."

Picard had no sympathy for the stranded ships. "How many vessels got through, Data?"

"Five, sir, including the *Fang*. I am afraid they will be in range of Pai within the hour. Have you alleviated the Dragon's doubts about the treaty, sir?"

"Not yet," Picard admitted. He stroked his chin, feeling stubble. His eyes burned for lack of sleep. He had hoped for a shower and shave before the wedding; instead, after spending nearly the entire night playing *ch'i,* eating inedible meals, and tracking down a run-away bride, he was no closer to convincing the Dragon to join the Federation. Never mind the treaty—he wasn't sure there was even going to be a wedding this morning.

"I hope there is the possibility of a speedy resolution, sir," Data said.

"You'll be the first to know," Picard promised. "Picard out."

The Dragon-Heir suddenly appeared in the doorway with Will Riker in tow. Sometime in the night, Picard noted, his first officer had exchanged his dress uniform for a much more impressive assemblage of Pai robes; he hoped this meant that Riker had made a good impression on the Heir and his associates. Right now, every little bit helped.

Riker, looking fatigued and a bit sheepish, approached Picard. "Sir," he began, "there's something I need to tell you."

But Picard had his eye on the front of the temple, where an angry Heir appeared to be confronting his brother. "Not now, Number One," he said. "We have a crisis on our hands."

Evidently, news of the Second Son's crimes had finally penetrated the Dragon-Heir's quarters. "Thief! Traitor!" Chuan-chi screamed at his younger sibling. "Not only the wedding gifts, but my bride as well! How could you be so dishonorable?"

Kan-hi did not shrink from his brother's accusing gaze. "I love Yao Hu," he said, "which is more than you could ever do for her. As for the wedding gifts . . . well, I confess I had debts to pay before I could provide for Yao Hu in the manner she deserves. Besides, the irony appealed to me. What a sham all these feasts and gifts are. No amount of treasure could ever sanctify this mockery of a marriage!"

"When I am Dragon," Chuan-chi snarled, "your execution will be my first act as Emperor." Reaching into the folds of his saffron robes, the Heir consulted a small timepiece. Looking on, Picard found this peculiar behavior for a man who has just found out that his brother tried to steal his fiancée. Chuan-chi stared up at the skylight. He checked his timepiece again. *What is he waiting for?* Picard wondered.

The old priest also looked to the skylight. "The sun is coming," he said, stamping a wooden staff upon the floor by the altar. "We must proceed with the wedding."

Would there still be a wedding? Picard held his breath, watching all the principals carefully as they hesitantly looked upon each other. In the end, he observed, and despite the best efforts of Kan-hi, Yao Hu, and the still-elusive assassin, everyone had made it to the church on time. But had the events of the evening torn Pai's fragile alliances apart?

"I suppose there must be a wedding," the Dragon said, "for the sake of the Empire."

Lord Lu Tung nodded. He walked over and looked at his daughter. "It is a matter of honor," he said gravely, as he helped the tearful girl to her feet.

Yao Hu choked back sobs. "Very well," she said, raising her chin up high. "In the name of peace, I will marry the Dragon-Heir, but my heart will always belong to my beloved Kan-hi!"

"So be it," Chuan-chi said. He seemed strangely unmoved by his bride's passionate declaration of love for another man. His gaze kept darting back and forth between the slowly lightening sky and his father, the Dragon. Minutes before his wedding, Picard observed, the Heir kept watching the skies—almost as if he was anticipating the arrival of an alien armada.

It occurred to Picard that Kan-hi, who had proudly proclaimed his guilt in the matters of the stolen wedding gifts and the short-lived disappearance of the Green Pearl, had never claimed responsibility for either of the assassination attempts on the Emperor. And why did Chuan-chi seem so convinced that he would soon be in a position to execute his brother? Suspicion gripped Picard. He took a few steps toward the Heir, then stiffened when he saw Chuan-chi reach once more into his robes. Perspiration had broken out all over the Heir's forehead. His eyes looked crazed. Picard didn't think he was going for his watch this time.

"Excellence!" he shouted. "Watch out!" The world seemed to segue into slow motion as he watched Chuan-chi draw what appeared to be a standard-issue, type-2 phaser from within his robes and aim it in the direction of his father. Picard lunged for the would-be assassin, even as he realized that he was too far away to stop Chuan-chi in time. *It's too late,* he thought. *I should have realized . . .*

Beverly, however, was already standing by the altar next to Yao Hu. Hearing Picard's warning, and reacting immediately, she kicked out her right leg . . . hard. Picard recalled that Beverly had once won first place in a dancing contest when he watched her powerful leg connect with Chuan-chi's arm, which snapped upward, letting go of the phaser, which went tumbling through the air until Riker leaped up and snatched it in midflight. "There you are!" he shouted.

Worf and Chih-li instantly charged the Heir, tackling him to the ground. Deprived unexpectedly of their support, Kan-hi tumbled onto his hindquarters. The Green Pearl shrieked and ran to her sweetheart's side. Lu Tung reached out to stop her, then threw his hands in the air, apparently overwhelmed by the shifting tide of events. The ancient priest fainted dead away, coming to rest in a bouquet of flowers behind the altar. The Dragon just stood there, blinking, as if unable to comprehend what had just transpired.

"Chuan-chi?" he said. "My son? My heir?"

On the floor of the temple, Chuan-chi struggled futilely to free himself from Worf and Chih-li's grasp. "You don't understand!" he cried. "I have to kill him before they get here! I promised them he'd be dead!" He slumped helplessly between the Klingon and the minister. "If I don't," he moaned, his voice fading to a whisper, "I'll be just another victim."

Troi wandered over to Picard's side. "The Heir," she said, shaking her head.

"Our assassin," Picard confirmed.

"I wonder why I never sensed it," Troi asked.

"You never had any contact with him," Picard pointed out. "You were just a woman, remember? Even at the banquet, you were seated far away and out of sight." Picard smiled grimly. "The Dragon almost paid for that social gaffe with his life."

Even the Dragon could not ignore this blatant an assassination attempt. Picard could see the full implications of his eldest son's actions sinking into the Emperor's consciousness. His ruddy face went pale. He could not bring himself to even look in Chuan-chi's direction as Chih-li dragged him away. Pale and trembling, he staggered over toward Picard.

"Dear captain, dear doctor," he said, glancing at Beverly, "I owe you my life, such as it is. At this instant, I am not convinced that I still value this mortal existence, betrayed as I am by both my sons." He sighed deeply. "But my tragedy does not in any way diminish the honor of what you have done here. If there is anything I can do to repay you . . ."

"Actually, Excellence," Picard said gently, "there is the matter of the treaty." Part of him felt guilty about taking advantage of the unfortunate Emperor's gratitude in this way. Still, Chuan-chi was correct in one respect; the G'kkau *were* on the way.

"The treaty?" the Dragon said absently. Picard feared he might be in shock. "Oh, yes, the treaty. Well, this changes everything, of course. Your selfless heroism demonstrates that your honor is at least equal to our own, so there can be no dishonor in melding your honor with the honor of the Dragon Empire. Where is that treaty anyway? I'll sign it this very minute." He glanced around the temple, as if expecting a scribe to instantly appear with the proper document in hand. "Mu!" he called. "Where is that man anyway? Never around when I need him. You'd think there was a wedding going on or something. . . . Wait!" A thought struck him, and he clutched his head between his hands. "The treaty's no good without the wedding, and how can there be a wedding now?"

*A very good point,* Picard admitted. Lu Tung could hardly be expected to marry his daughter to a confessed assassin who was no longer remotely in line for the throne. There seemed no way to unite the warring factions now, unless . . .

Riker interrupted Picard's musings. "I hate to bring this up at a time like this, but there's something you really need to know. It's about a poker game, which seemed like a good idea at the time."

"G'kkau ships approaching Pai," Lieutenant Melilli announced. She looked meaningfully at Data. "They *are* within range of our phasers, sir."

Data shook his head. "The Prime Directive remains in effect, until the captain informs us otherwise."

"It's a wedding," La Forge exclaimed. "How hard can it be?"

Data assumed the question was rhetorical, but answered anyway for the good of morale. "Captain Picard did suggest that there were unforeseen difficulties to be dealt with."

"Can't we just drop a few more photon mines?" Ensign Craigie asked.

"Not within the boundaries of the Dragon Empire," Data said.

"Besides," La Forge added, "I don't think they'd have any effect on the G'kkau's engines outside the nebula itself."

"But we must do something!" Melilli said. Her earring rattled angrily as she spoke with great heat. Data began to understand why earrings were not considered proper Starfleet attire, even though concessions were made to Bajoran officers on account of their religious beliefs.

"Indeed," he said, "we must do something extremely difficult in such a dire situation. We must wait."

"You won what?" Picard said. He couldn't believe his ears.

"Er, the planet, sir, and everything on it." Riker repeated. "It's a long story, sir."

"Well, the short version, Number One, is that *your* planet is in serious jeopardy, and this latest complication does nothing to ease the situation."

Picard paced in front of the altar, his mind racing to come up with a solution, any solution. There had to be a way to secure the alliance between Lu Tung and the Dragon, and thus fulfill the treaty between the Empire and the Federation, before the G'kkau rendered the entire planet a smoking ruin. All they needed was a wedding. . . . His head snapped up. "Will," he said urgently, "how much did you win again?"

Riker looked miserable. "Let's see, forty-two major properties in the Empire, a brewery dating back three centuries, about fourteen hundred indentured servants, and eleven full households, including wives and concubines. I've probably forgotten some of it, sir. And the planet, of course."

"Of course," Picard echoed. A plan was forming in his brain. It was a bizarrely convoluted one, but that probably made it perfect for the Dragon Empire. "That should be more than enough, Number One." He strode decisively to the center of the temple. "Excellence," he called out, raising his voice. "Everyone? If I can have your attention?"

"What is it, dear Captain?" the Dragon asked. All eyes turned toward Picard.

"A very simple matter, Excellence. I propose a marriage between my esteemed first officer, William Riker, and your granddaughter, the honorable Hsiao Har."

"What—!" Riker exclaimed. Hsiao Har's eyes lighted up as she stared at Riker with ill-disguised glee. Beverly and Deanna simply looked confused.

"At ease, Number One," Picard said. *Will's going to have to trust me on this, along with everyone else.* "I believe an exchange of gifts is appropriate at this juncture. As a brideprice fully worthy of the infinite prize of your granddaughter's hand, Commander Riker offers the planet Pai itself, which he has recently acquired from your son, the former Heir."

The Dragon's eyes widened. "Is this true?" he asked Riker.

"On my honor," Riker said, squirming a bit under the intensity of Hsiao Har's adoring gaze.

The Dragon shrugged. "Why not then? The world has gone mad already, and we might as well have at least one happy occasion to celebrate. A marriage between one of your people and mine is a fine idea. I should have thought of it before." He scratched his chin. "What sort of dowry are you asking for?"

"As a dowry," Picard said, "we request only a pardon for your Second Son, the misguided-but-honorable Kan-hi."

"A pardon?" The Dragon was visibly taken aback. He stared, scowling, at his younger son, who remained in shackles with Yao Hu by his side.

"Consider the matter, Excellence," Picard said quickly. "Kan-hi's errors in judgment were those of a young man in love. Once pardoned, he would be free to marry the Green Pearl in his brother's place, thus sealing your alliance with Lu Tung and fulfilling the terms of your treaty with the Federation." *And freeing the* Enterprise *to protect your Empire,* he added silently. "Assuming that is acceptable to you, Lord Lu Tung."

The dour warrior nodded his assent. "Better a thief than an assassin, I suppose. Although," he added, looking directly at Kan-hi, "if you disappoint my daughter in any way, know that you will answer to me."

Kan-hi gulped. "I understand, Lord Lu Tung. I love Yao Hu with all my heart. You won't regret this."

"I don't know," the Dragon said. "Everything is happening so fast."

"Please, Exalted One," the Pearl pleaded, never budging from her lover's side. "Don't you see? It's destiny. Our union is fated."

"Well . . ." the Dragon said, overwhelmed and undecided.

Troi took the Emperor by the arm. "Surely," she said, "a man so wise in the ways of love and romance cannot remained unmoved in the face of the obvious passion between your son and the Green Pearl of Lu Tung?"

"What?" he said. "I mean . . . no, of course not! Very well, Kan-hi is pardoned. Let the weddings begin!"

"Weddings?" Riker blurted, emphasizing the plural. Meanwhile, Hsiao Har was now holding on to Riker's arm as if she was afraid he would suddenly flee for the hills. *A distinct possibility,* Picard thought, *if this goes on much further.* He whispered in Beverly's ear.

"Excuse me," she said a moment later. "Before the

joyous nuptials between Lord Riker and Hsiao Har can take place, I must complete a brief medical examination." She approached the unlikely looking couple.

Riker was blushing bright red by now. "Beverly," he asked, "what's this all about?"

"Ssssh," she murmured while she ran her medical tricorder over him, humming thoughtfully at the results. Then she did the same to Hsiao Har. The girl didn't even glance in Beverly's direction, preferring to stare moonily at Riker. "Alas," Beverly announced. "It is as I feared."

"What?" said the Dragon, Riker, and Hsiao Har, in various tones of concern, anxiety, and fear.

"This wedding between Lord Riker and the Dragon's granddaughter is unhappily impossible," she said.

"Why?" asked the Dragon, Riker, and Hsiao Har, this time blending curiosity, hope, and despair.

"Because Lord Riker and Hsiao Har are incompatible. They can never have children together." Only Picard saw Beverly wink at Riker, who released a less-than-tactful sigh of relief.

"It is impossible?" the Dragon asked.

"Even the advanced medicine of the Federation could do nothing to make their union fruitful."

"That's all right, Grandfather," Hsiao Har said, practically jumping up and down. "I don't care. His second wife can give him all the babies he wants. They're smelly, disgusting things anyway."

The Dragon shook his head dolefully. "The Imperial bloodline must be continued. There must be heirs."

"Yao Hu will give you heirs," Hsiao Har insisted. "Lots of them! I just want Lord Commander Riker."

Troi couldn't help glancing at Riker, who looked positively crimson.

"No," the Dragon decreed. "We cannot allow any branch of our celestial heritage to wither on the vine. Nor can I deprive my granddaughter of the most noble calling any woman can have: that of a mother. This marriage cannot take place." He paused. "The gift exchange was without fault, however, so we will have to keep the planet Pai as compensation for this failed engagement."

"We wouldn't have it any other way," Picard said.

"Yes," Riker insisted. "Please keep everything, with all my goodwill."

Hsiao Har uttered a Pai curse which sounded unimaginably obscene.

"Which frees the Green Pearl and Kan-hi to wed," Picard said briskly. "Let them do so immediately."

# Chapter Fifteen

THE ANCIENT PRIEST could not be roused.

"Is he dead?" Picard asked apprehensively. Considering the man's obviously advanced years, it seemed more than possible that the excitement of the last fifteen minutes might have been too much for him.

"No," Beverly answered, bending over the collapsed priest. "He just won't wake up."

"Poor old Tsai-lung," the Dragon sighed. "He presided over my own first wedding, and my father's before me."

"Is he likely to come to anytime soon?" Picard asked.

"Oh, I doubt it," the Dragon said. "These days, he wakes up only once every year or so. It required several months of preparation to rouse him for this wedding."

Picard would have pulled his hair if he'd had any to pull. *I don't believe this,* he thought. "Aren't there any other priests available to perform the ceremony?"

The Dragon laughed. "My dear captain, does it look to you like I am running a religious retreat? Between you and me, I prefer to keep spiritual leaders at distance; they place too great an emphasis on celibacy and moderation."

"Perhaps we can beam one here . . . ?" Picard began. His comm badge chirped, establishing a communications channel with Data.

"My apologies for the intrusion," the android's voice said, "but the G'kkau ships have taken offensive positions above the planet's atmosphere. The *Fang* is directly challenging the *Enterprise.* Might I ask if there is any progress on the wedding front?"

"Mr. Data," Picard said brusquely. "I promise you, I will get these two married if I have to perform the ceremony myself!"

"In that case, Captain," Data replied, "I strongly urge you to do so promptly. The *Fang* is now charging up its disruptors."

Picard shook his head. "I wasn't speaking literally, Data. I just—" He froze as a sudden idea hit him with the force of phaser blast. *Why not?* "Data, prepare to beam the following individuals to the *Enterprise.*"

"Lower shields," Data ordered.

Melilli Mera gasped out loud. She hesitated, her fingers frozen above the controls.

On the main screen, the *Fang* floated against a backdrop of distant stars. The curved point of its crimson tip seemed aimed directly at the *Enterprise.* A smaller display, inset in the lower left-hand corner of the screen, provided a graphic schematic of the location of the other four G'kkau warships in proximity to both the *Enterprise* and the planet below. As a precaution, Data had ordered photon torpedoes locked on the coordinates of each of the G'kkau vessels. All he awaited was the authorization to fire them.

"Lower the shields," Data repeated, "for the fraction of a second required to beam the entire wedding party to Ten-Forward. Then restore the shields at full strength."

"Okay," La Forge said, manning the ship's defense station. "Do you think we'll get away with it?"

"Perhaps," Data said. His memory circuits reminded him of the wedding of Miles and Keiko O'Brien, during the preparations for which he had personally uncovered a Romulan spy. "Are all human weddings so hazardous?"

"Honestly?" La Forge said. "I've been to a lot of bad weddings in my time, but this one takes the cake!"

The floor seemed to shake beneath Picard's feet as he materialized aboard the *Enterprise.* At first, he assumed it was a transporter malfunction. Then he realized the floor really was shaking. The *Enterprise* was under attack.

"Hurry, everyone, take your places!" he instructed. Every human and Pai in the temple had been beamed aboard the starship, including the venerable Tsailung, now stretched out on the floor behind Guinan's bar.

Ten-Forward was literally deserted. Everyone was at battle stations, he realized, briefly wondering where

Guinan was. He quickly cleared a space at the front of the spacious lounge. Beverly, assuming the role of the bride's mother, hurriedly moved Lu Tung and the Pearl into place before Picard. Both father and daughter were gaping wide-eyed at Ten-Forward, not to mention the panoramic starscape visible through the lounge's windows, so Beverly had to physically drape Lu Tung's arm over Yao Hu's. Meanwhile, Riker stood to the left of Kan-hi, appointing himself best man. The groom's hands were still in shackles, but there was no time to deal with that now. Deanna held on to Hsiao Har's shoulders, lest the jealous teenager tried to latch on to Riker again. The Dragon, looking totally at a loss, collapsed into one of the many chairs scattered throughout Ten-Forward. The sturdy duranium-alloy structure sagged beneath his weight. "I don't understand," the Emperor said. "What are we doing here?"

"As captain of the *Enterprise*," Picard explained, "I am authorized to perform weddings aboard this ship. Right now, we need a wedding with all deliberate speed."

"Oh, that's all right then, I guess." The Dragon settled down at his table, apparently content to be a spectator from now on.

Another jolt rocked the *Enterprise*. The floor tilted abruptly, then righted itself. Riker grabbed on to Kan-hi, now the Dragon-Heir, while Beverly steadied the Green Pearl. Hsiao Har fell on top of Deanna, but they managed to untangle themselves without too much difficulty. Picard glimpsed a flash of green through the starboard windows. So far, the shields seemed to be holding up, but for how much longer?

"Captain," Deanna said breathlessly, "I recommend the short ceremony."

"Agreed," he said. Facing the young Pai couple, he cut straight to the chase. "Do you, Kan-hi, son and heir to the Dragon, take this woman to be your lawfully wedded wife?"

"I do!" Kan-hi said. He reached for Yao Hu, but his chains held him back.

"Do you, Yao Hu, called the Green Pearl of Lu Tung, take this man to be your lawfully wedded husband?"

"Most gladly!" breathed the bride. She seemed delirious with joy.

Green energy burst over the port side of the lounge, only partially deflected by the shields. Picard struggled to keep his balance, seizing the edge of a tabletop. Bride and groom fell toward each other, each one holding the other up. The overhead lights flickered briefly, then came back on again. The *Enterprise* was taking a beating, Picard realized. *Even a pack of lizards can take down a dragon—if the dragon is restrained and can't fight back.*

Here, at this moment, there was only one way to free the dragon. . . .

"By the power vested in me by the United Federation of Planets, in accordance with the temporal ruler of the Dragon Empire, I now pronounce you man and wife."

*That's it,* he thought. *The wedding is official, so the treaty goes into effect.*

He tapped his comm badge. "Mr. Data, fire at will!"

The wide front window of Ten-Forward offered him

a perfect view as half a dozen photon torpedoes shot forth from the bowels of the *Enterprise*. Two of those torpedoes converged on a G'kkau ship that was directly facing the front of the *Enterprise*. *That has to be the Fang,* he thought, feeling a surge of satisfaction as the torpedoes slammed into the G'kkau flagship. Bands of blue-white energy crackled like lightning over the hull of the *Fang,* leaving its gleaming green surface pitted and scarred. This "fang" was going to need a lot of dental work after the battle was over. He doubted if the G'kkau would be so quick to encroach on the Dragon Empire the next time they felt the need to expand their own territory.

The *Enterprise* followed its torpedoes with a bombardment of steady phaser fire. *Talk about fireworks,* he thought, wondering if Geordi could come up with anything to match this show. Picard turned away from the window to find Kan-hi and Yao Hu still staring at him expectantly. *What now?* he wondered. *I thought we were finished.*

At the back of the room, still holding tightly to Hsiao Har, Troi caught his eye, then puckered her lips.

"Oh, yes," he said. "I almost forgot. You may now kiss the bride."

"Really?" Kan-hi asked. He couldn't seem to believe his good fortune. Not too surprising, Picard thought, when you considered that he had gone from disgraced criminal to husband and future Dragon in less than an hour.

"Make it so," he said.

of *ch'i?* If so, Picard wished him both good luck and endurance. Drawing nearer, however, he saw that the Dragon's Minister of Internal Security was shuffling an ordinary deck of cards. "Greetings, honorable captain of the most honorable Worf," Chih-li said. "We have agreed to settle our duel by playing this game of poker. Lord Li Po informs me that it is an honorable game comparable to the clash of mighty armies."

"That's one way of looking at it, I suppose," Picard said. He gave Worf a warning glance. "Be careful, Mr. Worf. Be *very* careful."

Continuing down the path, he came at last to an wide, open courtyard full of Pai and Starfleet personnel. A raised dais, bedecked with hangings of silk and satin, had been erected on the southern edge of the courtyard. He recognized a few of the dignitaries seated upon the dais: the Dragon and Lu Tung, sitting side by side at last, as well as Geordi La Forge and Beverly. Chuan-chi, the treacherous former Heir, was conspicuous by his absence, as were the happy couple themselves, presumably for a far more joyous reason.

He was amused to see Master Kakkh upon the dais as well, his scaly body wrapped in bandages and coated with a smelly blue salve. Kakkh had had no choice but to throw himself upon the mercy of the Pai after the *Fang* lost its life-support capabilities. The rest of his crew was confined under house arrest in the murky tunnels beneath the Imperial Palace, which was actually the kindest place to keep them. As the senior ranking officer among the G'kkau, however, Master Kakkh had been "invited" (in the strongest possible terms) to represent the G'kkau at the wedding reception as a demonstration of the "new and lasting peace" between the G'kkau and the Dragon

Empire. Kakkh's tongue flicked miserably at the flying insects attracted by the glowing paper lanterns hanging over the dais. He did not look like he was having a good time.

"Captain!" La Forge cried out. "Hurry. You're just in time for the fireworks!"

Picard ascended the steps to the dais even as the first skyrocket zipped into the sky. It exploded in midair, throwing off a huge bouquet of gold and silver sparks and emitting a bang loud enough to shake the tea in his cup. More rockets followed, some whistling, some screaming like banshees before they detonated in a symphony of light and smoke and noise. The awestruck Pai oohed and aahed along with their Federation guests, reacting as much to the bangs and whistles, Picard noted, as to the colorful spectacle filling the evening sky.

"Listen to it!" enthused the Dragon. "The noise! The sounds!"

"Indeed," Lord Lu Tung agreed, holding his hands over his ears to protect them from the loudest bangs. "Most remarkable."

Picard sat down between La Forge and Beverly. "Congratulations, Geordi," he said. "Your show is an unqualified success."

"Captain, you have no idea." La Forge confessed, "I was really stumped there for a while. Then I remembered—what about *gunpowder?* Good, old-fashioned fireworks . . . like they used to make in the old days? The Pai have never seen anything like them, and neither have our people."

"Excuse me, Geordi," Beverly said, "but weren't old-fashioned fireworks banned sometime in the twenty-first century? I seem to recall that they were incredibly dangerous."

"And fighting carnivorous, spacefaring lizards isn't?" La Forge whispered conspiratorially. "Look, if you won't tell Starfleet, I won't."

"My lips are sealed," she said, "but let's not make a habit of this."

"Ah, Captain," the Dragon said warmly. "I see you've joined us. Good, I was wondering when we were going to hear your poem."

Picard choked on his tea. "I'm sorry," he said, clearing his throat. "My poem?"

He dimly remembered the Emperor saying something about a poem at the banquet the night before. In all the subsequent confusion, he had completely forgotten about it.

"Of course," the Dragon said. "It's tradition. The guest who has traveled the farthest to attend the wedding recites a poem at the reception, as does the priest who administers the vows. That's you in both cases. You have to do it. It's unlucky if you don't. Isn't that so, Lu Tung, my brother?"

"It is indeed a tradition, Nan Er," the former rebel confirmed.

"Hah!" the Dragon laughed. "No one else can call me by that name, but he's family now so that's all right. Anyway, you must recite a poem. I assume you've been working on one."

"To be honest, Excellence," Picard said, "I have been otherwise engaged for the last day or so." He paused, searching his memory. "The Federation, however, is home to many great poets. My own planet has had its share, all more proficient than I. If it is all same to you, I would be delighted to share the work of one of my favorite poets with you."

"Very well," the Dragon said. "It's all new to me. Proceed."

Rising to his feet, Picard coughed once and began:

"Let me not to the marriage of true minds
Admit impediments, Love is not love
Which alters when it alteration finds,
Or bends with the remover to remove.
O no! it is an ever-fixed mark,
That looks on tempests and is never shaken;
It is the star to every wand'ring bark,
Whose worth's unknown, although his height be
    taken.
Love's not Time's fool, though rosey lips and
    cheeks
Within his bending sickle's compass come,
Love alters not with his brief hours and weeks,
But bears it out even to the edge of doom:
    If this be error and upon me proved,
    I never writ, nor no man ever loved."

Picard bowed briefly to the enthusiastic applause of all but Master Kakkh. Then he regained his seat beside Beverly to find the ship's doctor dabbing at the corner of her eye with the hem of her sleeve. "Oh, I can't help it, Jean-Luc," she said. "I always cry at weddings."

He looked back on the past twenty-four hours. "I know exactly how you feel," he said.

# THE ART OF
# STAR TREK®

THE never-ending multimedia phenomenon that is STAR TREK has treated generations of viewers to a dazzling barrage of unforgettable images of the future. Bizarre alien beings, breathtaking extraterrestrial landscapes, exotic costumes, state-of-the-art special effects, and remarkably convincing futuristic sets and props have brought Gene Roddenberry's inspiring vision to life before the public's awestruck eyes.

- Over 1000 photos and Illustrations
- Hundreds never before seen

## By Judith and Garfield Reeves-Stevens

**POCKET BOOKS**

A Pocket Books Hardcover